Eternal Beloved

Also by Mary Ellen Johnson

Travels Across Time

Before I Wake

Eternal Beloved

The Moment I Kissed You

The Knights of England

The Lion and the Leopard

A Knight There Was

Within A Forest Dark

A Child Upon the Throne

Lords Among the Ruins

Flames of Rebellion

Eternal Beloved

TRAVELS ACROSS TIME
BOOK TWO

MARY ELLEN JOHNSON

ePublishingWorks!
...love what you read.

Book and cover design by eBook Prep
www.ebookprep.com

January 2024
ISBN: 978-1-64457-722-6

ePublishing Works!
644 Shrewsbury Commons Ave
Ste 249
Shrewsbury PA 17361
United States of America
www.epublishingworks.com
Phone: 866-846-5123

"In the garden of memory, in the palace of dreams... that is where you and I shall meet."

— LEWIS CARROLL

Part One

〜

CLARABEL LUCY

1980s–1990s

One

When I was little, my dad read me fairy tales. Snuggled against his enormous chest, with his powerful arms around me and holding the oversized book, I listened to his rumbling voice while running my fingers over the colorful pictures. My favorites were *Sleeping Beauty* because I liked the idea of being tucked away in brambly darkness until I'm discovered by a handsome prince; *Rumpelstiltskin* since the queen was clever enough to fool a nasty imp; and *The Princess and the Pea*.

Peas are my least favorite vegetable.

One fairy tale, *The Fir-Tree*, made me cry. At Christmas time, the tree is chopped down, carried into a manor house, and decorated with candles, ribbons, and shiny baubles. The children ooh and aah at its beauty and open their presents around it, which makes the fir happy. But once the holidays are over, the decorations are removed, and the poor tree is discarded in an attic until spring arrives. Then, with its branches withered and needles falling everywhere, it is hauled outside, cut up for firewood, and burned.

"Why are you crying, princess?" Daddy asked. (After watching *Snow White and the Seven Dwarfs*, I'd insisted on being called "princess.")

"It's so sad." I whimpered against his flannel shirt. "The tree didn't do anything bad, and yet they chopped it all up."

Daddy shifted position to better observe me. Raising my chin with the tips of his calloused fingers, he gazed into my eyes. "You can always change the ending. Tell me what *really* happened to our tree."

So, I did. The little fir is visited by a hideous-looking monster, who complains that he is tired and asks, "Might I rest beneath your branches?" When the fir agrees, the monster turns into an elegant prince who magically replants the tree, which eventually grows to be the biggest, straightest, and sparklingest fir tree in the entire kingdom.

"I like your story much better, princess," Daddy said. "That's the story we'll always tell."

"Yes," I agreed, feeling quite pleased with myself.

Even at age four, I was a sucker for happy endings.

~

Daddy, Dottie—my mother insisted everyone, including me, call her Dottie—and I lived in a ramshackle Victorian which Daddy nicknamed "the Duchess." The Duchess looked about right to house Casper, the Friendly Ghost, and his spectral trio of naughty uncles, though Daddy had started renovations, which involved a lot of tearing and hammering and scrapping of things. Located on one side of our massive stairway was a parlor, dining room, kitchen, and bath. To our left, separated by a velvet rope, was Ute Creek's Historical Museum, which, like much of the rest of the house, was pretty much a work in progress. Its lone occupant was Blix the Wonder Horse. Strong, stuffed, silent, and Ute Creek's most famous resident.

At one time, living, breathing Blix the Wonder Horse had enthralled audiences by solving math problems, spelling out names of objects with his nose, and even predicting the bombing of Pearl Harbor weeks in advance. Upon Blix's death, his owner had him stuffed and returned to Ute Creek, his original home. Forevermore, Blix, ears pricked forward, one foreleg raised as if pawing the air or pointing to a letter on an invisible block, held pride of place in the cavernous room.

Dottie was obsessed with creating an honest-to-goodness museum, though I had no idea why since her stated ambition was to be a "Hollywood Movie Star." Still, she gave her fundraising spiel to everyone she met.

"Ute Creek has *such* an exciting history." In addition to Blix, "the town held Chautauquas here every summer. Teddy Roosevelt...blah, blah, noise, noise, blah cattle drives...donations...tax deductible."

Dottie seldom had anything interesting to say, so even when I did understand her, I pretty much shut her out. Except when it came to a direct question, criticism, or a scream, "Clarabel Lucy, get over here!"

Yes, my name is Clarabel. Like the cow.

Mooooo.

Even as a kid, I sensed Dottie was nuts. Maybe not in the clinical sense, but in the sense that I really wished I could have chosen a different mother. A lot more like Cinderella's fairy godmother and a lot less like her wicked stepmother.

I was the outcome of an "oops" pregnancy, which had forced my parents to get married before Dottie's eighteenth birthday. As my mother reminded me from the age I could marginally understand such things, I was the reason she had been denied her destiny, which seemed to be time traveling back to mid-century Hollywood where she would be a nineteen-eighties version of her favorite actress, Debbie Reynolds. (How someone with no discernible acting or singing talent was going to be discovered in a tiny town tucked in a picturesque valley outside Colorado Springs is a mystery.)

After endlessly replaying her favorite musicals—*Singin' in the Rain, Unsinkable Molly Brown,* and *I Love Melvin*—in which she tried to recreate Debbie's dance routines and songs—Dottie often lamented, "If I don't get out of this one-horse town, I'm gonna lose my mind."

Even as a kid, I found that statement amusing for a couple of reasons: 1) My aforementioned assertion that Dottie Lucy had already lost her mind and 2) Setting aside the equines Old Man Pettigrew boarded on his ranch just beyond town limits, Ute Creek's lone claim to fame *was* one horse.

When I was five, Dottie decided to mold me into a contemporary version of Shirley Temple.

After examining a strand of my very average brown hair, she put two fingers beneath my chin, forced me to look at her, and emitted a long sigh. "We all have crosses to bear," Dottie said, after which she permed my hair until it looked like I had a workshop full of wood shavings glued to my head. Then, she enrolled me in Mrs. Grubner's Dancing Emporium (Ballroom Dancing a Specialty!), where I suffered through tap-dancing lessons.

Brush, strike, brush, strike...

I grew to hate terminally cute Shirley Temple, particularly her performance of "On the Good Ship Lollipop." Even then, I found the song creepy, with all those oddly grinning men on either side of some chubby kid with dimpled fingers and elbows strutting down the aisle in a dress that barely covered her butt.

Note to readers: Now, everyone involved with "Lollipop" would be arrested for kiddy porn, and Shirley whisked off to Child Protective Services.

By the time my perm grew out, Dottie declared me "hopelessly two-left-footed," which left me free to hang with my best friends, Ollie Scott and Lizzie Trahern. No matter what we were doing, however, every weekday at 5:30, I would be seated at the bottom of our sagging front porch steps, waiting for Daddy to come barreling down our drive. After exiting his old Chevy pickup, he'd scoop me in his arms, say, "There's my princess," kiss me on both cheeks and order me to tell him everything I'd done that day.

Daddy listened to my prattle as attentively as Dottie devoured her musicals.

I was indeed his princess.

Looking back, I believe this was the first and only time I actually felt safe—even though I had no concept of what "safe" meant.

Or sadness. Or betrayal.

But I would learn soon enough.

~

I never saw Daddy hit Dottie. Never saw the bruises. Or any physical evidence, really. The beatings were done in other rooms, late at night, after I was tucked in bed. Sometimes, my parents' voices drifted to me from the opposite side of our dilapidated mansion, sounding like some demented lullaby. Other times, they rose and fell like a summer storm before ending in one last violent crescendo. *Boom!* Thuds, noises I couldn't distinguish one from the other. Dottie sometimes screamed so loud the neighbors had to hear, though no one ever came knocking. Those were the times I wrapped my pillow over my head and distracted myself with stories about children wandering in scary forests and trolls that were actually princes who reverted to their proper form after a tenderhearted maiden kissed them, breaking the curse.

Afterward, the incidents were never addressed. (Later, so very much later, I realized that "battered wife" was simply another of Dottie's performances.)

Once Daddy went off to his job as a union electrician and Dottie retreated to her makeshift dance studio, I spent most days with Lizzie and Ollie begging mangled treats from Heavenly Smells Bakery, riding Old Man Pettigrew's Shetland ponies, playing Chutes and Ladders and Go Fish at Lizzie's house; or watching videos at Ollie's, which wasn't as exciting as it could have been since Doctor Scott was an economics professor and Ollie preferred titles like Milton Friedman's *Free to Choose* over *The Goonies*. We never, ever spent time at the Duchess, where Dottie holed up in the third story—an abandoned ballroom with bare wooden floors and scarred wainscoting—practicing dance steps to music videos playing on an endless loop.

If I thought about what happened after dark, I was afraid, so I just imagined I was caught up in some sort of spell. Once it was broken, everything would revert to the happy time before.

Two

S ix years old and enjoying my first day of summer. I'd rearranged my pillows and stuffed animals in order to better snuggle with my favorite picture book, *Haunted Castles of Ireland*. I'd discovered *Haunted Castles* in our library, which, like the rest of the Duchess, was in need of renovation, with books and magazines haphazardly stacked throughout its cavernous interior.

Haunted Castles of Ireland was how I learned to read. After Daddy tired of endlessly recounting the captions beneath each painting, he'd said, "Now, princess, your turn." First, he taught me to recognize each letter of the alphabet, then how to sound out individual syllables, and finally, to string the words together to construct the entire sentence.

"What a memory you have," he'd said after I'd quickly mastered my task. "I reckon you're the smartest five-year-old in all of Ute Creek."

I kind of figured I was.

What fascinated me most about *Haunted Castles of Ireland*? While I loved the exquisitely detailed paintings of those great piles of stone perched atop the surrounding bleak or barren or lush countryside, it was the castle ghosts who were most captivating. Sometimes, I fantasized the Duchess possessed her own specters, though, beyond her creaking wooden bones and intermittently drafty corridors, she appeared boringly "normal."

During one of our bedtime readings, I asked, "Why don't we have ghosts?"

Daddy shifted his attention from *Haunted Castles of Ireland* to gaze at the opposite bedroom wall as if scrutinizing the faded rose-patterned wallpaper. "Everyone has ghosts. Except, most of them are between our ears." He tapped the middle of my forehead. "Which might be the scariest place of all." After which, he ruffled my hair and flipped the pages to my favorite castle.

Castle by the Sea.

The first time I viewed Castle by the Sea, my breath caught. Its stones were the color of daffodils; its soaring turrets and pointy windows faced an expanse of water painted such a dazzling blue it looked like Colorado's sky fallen to earth. *The perfect place for a princess*, I thought, though the flag with the black bear standing on its hind legs hanging above its drawbridge was too mean for my liking.

But the main reason I was drawn to Castle by the Sea was its ghosts: the Knight and his Lady. The lady was drawn wearing a conical headdress exactly like those in fairy tales, while the knight was encased in so much armor he resembled Gort the Robot from *The Day the Earth Stood Still*, one of Daddy's favorite videos.

The caption beneath the drawing explained, *"This Knight and his Lady like to sing and laugh and play hide-and-seek, just like regular boys and girls."* I imagined the lady, the gauzy scarf atop her pointy hat trailing behind like a wayward kite, fleeing the knight, who clumped after her like a steel-encased Frankenstein.

"What song do you think the ghosts sing?" I asked Daddy, which led to another of our routines.

He immediately responded, "Down in the Valley."

"Sing it for me."

Ever after, Daddy ended our routine by singing at least my favorite verse.

Build me a castle forty feet high
So I can see him as he rides by
As he rides by, love, as he rides by

15

So I can see him as he rides by.

A knock on the door startled me from my daydream.

"Morning, princess." Daddy poked his head into the room. His eyes appeared bloodshot, and his smile flickered like a faulty neon sign. The leaden ball that settled in my stomach whenever I heard my parents fight abruptly returned.

"Why aren't you at work?" I nearly blurted, but when something seemed out of kilter, I'd already learned it was safest to pretend otherwise.

After Daddy gently lifted *Haunted Castles* from my hands, he sat on my mattress and gathered me in an embrace so tight I imagined my skin and bones being crushed into his.

Finally drawing back, I gazed into blue eyes everyone swore were twins of my own. "What's wrong, Daddy?"

"I've gotta go away for a little while, princess," he said, stroking my hair. "But I promise I'll be back for you."

"Why are you leaving?" I wanted to ask, but my pesky inner voice warned, "*You don't want to know.*" Besides, I sensed all the questions in the world wouldn't prevent my father from leaving.

"Everything's gonna be fine," Daddy said, pasting on another of his pretend smiles. "I've got a job a long way away, so I can only drive home on weekends. But I promise I'll call every night, and I'll visit as soon as I can."

I nodded. Daddy tucked me back in bed, returned *Haunted Castles of Ireland* to my lap, kissed me on the forehead, and left.

I never saw or heard from my father again.

~

"Did Daddy call yet?"

"Quit pestering."

That was the extent of my conversations with Dottie regarding Daddy's disappearance all that first summer. We stayed at Granny Grace's ranch house in Nebraska, where I carried around *Haunted Castles of Ireland* as my talisman and tried to stay out of Granny Grace and Dottie's way.

All those years later, after I learned the truth, I wondered whether Dottie and Granny Grace's behavior would have given them away if only I'd been able to decipher the signs. Did Dottie spend an unusual amount of time in the basement playing her movies? Was Granny Grace even nastier than usual?

I do remember my grandmother mocking me for carrying around my talisman, and when I said, "After I grow up, I'm going to live in Castle by the Sea," she'd replied, "Don't be ridiculous. Americans don't live in castles, and there's no such thing as ghosts."

I nodded, though, by the time we returned that fall to Ute Creek, I realized Granny Grace was wrong.

Ghosts were very real. And the Duchess was filled with them.

Daddy's absence festered, a wound refusing to heal. Sometimes, I swore I woke to him singing, *"Build me a castle forty feet high,"* or whispering through the fog of my dreams, *"Down in the valley...Down in the valley."*

I assured myself that was Daddy's way of communicating with me, that he would return when he could. I merely had to trust, to believe.

In the meantime, I wrote him letters that I hid in a box under my bed until the time I could personally present them to him or until I discovered an actual address.

That ended the day Dottie barged into my room, upset because she'd discovered my friends and I had hung all my toy Smurfs off the fireplace mantel. When she spotted the letter I was writing, before I could hide it, she snatched the paper, balled it in her fist, and bent down until her face was even with mine. "Listen, you little fool. Your father has another family. He's already remarried and has two kids. He doesn't want to see you, do you hear me? He doesn't care about either of us, so quit even thinking about him, understand?"

I can't say I quit thinking about Samuel Chaderick Lucy, but it would be many years before I mentioned his name again.

Three

When I was nine, Dottie remarried. My stepfather's name was Maurice Flack.

Maurice was another tall man, though where my real dad, with his shining black hair, big grin, and booming voice, was an unforgettable presence, Maurice had a way of disappearing into the shadows.

My stepfather was a human shrug. A "whatever."

I couldn't figure out why Dottie married Maurice. Apparently, men found my mother, with all her airs and ridiculous dreams, attractive. So I could *theoretically* understand why someone would want to marry her, but Maurice, who allowed himself to be moved about and rearranged like a cardboard cutout?

Maybe that was precisely the point.

When Dottie became mayor of Ute Creek, she started implementing her plans to improve the town's economy—all of which benefited her in some way. For my part, every summer, I wrote plays. Lizzie rounded up the talent and basically acted as producer—she could be quite bossy—while Ollie collected dollar bills from parents who showed up on our front lawn to watch their kids emote.

Sometimes, I imagined Daddy among the spectators. After hugging me and saying, "I'm so proud of you, princess," he would promise, "I'll never, ever leave you again."

Even then, I dreamed impossible dreams.

~

I was shocked—and privately annoyed—by the success of Hollywood Comes to the Valley, an annual event honoring some hotshot movie star with a bunch of hoopla climaxing with a showing of one of their movies at Ute Creek's retro drive-in. And let's not forget the fireworks since "Hollywood" was thrown on the Fourth of July. How could Dottie have a good idea? How could she implement it? How could people call her clever?

When the 1950s comedy duo of Jerry Lewis and Dean Martin was honored in my sixteenth year, I complained to Ollie and Lizzie. "To start out with John Wayne—I'll give Dottie he was a decent first choice—and end up with a couple of washed-up idiots is...why, it's... she's mental!" (I'd become quite the complainer.) Maybe not. Since Rosanne Barr and Rosie O'Donnell were currently hot commodities, Dottie had decided to become a standup comic. She'd even put together a routine, no doubt hoping Tim Burton or Robin Williams or Jerry Seinfeld would be in the audience.

One thing I'll say about my mother is that she was persistent.

This Fourth of July, I watched the festivities from the front porch of an Arts and Crafts bungalow overlooking Ute Creek Park. (Ollie and Lizzie had betrayed me by agreeing to man the cotton candy booth and collect entrance money.) The bungalow belonged to Susan McDermott, Ute Creek's librarian, who was about a thousand years old and wore orthopedic shoes with tire-track soles that squeaked with each step. Ms. McDermott seemed to know just about everything in the world, which I liked. I also liked the fact that when she'd discovered I could repeat entire poems or paragraphs verbatim after one reading, she'd been impressed. "You have a photographic memory," she'd explained. "Such a gift! Use it well."

The absolute low point of the afternoon was watching Dottie make a fool of herself on Ute Creek Park's stage with stupid jokes the stupid crowd seemed to enjoy.

"Dorothy"—McDermott was the only person I'd ever heard who called Dottie by her given name—"has a natural charisma, doesn't she?"

In my opinion, Susan McDermott was way too tolerant of Dottie—in the way you are of two-year-olds when they smear mashed potatoes in their hair. Mildly amusing so long as you don't have to clean up the mess. And while my mother might possess a certain superficial charm, so did psychopaths. I particularly hated the way she ridiculed my step-father for his "hillbilly" musical tastes, his "Goodwill" clothes, his table manners, his piss-poor job (he'd recently deep-sixed long-distance trucking to start a local taxi service), his fixation with growing Old Garden Roses along our veranda rather than keeping up with household repairs that would ensure the town council didn't slap a "condemned" sign on our front door and raze the Duchess.

"I've started working on my first novel," I said to change the subject. I had to raise my voice above the incessant cackling and screeching of Dottie's voice blaring from park loudspeakers. "It's called *Robin of the Rood*." Actually, I'd invented the title on the spot, but it rolled nicely off the tongue. I was still fascinated by Castle by the Sea and, over the years, had learned as much about its inhabitants, the DeLaMers, as possible.

"With your facility for writing plays and stories, that seems a natural progression," Susan McDermott said mildly. To my ears, she sounded dismissive. Not nearly as excited with this revelation as she should be.

I have a title for my book!

My thoughts drifted like the smoke from the barbecue cookers below. I would set *Robin of the Rood* in a fictionalized version of Castle by the Sea—though that idea had just come to me. Should I include a couple of ghosts? Name my hero after one of the names that ran through the DeLaMer family? William, Lucan, and Alaric were the most common. But during the period I was considering, the DeLa-Mers were always warring. I imagined them as enormous, hairy, lumbering creatures, waving their swords like Gort the Robot. And what sort of a name was Alaric? I wasn't interested in a moniker that evoked images of the Incredible Hulk. Alaric wasn't sensitive or noble sounding. If you said it just right, it sounded like a squawk. Or somebody being strangled.

Susan trained her opera glasses on the stage. "Tell me about your *Robin of the Rood*."

I sketched out the plot, improvising as I went along. Robin is a sensitive minstrel who falls in love with one of King Edward's daughters—I'd been researching Edward II—and because of the difference in their stations, they have to flee to Ireland in order to live happily ever after.

"I've been reading Gerald of Wales's *Topographia Hibernica*," I explained when Susan didn't comment. "You know, he's the monk who wrote all those fantastical tales about twelfth-century Ireland—talking animals, mythical beasts, and all the rest. Maybe I'll do a kind of mix, a historical fantasy—"

"Something along the lines of *Lord of the Rings* or *Game of Thrones?*" Susan interjected.

"Robin will be different." I was irritated she would compare what would be the greatest fantasy/historical novel ever written to lightweight commercial fare. "Instead of using brute force, Robin will solve problems via his wits. And musical talents."

When McDermott didn't seem suitably impressed, I finished with, "I'm teaching myself Middle English from *The Canterbury Tales* with the original text on one side and the modern translation on the other."

My gaze swung from the festivities to the red sandstone of Rojo Mountain peeking through thick stands of pine; and opposite, among trees and scattered rooftops, the Duchess's turret, topped by her crown of rusted wrought iron. From here, you couldn't see the scaffolding Daddy had erected more than a decade ago in order to paint an exterior that, like everything else about the Duchess, had continued its relentless deterioration. Way beyond the farms and ranches, past the Wet Mountains that bumped against our valley, was...*everything*, that endless, beckoning world of my imagination.

I couldn't wait to leave.

~

I didn't realize that this particular Hollywood Comes to the Valley would be the last time we Three Musketeers—Ollie, Lizzie, and I—would be together.

Following the showing of *Sailors Beware,* when fire flowers, Roman candles, and rockets boomed, blazed, and faded the way summer light-ning danced and flashed over the Wet Mountains, Ollie revealed his secret.

"I'm moving to Paris! Actually, my whole family is. I will miss you, *mon amies,*" he said in his Ollie-pretentious way.

Before I go any further, here's a good time to elaborate on Oliver Harrison Scott, who will feature so prominently in my tale. Physically, Ollie was short and alarmingly thin, with glasses that swallowed most of his face. He reminded me of that googly-eyed icon that popped up on some early computers, asking if it could help with some tasks. But it wasn't Ollie's looks that some found unsettling. He reminded me of an automaton impersonating a human being. Like he was attempting to blend into the human species and making a botch of it. Maybe it was because if you cut open Ollie's brain, you'd probably find a calcula-tor. And stacks of million-dollar bills. Still, Ollie was Ollie, and we'd always been friends. Of course, I would miss him, but to travel to such an ancient and romantic city?

"How lucky you are." I experienced a sense of *hurry, hurry* to get on with my life. I couldn't wait to backpack across Europe, crash in youth hostels, and fall in love with some dreamy-eyed Italian who murmured "Bellisimo" in my ear or a French artist who painted me in the nude and unsuccessfully tried to talk me into naughty threesomes.

As Ute Creek's show reached its climax, a multitude of colors painted our faces. Fairy lights danced and pulsed; pinwheels whirled and twirled; an enormous Catherine Wheel, white as bleached bones, rotated overhead. Even as I reveled in the magnificence of it all, I felt off-kilter. As though everything safe and comfortable and predictable was shifting before my eyes.

Ollie turned to me. "You will visit me in 'Gay Paree,' won't you,

C.L.?" The lenses of his glasses reflected dying trails of color from the fireworks.

"I promise." The very thought caused my throat to constrict with emotion. Knowing that in a little over two years, that would be me.

~

Ollie and I wrote a few times before thoughts of him just kind of drifted away like a lazy summer afternoon.

~

Following my high school graduation, I didn't go to France or anywhere magical.

I did go off to college.

Four

Sophomore year: While I took all the basics, I managed to sneak in a course on Anglo-Norman French, which might come in useful if I decided to become a professor rather than a famous writer.

The main thing I learned in college, though, was this: I, Clarabel Lucy, would never fall in love.

The closest I came was my crush on my "High Middle Ages" professor, who was small and slender and looked desperately in need of rescue. Maybe it was because his hair was generally unstylishly mussed, his clothes carelessly thrown together, and he sometimes wore mismatched socks. I liked to think of him as "haunted," casting us in the mold of Héloise and Abélard; only Professor High showed absolutely no romantic interest in me and, thankfully, from his point of view, did not risk castration.

My infatuation with Professor High ended when, after arriving for class, he started unpacking his briefcase beside the lectern. Only to discover it was a diaper bag.

"Father of triplets," whispered the student next to me.

Boom! Another fantasy shot to hell.

The summer before my senior year, I'd returned home to help manage Ute Creek's Historical Museum, which had become quite *the* tourist attraction, and to work on *Robin of the Rood.* I'd solidified my blueprint, which included (my admittedly brilliant) idea of creating dialogue in a mix of Anglo-Norman and Middle English (Two dead languages in one!).

Clarabel Lucy: Destined to blow up the publishing world!

Actually, no. How could my writer's imagination be so woefully inadequate when it came to reality? How had I never guessed that my mother, in her final attempt at stardom, had decided to run away with Bernard, the Living Waters Bible Church's choir director? As the Joyful Noise Duo, Dottie and Bernard were destined to take Nashville by storm.

Thus, Dottie, dressed like a low-rent Wynonna Judd, and Bernard, a smarmier version of Jim Bakker, informed me as I cooked my stepfather's breakfast. "It's time for you to grow up," Dottie said, wrapping up an explanation that highlighted both her narcissism and her delusion. I was tasked with "stepping up to the plate" and "doing the right thing."

Twirling a strand of her long, flaming red wig between her fingers, Dottie said, "You know Maurice won't take care of himself when I'm not here. His blood sugar and blood pressure are *dangerous,* and he just ignores them the way he does everything. If he continues abusing his body, he won't be able to support himself *at all.*"

By that time, my stepfather had entered the kitchen, looking simultaneously gaunt and puffy. He carefully ate the meal I'd prepared while watching the rest of us as if we were a mildly entertaining television show.

I didn't have to stay. I reminded myself of that a thousand times. I could walk away, return to school, and leave Maurice to take care of himself. But my stepfather had always been kind to me in his own way. And I could take online courses and work on *Robin of the Rood* in my spare time.

I acquiesced, as I so often did.
Readjusting my dreams didn't mean abandoning them.
Or so I told myself.

Part Two

Alaric DeLaMer

_1306–1307_

Five

'Twas said Edward Caernarvon was the handsomest man in England. I cannot speak to that, though our prince was big and strong and blessed with an easy laugh. But we were all of us young and gay and addicted to carefree pleasures. Fine clothes, fine jewels; elaborate meals and entertainments; days-long tournaments where we proved we could cross swords and break lances with the best of the old guard. And, saints be praised, the women! Though a few of us, such as Roger Mortimer, Baron of Wigmore, were married, more of us were like bees in summer, flitting from flower to flower.

Or like randy bulls.

The most important of our group, even then, was Piers Gaveston. Though he and Edward were of an age, the old king had brought Piers into the royal court to act as the prince's companion and teacher. Piers was lean, lithe, and graceful as a Greyhound with handsome features that could transform in a flash from saturnine to mischievous. Undeniably charming, Piers also possessed a wicked tongue, which he oft employed at the expense of his betters. Most importantly, Piers was an experienced soldier and jouster. Our old King Edward believed Piers Gaveston provided a perfect role model to prepare "Lord Edward, Prince of Wales" for his ascendancy to England's throne.

As a second son, I was lucky to be included among our prince's companions. I was comely—so said my conquests—and, as important, made myself amiable to all, good for a jest or ribald quip or to provide an interested ear. "Charming" was a word used to describe me, though that was an act. My natural disposition was more taciturn and solitary, but such would not gain me favor in Prince Edward's court. The world is cruel to younger sons, offering us few choices other than the priesthood or crusading, and the Holy Land was currently peaceful. Like Piers Gaveston, I was gifted at tourneying. My purse might be perennially empty, but tournaments only cost a few marks to enter, and the prizes were lucrative, allowing me to purchase rings to adorn my fingers, brooches to fasten my mantles, and velvet surcoats that hung just so in order to impress the ladies (as well as their maids or even those of coarser blood). We of the prince's entourage sang and flirted and dazzled with our silver tongues, conversant as we were in the language of courtly love. Though we'd no intentions of worshipping our *demoiselles* from afar. Rather, we tallied up our conquests the way tally sticks are used to settle accounts.

While my older brother Lucan and my father sometimes chastised me for my wastrel ways, I simply shrugged. This was who I was—carefree, merry, relentlessly superficial, concerned about the angle of my chaperon and the ability to woo maidens into my bed in French, English, or in a press, Latin.

"No wonder God, in His infinite wisdom, made you first-born," I said to Lucan during one of our related conversations. I meant that. From earliest memory, when I'd figured out Lucan was heir to the DeLaMer fortune, I'd determined I could do as I pleased.

My family's disapproval extended to the prince's court. Lucan and my father were vocal in praying that Edward Longshanks would rule another several decades. While I'd never be so imprudent to say so aloud, I hoped God would soon see fit to call our first king Edward to his final reward—or punishment, as may be. For Edward Longshanks was a harsh man with many sins on his soul.

However, England's primary problem, in my opinion, rested with the old king's indurate court and its adherence to outdated ways. The royal court stank of seriousness, of age, and needed to be swept free with a new broom. Furthermore, while King Edward still thought of himself as a lion, he might be able to manage a passable roar, but the blows delivered by the Hammer of the Scots had lost much of their force. Edward Longshanks was about war and subjugation, while we young cocks were happy to leave strife to the grizzled veterans of those campaigns.

We particularly enjoyed elaborate ceremonies where we could strut about in the form-fitting cotehardies introduced by the fashionable Piers. On Whitsunday of 1306, I participated in the most elaborate celebration of all. A mass knighting! Two hundred sixty-seven squires gathered in London. Never before had so many been dubbed on a single occasion.

While I suspected the old king's proclamation had more to do with providing new blood for his war against Robert the Bruce, I, at twenty-five years of age, had other priorities. Adoring crowds cheering me at the joust was one thing; long weeks chasing Scots across boggy moors held no appeal. Like our Prince Edward, I did not see the glory in or necessity of actual combat.

The night before our ceremony, we camped on the grounds of the Temple Church, which was the headquarters for the famed Knights Templar. Odd that the celebratory atmosphere awakened in me an unfamiliar feeling of melancholy, even revulsion. As if we were making merry at Stourbridge Fair rather than about to pledge our sword arms to God. It seemed blasphemous somehow. A longing, soon come and gone, stirred within. That I was called to be more than a courtier consumed by fashion and flirtation and amorous pursuits.

Overwhelmed by the weight of tradition, of duty, I experienced a wholly unexpected sense of shame. So often, I'd mocked the old king and his retainers for so wholeheartedly embracing their *raison d'etre*.

Might King Edward be right, I wondered, *to call us wastrels?*

❧

May 22, 1306: a huge crowd cheered us as we made our way from Temple Church to Westminster Abbey, where our dubbing would take place. Beside me, Piers Gaveston made merry with the ladies, dark eyes sparkling, compliments pouring from him like wine from nearby conduits. Normally, I would have joined him, but today was sacred. Plus, Jocelyn Goodknyght had recently become betrothed, and I needed time to mourn the crushing of so many dreams, as improbable as they'd always been.

Nay. No thoughts of a woman, not even Jocelyn.

Though minstrels would have it otherwise, I'd learned love was not the be-all and end-all.

Still, I did picture Prince Edward, dressed in full armor, kneeling alone in the chapel of Westminster Palace. His father, the king, would be in front of him, observing the ceremony. Beside our monarch, his oldest and most trusted lord, James Lackford, would lay the sword on the side of Edward's neck and dub him "Sir Knight." James Lackford, betrothed of Jocelyn Goodknyght. Old, Lackford might be, but he was a respected warrior, fierce against the Scots, gentle to his friends, and helpful to squires and pages without berating or manhandling us. No doubt Lackford had once been handsome—not that looks mattered—but his face was as lined and his hair as white as our sovereign's. Still, he looked healthy enough to sire a passel of sons off his bride. For his sake, I wished that would be so.

I could not hate Lackford, who'd taken up the crusader's cross as a young man and fought beside His Grace throughout the Welsh and Scottish wars, for wedding my heart's desire. Or Jocelyn Goodknyght for eagerly embracing the match. To Jocelyn, I was a longing, a wish. And we all know the saying *If wishes were thrushes, then beggars would eat birds.*

Upon nearing Westminster Abbey, Roger Mortimer cut into my wayward thoughts. "The new chivalry of England," he commented, his gaze sweeping the rows of gleaming armor before us. Though Mortimer, like Piers Gaveston, could have a wicked tongue, he spoke without irony.

Roger Mortimer, Lord Mortimer of Wigmore, and I were childhood friends, though I was privately in awe of him. While he was lord or overlord of so many towns and baronies, I could not count them all; he'd have made his mark even if he'd been born landless.

Roger Mortimer was fearless, shrewd, eager enough for battle, and good at it. Oddly—or perhaps because our destinies are ruled by the stars—Mortimer and Prince Edward had both been born on the Feast of St Mark. Might that partially account for their closeness? Mortimer was fiercely loyal to his prince, while Edward sought him out nearly as often as Piers. Though some astrologers proclaimed St Mark's to be a day of bad omen, I scoffed at such hoary naysaying. Since one man would inherit a kingdom and the other, who was already one of the richest barons in England, had recently married a woman with estates in Gascony and Ireland, I cursed my poor luck for having been born on Midsummer's Eve.

Tonight, we, who had begun the day as squires and finished it as knights, feasted at Westminster Palace. The wine was good, though I had vowed to be abstemious, and my peculiar mood persisted. Course after course was presented until the beeswax candles burned low, and my body felt the weight of last night's vigil and today's ceremonies. Eighty minstrels, picked by our prince and Piers, serenaded us throughout. The sprightly tunes jarred with my mood. Especially when I raised my gaze to the dais where James Lackford was seated close to the old king while Lackford's fiancée sat at his right hand. *My Jocelyn.*

She never belonged to you, I reminded myself, though once I'd deluded myself otherwise. Aye, I was lovesick, which might be a romantic state in songs and courtly games, but now it simply hurt.

Over the rim of my goblet, I stared at Jocelyn, sitting still and silent and exquisite as the Madonna. Hair like liquid sunshine, eyes as blue as the River Wye on a cloudless day.

For the feast, Jocelyn wore a surcote of the deepest green, edged in silver. Her hair, which I'd often arranged around her breasts after lovemaking, was threaded with pearls. Ahh, *mon cœur*. Even after I'd learned her secret, that Jocelyn Goodknyght's heart was as cold as the ice glutting the River Thames in winter, I still loved her.

And feared I always would.

This was the night I learned what it meant to be God's avenger. To realize that, while I might be a second son, more importantly, I was a *knight*.

When festivities were nearly done, and I was dreaming of my pallet, King Edward, white-haired, white-bearded, and arrayed in white, rose to address us. First, His Grace spoke of bravery, honor, courtesy, faith, valor, and gallantry toward women. Familiar words, yet tonight, each was like an arrow unleashed from a longbow, piercing my heart.

I am called to this. To live by this code. As are all knights.

His Grace's words soon took a darker turn. Robert the Bruce had committed an unspeakable crime, he informed us, this one on consecrated ground. Before the high altar at Greyfriars Kirk, Bruce had stabbed his rival for Scotland's throne, after which he'd crowned himself Scotland's rightful sovereign.

Even I was not so jaded as to shrug aside such sacrilege. When King Edward swore we must avenge the rival's death, our answering huzzahs seemed to shake Westminster's very roof timbers.

A knight for a day, and I had already been called to dip my sword in the blood of our enemy.

Such I would do with relish.

~

Jocelyn Goodknyght tracked me down inside the nave of Temple Church, where head bursting with King Edward's speech and our forthcoming campaign, I'd been contemplating the effigies of several crusader knights.

"Nothing need change between us," Jocelyn said, as if resuming a conversation we'd not actually had. My former paramour rubbed against me like a cat, a disgraceful act within such a sacred—and busy—place.

"Do not." I looked around, fearful someone might carry scurrilous tales to Lord Lackford.

"What is wrong, Sir Knight?" she asked, teasing me with my new title. Jocelyn ran slender fingers up my forearm. Even through the material, I was thrilled by her touch.

"I do not bed married women," I said bluntly, though that declaration had only been true since last night and my newfound embrace of more chivalric virtues.

"I am not married." Jocelyn stuck out her bottom lip in a simulacrum of a pout. I'd always found that particular mannerism arousing. 'Twould not be as easy as I'd hoped to purge Jocelyn Goodknyght from my blood.

"The banns have already been called," I said, gazing down at her slender fingers, those hands a little larger than a child's. "'Tis done." My voice was as strong as my resolve, though it was not easy. My heart was bruised. Nay, more than that. Pierced. But I would learn to live with that, and in time, such a wound might heal.

The blue of Jocelyn's irises had turned a sea-green, as they did when she was angry. Jocelyn Goodknyght did not like being denied.

"Since we've slept together," she said, "I could make the case that you and I are already married."

I felt a flash of such rage my breath stuttered in my chest. I'd been a page in the Mortimer household when I'd first glimpsed Jocelyn. She'd been younger and bossy even then. I'd not given her much thought until she'd ripened into a beauty worthy of endless lovestruck sonnets. When I, so young, naïve, and in the throes of first love, had asked for her hand, she'd batted my plea aside the way a cat toys with a wounded bird before the kill. Technically, it was true that two people who'd indulged in intercourse might later be declared married. However, if we applied that standard to Prince Edward's court, most of us would be married ten times over.

"James Lackford is a knight *nonpareil*," I said, noting how exquisitely the light caressed the spun perfection of my former lover's hair, the alabaster column of her throat. "He will give you everything your heart desires."

"But my heart desires you," Jocelyn cried.

I could almost believe her, though even then, I realized Jocelyn Goodknyght loved only herself.

King Edward exacted vengeance in his usual brutal fashion—imprisoning various of Robert the Bruce's relatives in cages and hanging, drawing and quartering one of Bruce's younger brothers. Yet, oft times during this, his final campaign, the old lion was so weak he had to be carried in a litter.

On July 7, 1307, Edward Longshanks died of dysentery.

On July 20, Edward Caernarvon ascended England's throne.

Part Three

~⚬~

CLARABEL LUCY

Early 2000s

Six

"**N**ow you and I will be together forever, my eternal beloved."

I leaned back in my office chair, gazing at the words on the computer screen. Finished. In some form, *Robin of the Rood* had been a part of my life for nearly seven years. Maybe that accounted for the tears stinging my eyes. Like bidding farewell to an old friend.

Beyond the pool of light created by the glowing screen and desk lamp, my makeshift office was a fuzz of black. Between bouts of his increasingly frequent "spells," Maurice had renovated the Duchess's turret, and I fancied myself a contemporary version of Rapunzel—minus the long hair or handsome rescuer prince. And, while Rapunzel's vocation appeared to be singing, I had created what would become the most unique bestseller in the history of the world.

Note to reader: (Yes, I realize I'm hyperbolizing since I haven't read every bestseller.)

While Susan McDermott encouraged me to work on *Robin of the Rood* during slow times at Mountain High Library, where I'd been employed this past year, I was most productive after Maurice had retreated to his bedroom, and I was ensconced in my turret, creating an entire world with only my brain and a machine as my tools. A magical process.

But now it was over.

Already, I missed Robin. Conjuring my minstrel as I had out of my longing and loneliness, I'd fashioned my ideal man. Besides looking remarkably like the ancient print in my bedroom depicting a golden-haired, non-threatening, vaguely androgynous guardian angel guiding adorable children across a dangerous bridge, Robin was erudite, sensitive, resourceful, musically gifted, and forever complimentary to his adoring Lilith. Because Robin was so delicately beautiful and preferred solving problems with a song or clever turn of phrase, boors like my antagonist Alaric, the Beast, forever underestimated him. The Beast, whose pea-sized brain deduced that the solution to life's problems was hacking all and sundry to pieces, was ultimately tricked by Robin into tumbling down a magic well, where he was dispatched by a school of fish with golden teeth, thereby providing my lovers their happily ever after.

Robin of the Rood was my subtle thesis statement: the arc of mankind bends toward brain rather than brawn.

While I dared not utter my truth aloud, I **knew** *Robin of the Rood* was a masterpiece. I imagined the jacket blurb: **Breathtaking blend of romance, fantasy, and hardcore history!**

So far, the responses to my queries had been discouraging, but it was merely a matter of time before an enlightened agent or editor grasped my vision.

Each night, after turning off my computer, plodding back down to the second story, and crawling into bed, I imagined my future. I visualized the hell out of it, just like that New Age bestseller, *The Secret*, instructed. Never doubt, never allow negative thoughts lest the law of attraction gets confused and hands you your worst nightmare.

I didn't. I wouldn't.

My vision would not fail me.

◦◦◦

The book signing of (self-published) *Robin of the Rood* was a "triumph," according to the article in Ute Creek's *Town Crier.* "*Half the town showed up! Congrats, Clarabel, for selling more than two hundred copies of your exciting, wonderful book,*" gushed Lizzie Trahern-Wahlberg, administrator of Ute Creek's Facebook page. Though I doubted anyone would actually *read Robin of the Rood*, I was grateful for the town's ongoing love and support.

Still, when I climbed the turret stairs to sit before my lifeless computer screen since, you know, *Robin of the Rood* was finished in more ways than one, my mood was as black as the surrounding shadows. *Robin of the Rood* had simply been an amateurish bit of escapism, necessary to pull me out of life with an ailing stepfather and to forget dreams that had been crumpled and tossed aside like used Kleenex.

Those three o'clocks in the morning were killers.

That fall, Maurice was hospitalized for the final time. His muscles had atrophied so badly he couldn't stand or walk unaided. He slept most of the time, though when awake, he didn't complain. I marked his weight loss by the increasingly prominent bones beneath his parchment skin.

Since Maurice preferred to die at home, we converted the Duchess's dining room. Under the supervision of our hospice nurse, a trio of high school friends and I moved our oversized Victorian furniture off to the side before setting up all the necessary equipment to keep Maurice comfortable.

I braced myself for the inevitable.

Over the past three years, I'd grown fond of my stepfather. Maurice was always pleasant and expressed gratitude for the smallest acts of kindness, which were really no more than common courtesies. He'd asked for so very little and had deserved better than Dorothy Lucy-Flack. Far from being a man with nothing to say, Maurice's silences signaled someone who kept his own counsel. A "still waters run deep" type, he'd quietly woven himself into the fabric of my days. I just wished he'd chosen his life rather than simply fallen into it.

Each evening, I kept watch beside his hospital bed, propping my latest romance atop *Haunted Castles of Ireland*, which I used as a makeshift table. While Maurice slept, I lost myself in a world where gorgeous men and beautiful women fall in love, enjoy sex that's sometimes steamy, sometimes sweet, and live happily ever after. If someone gets sick, they recover, or if they die, it's long in the past and relevant only so the writer doesn't have to juggle too many characters.

Nothing, however, could long distract me from the fact that Death shared our room. According to tradition, deceased family members had once been laid out on our massive dining table, their corpses washed and tended before being publicly displayed. I imagined all the Lucy dead waiting deep in the darkness, readying to pay their respects. Is that why I sometimes shivered from a sudden coldness, an impossible downdraft, heard an unexpected creak of a floorboard, susurrations from the direction of the sideboards, scamperings that couldn't be dismissed as wayward mice?

I thought of other ghosts, of the Knight and his Lady, playing hide-and-seek in Castle by the Sea.

I am Castle by the Sea's chatelaine. I am dressed in a brocade gown, with my candle raised high, because I'm apparently addicted to midnight wanderings rather than sensibly snoring the night away beneath a mound of blankets. Is that the train of my gown scraping behind me? Or ancestral voices, generally tucked away in manor walls, coming out to play? Teasing me with whispers and murmurings and maybe even calling my name, so that I turn with racing heart, angling my candle flame, unsuccessfully attempting to penetrate the gloom.

"No, that must be the wind," I mutter. Or "My, how these old castles moan and groan, don't they?"

I shivered and returned to my Death Watch.

～

Who were you before you met Dottie? I wondered, watching the gentle rise and fall of Maurice's chest. *Where did you grow up? Why don't you ever talk about anything or anyone from your past?* Other than mentioning his stint in the Army, which explained his VA disability, Maurice might have been conjured out of a wizard's spell the day he'd arrived in Ute Creek.

"Something to tell you, Clarabel."

I raised my head to view my stepfather, who had struggled awake. "Will," he croaked.

"Will?" I repeated, frowning. "Do you mean like the legal document?"

Faintest of nods. "With Chuck." Our attorney, Chuck Watkins?

"Okayyyy." No idea where this was going. Nor did I want to discuss financial matters. I couldn't, wouldn't worry about what would happen following Maurice's passing. If I had to sell the Duchess, so be it. The rest, pressing a dying man about my needs, my worries was too ghoulish. Since Maurice and Dottie had never divorced, I assumed she would automatically inherit everything.

"Watkins," Maurice repeated. "He's always known. Trust." His eyelids drooped before he rallied and trained his gaze on me. "Your daddy didn't abandon you."

I startled. *What?*

Between starts and stops and hesitations, Maurice revealed what had really happened that terrible, awful year my father disappeared.

"Your daddy...on his way to you." Maurice's rasp was the only sound in the tomb-like room. "I-76 straight as a stick...Favorite route for long-haulers...Dust storm came out of nowhere. Cars inching along."

It had only taken one car, driving too fast, to cause one vehicle to run into the other. Like dominoes falling. Maurice had been one of the truckers who'd parked alongside the highway to wait out the storm.

"Pulled your daddy out of the wreck," Maurice said between long pauses. "Died at the scene."

Died? No, that couldn't be. I alternated between a feeling of numbness and such rage I was capable of raining down destruction on the entire universe. I only half-listened, and yet I heard and felt *everything*.

There had been no other family, Maurice told me. Dottie had lied about that, the same as she'd lied—by omission—about Daddy's death.

No, No, NO!!! Screaming internally. Which was worse, thinking your father abandoned you or knowing he's dead? An awful hammering in my chest; my heart threatening to break free.

"I would have known," I cried. "I would have felt it!"

"Tracked down your mother. Already knew. Because of the paperwork to collect survivor's benefits...and the rest. 'Our secret,' she said.

'No purpose,' she said. And since it happened out of state...easy enough to keep out of local papers, to pretend."

Daddy couldn't be dead. This was some horrible mix-up, some hateful joke. Maurice wouldn't lie, but how could he be telling the truth? And why would Dottie do such a thing? How would keeping Daddy's death a secret benefit her? Why hadn't she told me?

"Your mother and I weren't... friendly until way later." My attention returned to Maurice. "Couldn't get your daddy out of my head. So sorry for you both."

Pulse thundering in my ears; mind tumbling and turning like some demented acrobat.

"The will, Clarabel. Trust. Don't let Dottie contest. Bully you. Yours. All of it."

With that, Maurice sank back into the pillows.

The next day, he slipped into a coma.

The day after that, Maurice Flack died. Peacefully.

Shakespeare's Calpurnia said, *"When beggars die, there are no comets seen; The heavens themselves blaze forth the death of princes..."*

I, at least, marked my stepfather's death. As did the town. Wreaths. Funeral. Expressions of regret. A polished granite headstone with his full name and, beneath the dates of birth and death, a single rose.

But who had mourned Samuel Chaderick Lucy? I didn't even know where Daddy was buried.

Seven

∽

Perhaps it was the craziness of the day—that I had emerged from Chuck Watkin's office an astonishingly $567,000 richer, thanks to Maurice's life insurance policy and a trust fund Daddy had set up for me. Watkins also handed me the deed to the Duchess. The mortgage had been fully paid off in accordance with the terms of the fund.

While awaiting my mother's arrival—for I knew Dottie would show up this evening as surely as she'd shown up for the reading of the will—I felt as if I were floating. Gazing down at myself from a corner of the twelve-foot ceiling.

This, nothing, seemed real.

The front screen door squeaked. From my seat at our battered kitchen table, I awaited my mother's appearance in the archway.

Say it. Tell her. "You lied about Daddy hitting you. You lied about his other family. You lied about his abandoning me. You lied about his death. You lied about everything."

I did.

"I want to develop this property," Dottie said as if I hadn't spoken. "I have a good head for real estate. I'll make us both rich. You owe me that much, Clarabel Lucy."

The unflattering overhead light brutally displayed the flaws in

45

Dottie's makeup, the lines in her face. I fancied I could see the humiliations she'd suffered since fleeing her responsibilities and bombing as a country/gospel singer.

"Get out," I said. "You're trespassing. If you don't leave immediately, I'll call 911."

"You wouldn't dare."

By the time the police arrived, Dottie Lucy-Flack had scuttled back into the shadows like the cockroach she was.

∼

What now, Clarabel Lucy?

Destiny arrived in the form of a low-slung convertible encased in red metal so dark it appeared black. From my position on the Duchess's front porch swing, I monitored the vehicle's approach. (A Ferrari, I was soon informed, along with its cost, which nearly equaled my inheritance.) I'd been surveying my legacy—shaggy grounds, carriage house in need of a new roof and siding; the rose petals from Maurice's bushes blanketing the area below the porch like breadcrumbs leading fairy tale children back home.

The owner of the Ferrari was Ollie Scott, returned from France. At first, I didn't recognize him. Ollie's dishwater blond hair was immaculately cut and gelled; his complexion fairly glowed with exotic skin care products and an expertly administered fake tan; his hands were soft and manicured. He wore butt-hugging skinny jeans, a black T-shirt sporting a Gucci logo, and, to complete his ensemble, a giant leather bag slung over his shoulder. What we locals would call a purse.

Goodness. A metrosexual, right here in Ute Creek.

After settling beside me in the porch swing and bragging about the fortune he'd made in marketing, Ollie said, "Been following you and this old town on Facebook. Been thinking how to position you, determine your niche."

When I said nothing because I had no idea what he was talking about, Ollie moved to close the deal. "Give me ten years, C.L., and you'll be the richest writer in America. Or publisher, or screenwriter, whatever I decide. Trust me, I'll make all your dreams come true."

Trust somebody I hadn't seen in a decade? On the other hand, why not embrace something new? Hadn't I paid my dues? Didn't I deserve an adventure?

I thought of that silly book, *The Secret,* with its New Age nonsense about manifesting your dreams. Was this some sort of delayed response to all my positive thinking?

Ollie nudged me. "Speak up! What're you thinking? Shall we do this, C.L.?"

Part Four

Alaric DeLaMer

1312–1313

Eight

❧

Though our King Edward's favorite, Piers Gaveston, was the architect of his own fate, the manner of his death was still a terrible thing. God has imbued man with free will, which includes the ability to stopper our ears against what we do not wish to hear and to embrace our most destructive delusions. Both of which Piers did. The Gascon was exiled three times, the last with the warning that should he return, he'd be branded an outlaw. The barons he'd so relentlessly mocked even threatened Edward Caernarvon's kingship, warning a monarch's power was not absolute.

Yet Edward and Piers behaved as though they were protected by some enchantment.

Would that were so, for I loved them both. Piers was a brother-in-arms, and King Edward, while infelicitous in his political decisions, possessed a far more pleasing nature than his father. Although a winsome personality, hearty laugh, and an ability to tell risqué jokes do not make for a successful monarch, Edward Longshanks had been a harsh taskmaster, a man of violent temper, and a vicious, sometimes unchivalrous warrior. A king universally respected, admired, and feared among his subjects but largely unloved.

However, our first King Edward's every thought, every action, every calculation over nearly four decades could be summed up in one word: England. Whereas even when he reached an age to know better, our second king Edward's obsession was not a kingdom but a man.

While still prince, Edward over-indulged his Piers, responding to his every whim the way a father would his spoiled son, showering him with revenue and crown lands in both England and Ireland. His Grace behaved as though laws, traditions, and the mundanities of governing were choices to be made or disregarded, depending on his pleasure. Depending on how it might please—and enrich—his "brother."

Do strong fathers beget weak sons? It was not only Edward Longshanks' height that cast a long shadow. But if that were so, what did that say about my own sire? Since a decade separated me from my older brother Lucan, I'd not really known my father before he'd become middle-aged and querulous, complaining about old campaign wounds, crushing taxes, and men whose word meant less than a mouthful of spit. Weak? Strong? What did it matter? Because I was a second son, my father had never considered me more than an afterthought anyway. All his ambitions were poured into Lucan, who deserved the attention. Lucan DeLaMer, I knew, would do our legacy proud.

But Piers Gaveston was also a second son...

And I ramble...

To be king is a lonely business. Which might seem strange since our sire was always surrounded with moments of privacy dearly bought—including in the bed chamber. Still, even when he'd been prince, I'd sensed Edward's loneliness, the sadness sometimes leaking through his love of japery, dancing, music, and other merriments. Even more peculiar, Edward was a man of the people. He enjoyed mixing with them, sometimes acting as the farmer and thatcher and reveling in physical labor. Still, if he thought to earn their camaraderie, he was a fool. Such were not the proper hobbies for a king. His magnates despised him for it, while the common folk were befuddled and uneased.

Besides, England possessed one king. Which meant Edward Caernarvon was unique. While longing for unconstrained friendship might be a natural wish, he was in no position to indulge it.

Near the end, I tried to warn Piershe was courting disaster. "You are like a fox who doesn't hear the baying hounds on his trail."

Piers shrugged me off, calling England's most powerful lords "fopdoodles," mocking their looks, their intelligence, their martial talents —every way in which they were inferior to him.

Helpless, I watched the tragedy unfold. Like *The Fall of Lucifer,* the mystery play I'd viewed at Eastertime, with Edward being God and Piers the devil. The ending had been written long ago, and none could change it. The Morning Star had been cast down from heaven.

Ah, Piers. How could you have thought your fate would be any different?

Everyone, save Edward and Piers, knew how this tale must end. Edward, because he had too much faith in his power, and Piers because, well, Piers had a long history of biting the hands of his masters, forgetting he was the dog chained to the post.

By March 1312, the now excommunicated Piers had settled at Scarborough, a magnificent royal fortress and another gift from our sovereign. Scarborough Castle sat on a promontory overlooking the North Sea, its town spread below like a lady's skirt. During the old king's reign, we'd attended its Scarborough Fair, where I'd strutted about like the foolish coxcomb I was, wearing clothes and jewels I could not afford and sarding maidens whose names I'd not even bothered to learn. The memory caused me to cringe, but I soothed my conscience by rationalizing that with the ending of my youth, I'd become a better man. Or at least a more discreet one.

Surely, Piers realized freedom was trickling like sand through his fingers. When his enemies arrived at Scarborough Castle, his surrender, like his fate, proved inevitable.

Despite King Edward's frantic pleas for "negotiations," only the manner of Piers' death remained to be determined. Should Piers be hanged as a thief? Drawn as a traitor? Finally, his captors decided that "as a nobleman and Roman citizen," Piers Gaveston would be beheaded.

At Blacklow Hill—more a gentle incline, for certes—Piers was run through with a sword by one waiting Welshman and beheaded by a second. The most difficult for those of us who mourned him was the execution's aftermath. Because Piers had been excommunicated, he was denied a Christian burial. Rather, he was left at Blacklow for the forest animals to feast upon.

Piers Gaveston no longer belonged to God.

He belonged to the Morning Star.

King Edward, his queen, servants, men-at-arms, and all those who made up a pared-down version of the royal court had moved to Burstwick Castle. June was nearly past, Piers was already dead, and we, tucked away in East Riding as we were, did not know.

Burstwick Castle was one of the most important royal manors in the north. It possessed a charming manor with a large garden, now lush and green, and parks where Edward enjoyed hawking and hunting. I sometimes saw the king and his queen, arms linked, walking beyond the squared moat or lounging on one of the benches by the fishponds.

It is custom to pretend our monarchs are always handsome and their consorts beautiful; in this case, 'twas so. When Edward and Isabella were together, they dazzled the eye. He, tall and well formed, hair bright as molten gold; she, slight and graceful, her features more finely cast than those of the statue of Our Lady of Walsingham at the shrine of the same name. While I seldom thought of Isabella of France as a "woman" but rather as England's queen, she, with her beauty and dignified manner, did us proud, particularly now she carried their first child, which was a treasure more precious than all the kingdom's gold.

These were soft days filled with idyllic scenes. But tension lurked beneath the merriment. Sometimes, in the dead of night, when I couldn't sleep, I imagined the sound of war drums, though it was only the thundering of summer storms rolling in from the North Sea. Still, while we pretended, we could not escape. A few of the powerful, like Roger Mortimer, remained fiercely loyal to Edward and his favorite, but even I realized Piers had tweaked the ears of his enemies so long and brutally that his own were in danger of being cut off in return.

Still, we chose to believe Piers remained safe, that he would soon rejoin Edward and us, his handful of friends.

While wild animals picked apart the headless corpse of Edward's favorite where it had been discarded in the high grasses of Ludlow Hill.

29th of June: Trumpets blared from a watchtower, announcing a messenger's arrival. My squire and I were crossing the courtyard in the direction of Burstwick's great hall, close enough to see the dirt on the rider's gambeson, the sweat on the flanks and neck of his mount. My throat immediately felt dry as dust, and my fists clenched as if ready to deliver a blow. We all knew what the messenger's appearance foretold.

With Isabella and two of her ladies trailing behind, Edward approached the man. Mayhap, it was my imagination, but as the pair conferred, the air around us stilled. So quiet I could hear the cooing of pigeons from a nearby dovecote and the occasional flap of wings or jangle of hawk's bells from inside the royal mews.

We all tensed, waiting for Edward's reaction, which came in the form of one of his favorite oaths. "By God's soul!" he shouted. "If he'd taken my advice, he would never have fallen into the hands of the earls... This is what I always told him not to do..."

While Edward ranted and paced, Isabella stood nearby, clutching what looked like a book to her swelling belly, for our queen was a great lover of romances. Her face, which had been glowing with health, had turned pale as the white of the veil thrown over her crespine.

His Grace continued raving, though once his fury wound down, I knew the pain would overwhelm him. When he realized what he'd lost... well, Piers had only been a companion, yet my emotions were like a weathervane in a windstorm, twirling every which way until they settled on anger at Piers himself. He'd wooed his fate like a lover when all along, he'd known it to be a fickle whore.

The birth of King Edward's first child, born on November 13, 1312, temporarily banished the specter of Piers' death. Across the kingdom, church bells rang, not to mark the hours of the day or to chase away storms and demons but in a frenzy of rejoicing. Queen Isabella had ensured a smooth succession to England's throne. Aye, and Edward of Windsor, we were assured, was strong and hale and as handsome as a prince could be. We interpreted this happy news as proof of Divine blessing, that the bad days were past, and that God once more looked upon us with favor. Lord and commoner alike, we wept with relief.

The kingdom would survive and thrive. Surely, that was reason enough for happiness. Yet, melancholia clung to me like an irascible child. While I smiled and joked and participated in all the elaborate celebrations, inside, I felt as hollowed out as a wooden trough. Never had I been so troubled, not even when my beloved Jocelyn had announced her betrothal. Worst of all, I could not puzzle out the origins of my misery.

How could I banish my restlessness, this faceless and formless longing, when I remained ignorant of its cause? I imagined myself both Dominican Inquisitor and penitent, the inquisitor asking, "What do you seek, Alaric DeLaMer?" And I, standing mute before myself, vainly groping for an answer.

For the first time, I pondered traveling to other lands or at least to my birthplace of Castle DeLaMer. Perhaps a change of environment would banish my ennui.

Some of my fondest childhood memories involved gathering around the fire in Wendsbury Castle, listening to Lucan read aloud *Topographia Hibernica*. I was simultaneously frightened and fascinated by Ireland, which teemed with evil spirits, hermaphrodites possessing half a face and half a body male and the other half female; yew trees that could raise corpses from the dead so they might become servants of the living, and countless other freakish marvels.

By the time Lucan was a squire and I a page at Wigmore Castle, I'd grown mildly embarrassed by my brother. Lucan's temperament seemed more suited for a philosopher or theologian than a first son. Still, out of respect, I pretended interest during the infrequent times he shared the peculiar ideas rattling around inside his head.

"God can do as He pleases because He is God," Lucan had ruminated more than once. "If He chooses to create a second world just like this one in a totally separate universe, He could do that."

"Other universes?" I'd echoed. "Could that mean other lives we are living, just as we are right here, right now?

"Aye," said Lucan. "But in distant, distant places. And we would never even know."

Scientists taught there were infinite levels of existence between God and man. That those levels were peopled by beings who were more incorporeal than we humans, though far less so than Our Creator. Could that be true? That there were other earths, other universes?

"Peopled by you and me," Lucan mused, "in some form or fashion."

In my current distress, I pulled up those conversations and spent many unproductive hours trying to reason through the concept of me —or some version of me—inhabiting an identical environment existing somewhere beyond the Earth, the seven planets, past the heavens, into other universes. In such worlds, would I be feasting on peacocks and eels in a duplicate banquet hall? Gambling and racing horses in another Smithfield? Inhaling wood smoke from the pollution hanging over London and the stench of the Thames? Or would those other worlds be ever so slightly altered? Totally dissimilar? Perhaps somewhere else, I was, at this very moment, making different choices leading to different outcomes. Would I be a ne'er-do-well second son thwarted in love, or would I be awash in titles and wealth and wedded to a woman whose ambition did not extend beyond treasuring my company?

I wished I could discuss such matters with Lucan, but he'd become a husband and father, fulfilling his duties many miles away.

Eventually, my peculiar mood lightened, and I returned to the old Alaric DeLaMer.

Or someone quite like him.

Part Five

CLARABEL LUCY

AUGHTS

Nine

Looking back from what seems like the vantage point of forever, I liken yours and my relationship to a work of string art, with the necessity of "us" creating the pattern. Thread from the ball of yarn winding around one nail leading to the next and the next until everything connects, with you and me at the heart of it all. Finding *Haunted Castles of Ireland* as a child leading inexorably to Castle by the Sea itself. What seemed like detours—my learning of an arcane language, *Robin of the Rood*, and certainly Ollie Scott's return to create Bella Publishing—all of that led us inexorably to each other.

To you, my eternal beloved.

Camelot Faire was one of those indispensable nails, though I did not realize it until much later. At the time, I attempted to explain away what happened that afternoon in Old Man Pettigrew's riding arena as a brain misfire, a hallucination, or even a time glitch. Later, I minimized it so completely I could pretend it never happened. Which didn't stop the thread from continuing to connect nail after nail after nail on its way to completing our pattern.

Ollie Scott had kept his promise and more. "Bella Publishing will be about escape," he'd explained when laying out his initial vision. "Like eating comfort food or a favorite dessert." And later, after our early successes, "We're selling Hallmark movies on paper. And we all know how much you ladies love Hallmark."

Despite Ollie's frequent tone-deaf, sexist, or simply irritating remarks, he'd proven himself a marketing and organizational genius. I was CEO with all attendant duties. Whenever possible, I employed local talent. Lizzie Trahern-Wahlberg was our scheduler, as well as one of our graphic designers; her laid-back husband Brandon—former Wrench singer, an actual garage band from our teens—had been hired as our official videographer and social media whiz. Bad Boy Max Dockerty, Wrench's one-time guitarist (who'd carefully reglued his instrument after smashing it during performances), authored our motorcycle series under the pseudonym Duke Rocker. *Harley Hellraisers* and *Knights of the Backroads* were fan favorites. Okay, Max didn't actually write anything other than the sex scenes, which were heavily spellchecked and edited but still quite...inventive, and pose for all related covers, but we'd hired an excellent stable of ghostwriters. Susan McDermott penned cozy mysteries solved by a no-nonsense librarian; Old Man Pettigrew provided colorful dialog and knowledge of horses to lend authenticity to our Western lines. Regardless of the series, our books overflowed with love, love, love! And always ended with a happily ever after.

Which brings me to Camelot Faire. Because of Bella Publishing's outsized influence with Ute Creek's town council, we'd been able to combine Hollywood Comes to the Valley with Camelot Faire. Ollie'd scheduled it for Midsummer's Eve rather than the Fourth of July, declaring, "Midsummer's got that Merlin vibe. Kinda mystical and pagan."

Today, Ollie was dressed as Phantom of the Opera in Sunglasses—don't ask—while I wore a vaguely medieval-looking gown. My long brown wig was topped by a circlet which Guinevere, who had probably never existed and, if she had, would never have worn. While we strolled among the tents and entertainment, I bestowed upon all and sundry a dignified royal wave, not the least bit envious of so many seemingly happy couples and families. While it would be too cliched to say I was married to my career, I really didn't have time. Besides, I lived with romance every hour of the frigging day—book covers sporting bicep-bulging hunks in various poses and costumes, some embracing voluptuous heroines, some needing only their own fine selves to entice readers. My days and nights were crammed with editing, creating, and overseeing various sweet or spicy lines or writing my own historical romances. (Not sure you could call what I did *writing*. It was all formulaic—with pirates or highwaymen or regency dandies or civil war soldiers pursuing their hearts' delight against a sketchy backdrop of cannons, swords, famines, revolutions, or drawing room trysts.)

Throughout our stroll, Ollie had remained glued to his Blackberry, barking orders, making sure everything was running smoothly, and "subtly" monitoring the surprise I already knew about.

For whatever reason, Lizzie had thought Guinevere, aka me, needed to be entertained by something called the Rumbler Revue. After eavesdropping on a related conversation, I'd Googled "Rumbler Revue," which appeared to be some sort of vaguely medieval Chippendales troupe. The admittedly easy-on-the-eyes dancers sported lots of black leather—well, not lots since they were nearly naked—and wore Viking helmets because horned helmets are a nineteenth-century fiction.

So, of course.

Because nothing about Bella Publishing made any pretense of being authentic.

Not that I was complaining. Sure, I worked hard, but the money rolled in just the way Ollie'd promised. And, as much I hated to admit it, I'd inherited Dottie's "ham" genes. I enjoyed playing dress-up. At conventions and book signings, I assumed the persona of whatever pseudonymous author we were promoting at the time. During the mystery dinner theatre productions we regularly held at the (fully renovated) Duchess, I might be Diabolical Blackmailer, Murder Victim, Psychopathic Killer, or Sassy Suspect.

Like playing dress up with way better costumes.

I was living the dream.

Yet, today, something seemed off. The dazzling sky reminded me of the Irish Sea. Would it be as blue in person as in my *Haunted Castles of Ireland* painting? Once I actually visited Castle by the Sea, would I be disappointed? Would I wander through its rambling rooms, wringing my hands and lamenting à la J. Alfred Prufrock, *"That is not what I meant at all; That is not it, at all."*

Stop it. This is everything you've imagined, visualized, and yearned for.

Ollie had set up a book signing for *Robin of the Rood,* which he insisted on calling *Roger and his Rug.* He'd marketed *Robin* as a collector's item in order to triple the price. Unsurprisingly, we sold out. Not that anyone would actually read *Robin of the Rood*, which was a relief, actually. Over the last five years, I'd learned a lot about the craft of writing. Dear God, what had I been thinking?

After completing the signing, I headed for Old Man Pettigrew's riding arena, and my surprise.

Which, as it turned out, had nothing to do with half-naked men wearing horned helmets.

When I first saw the knight kneeling in the center of the arena, I was seated under a canopy stamped with Bella Publishing's logo. I initially assumed the knight was part of the Rumbler Revue's opening act, but he was no Chippendale-style dancer. That much I grasped before an impenetrable fog abruptly erased the scene, obliterating him and his surroundings.

I'd always assumed if I were caught up in a paranormal encounter, I'd automatically react—breaking out in goosebumps, gasping, screaming, or maybe even fleeing in terror. However, I'd entered this foreign country so casually—a kneeling knight where he did not belong; a weather anomaly—the extraordinary felt ordinary.

As sometimes happened, I found myself separated—me and not me—sitting upon a fake throne while simultaneously hovering above the crowd, the knight, and the arena before that grey woolen blanket had been tossed over it all.

What is happening? What does this mean?

The me upon the makeshift dais groped to fashion a logical explanation. Ollie had played some sort of trick; he'd projected a clever hologram onto the field and spiked my water bottle with shrooms. But this me, still tethered to the Earth, didn't feel any different, not really.

Yet I found myself thinking of Limbo, a concept I'd discarded with my childhood, wherein unbaptized infants drifted through an endlessly grey landscape located somewhere between heaven and hell.

My vision darkened. I wouldn't say I felt panicked exactly; more concerned. Why was I thinking about heaven and hell? And Limbo, with all those wandering babies? Had I suffered a heart attack? When the two *me*s had separated, was that a sign I'd died and shed my physical body?

I squeezed the arms of my makeshift throne, half expecting my fingers to pass right through. No, solid wood. At that moment, the hovering me slipped effortlessly back into my body.

Here I was then, Clarabel Lucy, obviously alive and caught up in...something.

The way a kitten chases a ball of yarn to see where it ends, maybe I needed to do the same. Play this through to its conclusion. Leaning forward, I stared into the fog. "Where are you?" I whispered. "Show yourself. Let me see you."

As if by my command, the fog disappeared. I was aware of an unusual stillness, reminiscent of those moments before sunrise when the earth has yet to stir itself awake.

There he was again, my knight. He appeared frozen in place—one iron-clad knee on the ground, one leg bent, bare head lowered as if in obeisance. The figure of a cross, at least three feet in height, was planted in the earth before him.

Abruptly, the rational, reasoning part of my brain clicked off. My mind, always whirling, jumbling with thoughts and plots and a million other things, quieted. My total concentration was laser-focused on the knight, on his blue surcoat that was forked in the front to expose the poleyn protecting his exposed knee; on the chausses covering his leg; on the spur strapped upon his ankle. I noticed that his scabbard, which was attached to his waist by a leather belt, was missing its weapon.

I then realized the cross planted in the ground was actually a broadsword. An entire class's *raison d'etre* embodied in forty inches of tempered steel—destroyer of worlds; protector of the Church. Born to serve both the Christian God and the God of War.

"Real!" I breathed, thrilled by the miracle unfolding before me. For

some inexplicable reason, I'd been granted this glimpse into an important moment: a medieval warrior preparing himself for battle in the
manner of all such warriors—by beseeching God to bless his cause. I
understood his thoughts as clearly as though I were in his head,
hearing them as my own. Victory, should God so will it. And if He did
not, at least, a valiant death. And because the knight had already been
granted absolution by his battlefield confessor, he prayed for immediate entrance into heaven.

Silently, I addressed the knight. *What year? What battle? Who are you?*
And...

Look at me. Let me see you.

The knight immediately raised his head. His hair, which was long
and tousled from where it had been freed from its coif and cap,
partially hid his face. Until he raised his head to meet my gaze.

My breath caught.

I wouldn't describe the knight as "handsome," an adjective so over-
worked as to be meaningless. Strong. Compelling. Bold. Those were
the words that popped up in my mental thesaurus. Powerful. Charis-
matic. Dangerous.

The knight rose from his kneeling position to his full, formidable
height.

*Blue surcoat with a sable bear rampant. I know that bear. I've seen it before.
But where?* My vaunted memory appeared to have failed me.

With his mail-clad legs planted firmly apart, the knight reminded
me of a giant oak, centuries rooted to the earth. His huge fists, free of
the mittens attached to his hauberk, were balled at his sides. And his
gaze? All that power, that concentration, was directed at me.

The air thickened; a pungently sweet odor invaded my nostrils. I
imagined a cosmic shift—tectonic plates smashing against each other,
causing earthquakes and volcanoes to spew fire heavenward. The hairs
on the back of my neck stood on end, the way they did when lightning
storms blew into our valley.

Without warning, an electrical current pulsed between us. Impossibly powerful, like the arc flashes that sometimes occur between
power lines, flashes capable of plunging entire cities into darkness.

Cosmic circuits blown; boundaries melting. I sensed it, felt it as if the knight and I had been ineluctably fused together. That there was no separating where he ended and I began.

That I, that other Clarabel Lucy, had ceased to exist.

A sudden blare over the loudspeakers startled me back to a midsummer afternoon, where the nine beefy beauties who comprised the Rumbler Revue performed the most "unique" dance routine I'd witnessed in my three decades on the planet.

From a great distance, I watched. I was aware of the roar of the crowd. I could even contemplate the high-energy hunks jumping around in some sort of synchronized rhythm, pumping up the crowd.

Real and yet not. My gaze drifted behind them to the spot where my knight had stood.

"What d'ya think, Guinevere?" Ollie said in my ear. "How d'ya like your King Arthur? This is all being filmed, so smile!"

I forced myself to refocus. Fake Arthur, the only dancer who wore a crown, certainly had lots of tanned, muscular, and well-oiled body parts on display.

"Very nice," I managed, which was true. And, yeah, there might not be anything even vaguely medieval about Arthur, but he...they...obviously worked out. A lot.

With the start of Nine Inch Nails' "Closer," the troupe jerked off their black leather pants in one expertly synchronized motion to continue their routine attired in a mesh metal "man pouch," combat boots... and nothing else.

The crowd, at least the female portion, went wild, particularly after the dancers gyrated through an open gate to mix among them. King Arthur strutted and writhed his way up the steps to the dais where I sat, a seductive smile on his perfectly proportioned face.

My, Arthur's teeth are white! And the rest of him? A queen always maintained her dignity, and in real life, this Guinevere would have found such antics laughable.

Yeah, but when Arthur began a kind of standing lap dance with his man pouch pretty much at eye level, what else could a queen do but sit back and enjoy the view?

∽

I said goodbye to Arthur, aka Jimmy, and the other members of the Rumbler Revue at their van. Jimmy, a happily married father of twins who'd recently started his own custom furniture business, leaned in to kiss my cheek. "I hope you find your Arthur someday, lovely Guinevere," he said before disappearing inside.

Even as I waved goodbye, my thoughts careened away, as if *they* were the illusion and my knight the reality.

It was then my photographic memory finally provided the delayed response to that *sable bear rampant* upon my knight's surcoat. I remembered where I'd seen it before—on the coat of arms belonging to the DeLaMers, the family who had inhabited Castle by the Sea for eight hundred years.

Part Six

ALARIC DELAMER

1314

Ten

What does it do to a man's soul when his every movement, decision, and opinion is mocked? Our King Edward's barons nipped his heels like pesky Corgis, intent on herding him in their direction, regardless of where he planned to go. For seven years, no matter His Grace's choice, it was the wrong one. He spent too much, too unwisely, too lavishly on frivolous pursuits; not enough on building and defenses, nay, too profligately on everything. He was too haughty, too friendly, too indifferent to his queen, too obsessed with her and his first-born son, our prince. Whatever his foreign policy, it was flawed. When Edward did obey his lords' counsel, they groused he did so gracelessly or switched their opinion the moment he agreed. I, more observer than an insider, was reminded of owls who swivel their heads around until their necks break.

I was happy to spend most of my days tucked away in a remote part of Shropshire with my bride, Katrin. A simple country life I'd once despised now filled me with contentment.

Because Edward Caernarvon did not roll in war the way a dog rolls in shite, his lords labeled him a coward. A monstrous charge for any man, but particularly a king who often displayed personal courage, not to mention restraint. Had Edward been the reprobate his lords claimed, he'd have chucked England's laws and ordered all those who'd participated in the murder of his Piers to be divested of their own heads and left to rot on some godforsaken hill.

Edward Caernarvon had proven himself to be the better man, for all the credit it won him.

~

June 1314: We, England's army, trooped north.

Our destination: Stirling Castle.

Our enemy: Robert the Bruce.

Stirling Castle, the key to Scotland, would be forfeited on Midsummer Day if we did not appear to claim it. Therefore, we marched. The royal arms of England, with its trio of snarling gold lions, played hide-and-seek through the interminable dust raised by two thousand men-at-arms, sixteen-thousand foot soldiers, and a supply train of two hundred wagons, many gilded and painted and carrying luxuries deemed necessary by the wealthiest lords. When we camped, our foot soldiers, who were forced to fast walk through the piss and shite of thousands of animals, collapsed beside the road, too exhausted even to eat. After our servants set up our tents, we, the privileged, dined off gold and silver plates, lounged upon pillows and carpets serenaded by the minstrels brought along for entertainment, told war stories, and strategized various ways to crush our enemy.

I will clarify that. Despite the DeLaMer name, my older brother's frugality meant we seldom participated in such activities. Weather permitting, Lucan and I preferred to roll our mantles around us and sleep in the open. This was the longest stretch we'd spent together since our shared time at Wigmore Castle, and I found I enjoyed Lucan's company.

My brother's observations were concise and insightful. Lucan had never been more than an indifferent fighter, but Wendsbury Castle was close to one of James Lackford's Shropshire holdings, and the old knight was like an Oxford master intent on improving the minds of his pupils. Lucan might be moving his mouth, but the wisdom behind it was Lackford's.

Nothing he said eased my mind.

"Most of the Scots are related to each other." Lucan mused one even. "They've grown up together, fight together, drill together even during peacetime, and obey not some strange commander but their individual lord. They are like a large family. A large, deadly family."

I stared heavenward, contemplating stars just blinking awake. The Scots were a motley bunch—reivers haunting the borderlands harassing whomever they pleased; vagabonds and brigands; wretches swathed in little better than rags. Still, their martial prowess could not be dismissed. Since it took great skill to be proficient with a longbow, our archers were deadly, but our regular soldiers, who were only obligated to serve forty days before returning to their occupations, were not.

Throughout our long march, Bruce's scouts had shadowed us like wolves. Surely, the mere sight of our force, stretching twenty miles along the old Roman road, must turn their bowels to water. Sheer numbers alone guaranteed us victory.

Lucan spoke again. "I would prefer a quiet life surrounded by books." He did not add "to having my brains bashed out on a summer's day," though that was clearly his meaning. Feeling an unexpected nostalgia for those nights he'd read us *Topographia Hibernica,* I shifted my position on the merciless earth to better study him. Where my eyes were more a dark grey, or so I'd been told, his were the deepest brown. Had a sadness taken up residence in their depths, or was that my imagination? Lucan had inherited our mother's fair coloring and slender build, his muscles more like those of a runner. Often, our father mocked him for being the "runt of the litter." True enough, I suppose, for by the time I was fully grown, I towered a head over both my brother and our sire.

Still, with two sons, 'twas a mighty small litter about which our father complained.

"I crave quiet," my brother blurted. I remembered his musings about alternate universes, his propensity for contemplations I was too dense to comprehend.

"You've chosen the wrong profession, then."

Our present world consisted of row upon noisy row of steel—thousands of human tributaries flowing inexorably toward Stirling Castle. At home, my brother had sired an actual litter of three girls and two boys.

All in all, Lucan DeLaMer had a better chance of changing moonlight into moonstones than finding tranquility.

~

Midsummer's Eve: the night before the battle. Bonfires, like stars fallen to earth, dotted the hills around Stirling Castle, which sprawled in the distance like an indolent giant. This shortest night of the year, mischief was afoot, including dragons who prowled the countryside poisoning wells and springs. Last Midsummer—Katrin's and my first as husband and wife—we'd watched similar fires from the roof of our keep. My arm had been around her, her head nestled against my chest, the voices of revelers drifting to us across our fields.

"Magical," Katrin had murmured. My wife's placid temperament reminded me of the ocean, deep and mysterious and endless. Unlike my past dalliances, which had been fast and wild and shallow. Even Jocelyn, though she would ever occupy a place in my heart.

"Magic," I'd echoed."Of the best kind."

After which she'd given me a birthday kiss, for it was my thirty-third birthday.

Tonight, that seemed like a memory snatched from a stranger.

We had set up camp on the carse between Pelstream and Bannockburn. The Burn of Bannock, while not particularly wide, was deep and swift running. Since its embankments were steep, King Edward had earlier ordered soldiers to tear down houses from a nearby deserted village and utilize the scavenged wood to construct a bridge. We were then supposed to cross the Bannock or, at least, the tents and wagons meant to service us lords. The result: two different encampments with knights on one side, while the bulk of the army was jammed together on the opposite, which was largely peatland and too boggy even for a campfire.

Beside me, Lucan shifted. Around us, the tents of our fellow knights had been set up, allowing King Edward and all the rest to relax in their usual luxury. I hoped Edward's war council, in particular James Lackford, was strategizing about tomorrow's battle. We'd had a taste of calamity with an earlier skirmish in which one of our knights had been killed by Robert Bruce; I did not wish to consume an entire meal.

Shouting, quarreling, and snatches of conversation drifted from the soldiers' encampment. King Edward had insisted foot soldiers were crucial in a win against Robert the Bruce because Scotland's terrain was better suited to fighting on foot than mounted. If that were so, why were they clustered behind our supply wagons, bedded down in a boggy morass without campfires for warmth or cooking or to keep swarms of mosquitos at bay? Where a man could wander off in the dark and drown in the River Bannock?

Malfeasance, I thought. How were exhausted, hungry men supposed to rise on the morrow in top fighting form?

I stared up at an impossibly black sky. Not a star to be seen. Perhaps they really had tumbled to Earth and come to rest upon the hills.

"None of this makes sense," I said aloud. Immediately, I regretted speaking. Doubt weakened one's confidence, potentially tipping the scales from victory to disaster. I was relieved when Lucan did not respond. He must already be asleep.

Eventually, I, too, drowsed, though I experienced the oddest notion—that I might already be dead, that I was hovering between two worlds with a soul that had not quite slipped free of its body.

Will I be killed on the morrow? I wondered sleepily.

I thought about Katrin, barely eighteen and so delicate I sometimes felt like a devil for touching her. Would my wife soon become a widow?

"Have you ever thought," came Lucan's voice, startling me from my dream state, "that Bruce has had months to pick the landscape on which he would fight? Have we been drawn into a trap?"

I remembered the uncertain soil, churned into muck by thousands of hooves and boots and wagon wheels; the two streams on either side of the carse that could theoretically trap us with no real way out. However, Lucan and I, all of us, had trained for war since childhood.

We were part of the finest fighting force in Christendom. That would —must—make the difference.

After making the sign of the cross, I groped for my brother's hand in the dark and curled his fingers around mine. "You will do the DeLaMer name proud tomorrow," I whispered.

Silence.

A deep inhale, almost a sigh.

"We both will," said Lucan, with a final squeeze of my hand.

Then he turned on his side, away from me, and pretended to sleep.

We had entered hell without dying. The smoke from last night's bonfires drifted overhead like confused souls that could not possibly have been loosed from bodies that mere moments before had been safely encased in steel.

Yet they had been.

Dead. Dead. Dead.

We were slaughtered like animals in an abattoir. Trapped between the Pelstream and the Bannock, as I'd worried. Because we could neither fight nor flee, our superior numbers ensured our annihilation. The Scots, with their circular schiltrons shaped like giant hedgehogs, were impossible to puncture. Our destriers balked at being speared in the breast or gutted by those pikemen who knelt and angled their spears so they could penetrate any exposed belly. The pikemen's goal was to dispatch our mounts, for once we knights toppled to the ground, we were easily finished off.

While our panicked mounts reared and kicked and unsuccessfully tried to avoid the Scots' deadly spear tips, the knights behind us, blind to our plight, pushed forward. In the back of those knights, our foot soldiers also pushed. The result? Our second line of cavalry pushed into the first. Pushed and pushed until we were pressed closer together than pages in a bestiary. Schiltrons in front; Pelstream to our left; Bannockburn to our right; our own soldiers behind. Nowhere to go; no way to escape.

After each cavalry charge, the Scots took a few steps forward within their formation, pushing us farther back into our advancing line. When our archers loosed their arrows, they ended up killing more of us than the enemy. Sometimes, I'd not room to wield my weapons or my mount to move. Still, I fought like a man possessed. I'd lost sight of Lucan during the first charge, and if he hadn't survived... By the rood, I couldn't allow my father to lose both his sons.

Though there were other fathers that day who did.

By noon, the battle, which had begun at dawn, was a rout. I do not blame our king. If one man could have changed the outcome by sheer force of will, it would have been Edward Caernarvon. His Grace fought with superhuman courage, always in the thick of the press, wielding sword and mace with the strength of a dozen. When his first destrier was killed beneath him, Edward commandeered a second and plunged back into the butchery.

Only after the battle was truly lost, only after so many of us had been killed we could cross much of the Bannock using corpses as our footbridge, did Edward allow himself to be led from the field. He had no choice. The only thing worse than this killing field would have been a dead or captured king.

In the end, hundreds of our men-at-arms were slaughtered and more than ten-thousand regular soldiers. Two enemy knights were lost, along with pitifully few common men. Only after Robert the Bruce knew the battle was won did he allow his men to capture and hold knights for ransom. Before that, he ordered us killed—as if we were of no more consequence than footmen.

I was not captured, though I would have made a lucrative prize since Lucan had indeed perished in the first charge. Which left me, Alaric DeLaMer, heir to the vast DeLaMer holdings.

After the Battle of Bannockburn, nothing was the same. 'Twas not only Lucan DeLaMer who lost his life.

Alaric DeLaMer died that day as well.

Part Seven

CLARABEL LUCY

2015+

Eleven

If I told you I was relaxing on a wrought iron veranda located on the third floor of a quaint hotel in Napoli, you'd no doubt assume I was still living the dream. While I was captivated by Italy, I was even more captivated by the Italian men—compact and trim and looking like they spent most of their time running around a soccer field. Oh, that olive skin and dark hair! Those eyes! I'd found a new stereotype to rhapsodize over in yet another series. How about *Amore in Roma?*

No, not thinking about work.

This was the first non-business-related vacation I'd taken since founding Bella Publishing. I wasn't about to ruin it.

If money was the sole yardstick, Bella Publishing remained phenomenally successful, with profits rising as steeply, as inexorably as Vail Mountain, near the town of Vail, where we'd recently purchased a second home/satellite office.

Where had it all gone wrong? was a question I asked myself whenever I could slow my world long enough to carve out a moment of reflection. I would re-shuffle my past the way one does a deck of cards, endlessly laying out events that had led to my current crisis of the soul. At thirty-four, I, as Bella Publishing's #girlboss CEO, had been written up in countless articles and magazines and interviewed on regional and national television. I'd even appeared via satellite on "Dublin in the Morning" when our Lily o' the Shillelagh series had topped a *Dublin Times* poll as the most popular romantic series. Its male host, who possessed the most arresting brogue, had promised that should I ever travel to Ireland—and I simply *must*—he would personally escort me to Castle by the Sea. *"I do know Sir Lucan. Quite an interesting bloke."*

Not Ireland, but Italy, which was even more enchanting than I could have imagined.

Sipping a *Campari,* I enjoyed the exotic—at least to me—view. The apartments across the way all possessed balconies adorned with colorful potted plants and floor-to-ceiling shutters sporting primary colors. My room overlooked a side street opening onto a teeming piazza where locals strolled arm-in-arm, shopkeepers lounged in door-ways, and *camerieri* hovered near outdoor eating areas adorned with fancy tablecloths. Everything was so vibrant and unrestrained that I was soon lost in the rhythm of it.

Even the graffiti was colorful.

We'd been in Napoli for nearly a week, with day trips to sites like Pompeii and Herculaneum provided by Seraphina, our relentlessly professional tour guide. Ollie remained rudely unimpressed through-out, continually complaining about the *impossibility* of conducting busi-ness from five thousand miles away.

To which I replied, "Not talking shop. Don't even bother."

"I can't wait to get to Capri," he said after yet another "important" phone call had been dropped. "If the cell phone service doesn't improve, I'm gonna charter a private plane right back to the good old US of A."

I suspect Ollie, with his talk of private planes and multimillion-dollar deals, was trying to impress our tour guide. Seraphina was a pretty, petite blonde who wore her hair pulled back in a casual knot. Her dress was simultaneously sexy, elegant, and casual in a way that appeared to be endemic to both Italian women and men. Throughout, she'd remained immune to Ollie's attempts at flirting. Until she over-heard a conversation in which he mentioned one of Bella Publishing's perennial favorites, *Harley Hellraisers.*

"*Che bella sorpresa!*" she cried, grabbing my arm. "You know the Duke Rocker? He is one of your authors?"

Oh, no. Another Bad Boy Max Dockerty fan. "He is," I replied reluctantly. While I didn't even want to utter the words "Bella Publishing," Seraphina was so excited I couldn't be rude.

"I've read every one of Duke Rocker's books," she gushed. "He is a very wicked man, is he not?" Dimpled smile.

When I told Max, aka Duke Rocker, about his pretty Italian fan, he would shuck his Bad Boy persona and grin like a schoolboy. "If you ever visit America, I will personally introduce you to our real Harley Hellraiser," I said, never imagining the repercussions of that promise.

After that, Ollie, Seraphina, and I were off to Capri.

Where I, Clarabel Lucy, fell in love.

Ollie and I were seated inside a lovely, glittering white restaurant plastered to a cliff overlooking the Tyrrhenian Sea. Halfway through lunch, he excused himself to "take an L.A. call," leaving me to imagine Neptune and his horses rising out of its watery depths.

"*Mi scusi, signorina.*"

I was dragged back to reality by a lilting voice, which immediately turned my insides to mush. Looking up, I gazed into the most meltingly beautiful brown eyes I'd ever seen.

His name was Raphael Accardi.

Il mio Raffaello.

Raphael was blessed with gorgeous coffee-cream-colored skin, close-cropped black hair, and an irresistibly lissome physique. His effortlessly stylish outfit was topped by a lightly patterned summer scarf, which no ordinary American male would wear and which looked fabulous on him. And that voice! After Ollie returned and they conversed, I absorbed their interplay, mesmerized by the way Raphael gestured with his artistic hands topped by slender fingers; the way those smiling eyes with their impossibly long lashes kept cutting back to me.

For the first time in years, I thought of my Robin of the Rood, and while Raphael was dark where Robin had been light, they were both gentle, poetic, and possessed of sensitive natures. (All of this I determined by spending a few minutes in the presence of Raphael, but the heart knows.) He was a professor at Sapienza Università di Roma, and beyond his charming but uncertain English and my non-existent Italian, we were content to find other ways of communication.

By the time Seraphina announced we were bound for Rome, there was no question Raphael would accompany us.

When I gazed at my Raphael, I didn't see the grandeur of Imperial Rome but of the Renaissance with its sensitive painters and poets like Dante, who'd pledged his eternal love to Beatrice after only two meetings.

That was Raphael. Passionate. Intense. His whispered endearments were far sexier than anything uttered by my fictional heroes, his voice as much a caress as those skilled, graceful hands.

When our official tour ended, I informed Ollie I wasn't ready to return to the U.S. He cocked his head, studying me. "What about you and I drive to Milan? Perfect time for some new suits. And top-notch jewelry. I'll buy you a necklace with your birthstone. Sapphires. And diamonds, too. "

When I declined, Ollie licked his lips, frowned, smirked, and threw in a few new facial expressions. "Look, I can only change our flight so many times. Bottom line, we've got a business to run, and I can't do that over Skype." He yammered on about juggling deals for a limited TV series, a podcast focusing on the "magic of love," revamping our YouTube channel, blah-blah...influencers...focus groups...expanding our footprint to create a children's series similar to *Diary of a Wimpy Kid*...

The only thing I cared about was that I had another week with Raphael. Since he shared his small apartment with his younger sister and her daughter, we holed up in my boutique hotel.

Look, I know all about vacation flings. I realize being plunked down in a dazzling Mediterranean environment, fairly screaming of love and enchantment, surrounded by ruins in turn romantic and grandiloquent, is hardly a basis for lasting relationships. I wasn't going to rent a villa on the Amalfi coast and ask Raphael to move in with me.

But I was captivated by the less hectic pace of life even in a city of millions, the sweetness of endearments I did not understand, the rightness of falling asleep in Raphael's arms.

Ollie returned from his side jaunt with three bespoke suits, an exquisite sapphire and diamond necklace, and an attitude. We were at one of those lovely outdoor cafes where you sit and chat and people-watch long into the night. Raphael had gone into the tiny *ristorante* while I finished my *cacio e pepe* to see whether he could purchase one of those heavenly citrus slushies I'd inhaled in Capri and Sorrento.

"We gotta wind this up," Ollie said, running his fingers along the stem of his wine glass. Under the guise of tasting all the wines with unpronounceable names, he'd been imbibing more than usual. "We're way behind, and the launch of our "Stetsons and Chaps" series screams disaster..."

Stetsons and Chaps? What was that? Oh yeah, our sweet cowboy line set on a Colorado Dude Ranch where the only steamy thing was the fog rising from the pond near the sprawling main log cabin; where innocent gals with names like Amy, Emily, and Sarah with sunshiny hair and cornflower blue eyes fell in love with hunky but shy wranglers called Lash or Col or Rawhide...No, Rawhide made his sex-on-a-stallion appearance in our "Heat on the High Plains" series, which was way more heat than sweet. Another template I'd written on autopilot—

While Ollie continued yammering, I studied him in the buttery light cast from nearby wall sconces and café windows. Really studied him. Why had he chosen a hairstyle that made him look like a rooster? Had he done something to his nose? Started waxing his forearms? *Aren't we too young for botox?*

Contemplating my childhood friend, my *former* friend, I felt something shift inside me. I was grateful to Ollie, I was. His dreams had turned out to be so much bigger than mine. Maybe I hadn't even had dreams, more like ill-formed concepts. But surrounded by the enticing aromas of a summer evening in Roma, where conversations rose and fell around us like the breath of the city, and with the touch of my lover still warm on my skin, I wondered whether *my* dream might consist of finding my heart mate and loving him into eternity...

"Are you paying attention, C.L.? Why do you have that ridiculous expression on your face?"

"When did you become my warden?" I wanted to retort. Instead, I shrugged and craned my head for a glimpse of Raphael, who appeared to be having a spirited conversation with the cameriera stationed behind a glass display case.

Is this my moment of reckoning? I wondered. To face truths I'd chosen to ignore? I didn't like the way I'd fallen into the trap of believing you can never be too rich or too thin or have too many hair extensions or designer duds. I didn't like the way wealth could obliterate one's conscience, causing you to rationalize or ignore things that shouldn't be rationalized or ignored. I didn't like the way Ollie had undermined Bella Publishing's original employees, who'd been the driving force behind our early success. I didn't like the way he'd staffed Bella Publishing II—hiring *wunderkinds* with Ivy League pedigrees who spouted mindless jargon and had less business savvy than Blix the Wonder Horse. I didn't trust Ollie's moral compass, and hiring the best accountants, attorneys, and internal and external auditors was more rationalization than solution.

Bottom line, while the public image of Clarabel Lucy might be a figure of envy, the actual Clarabel Lucy was miserable.

Leaning back in my chair, I folded my arms. "I'm done," I blurted, holding his gaze. "I quit. Buy me out. Don't buy me out. I don't care. My heart isn't in this anymore, and I can't do a good job for anyone when I'm only going through the motions."

Ollie's face paled beneath its vacation tan; his eyes narrowed before he arranged his features in a neutral expression.

"I want to live. To fall in love." I leaned forward, narrowing the gap between us, my body language imploring. "To enjoy my actual life rather than some fantasy. *Real* memories, Ollie, not silly plots and fake romances with perfect people who don't act like human beings—"

"You can't just—"

At that moment, Raphael returned. *"Cara mia,"* he murmured, kissing the top of my head before presenting me with my slushie.

I smiled up at him. *"Grazie."* In six months, while Raphael and I were tucked away in my yet imaginary villa, I'd be speaking Italian like a native.

For the rest of the meal, I was so caught up in Raphael's attention, his flashing eyes, and caressing voice that I nearly forgot all about Ollie. He could frown at us over the rim of his wine glass all he liked.

Clarabel Lucy was beginning a new chapter in her life.

Get over it.

Apparently, I was the one who would have to get over it. The following morning Ollie called me into his spacious suite, which was plastered with murals of reclining gods, goddesses and nymphs framed by Doric columns and lots of urns.

Snatching a wad of credit card statements off a nearby desk, he waved it in my face.

"You need to know the truth, C.L."

As my business partner cut out my heart and fed it back to me piece by bleeding piece, I may have disassociated. My gaze drifted to the picture window behind Ollie's desk, which displayed an impressive view of ruins flanked by cypress trees, straight as a formation of legionaries.

"The cypress is a symbol of death," Raphael had once explained. "And the underworld also."

Since Rome was a city of ruins and cypresses, I assured myself this wasn't a bad omen. Not at all. The truth, it turned out, was much worse: the strangulation of my dream in its bloody, fucking cradle. Ollie had paid Raphael Accardi an impressive sum of money through Premium Escort Services to act as my gigolo. "Seraphina arranged everything," he concluded dramatically. "I just wanted your vacation to be memorable. But then it got out of hand. You know how it is when people get greedy."

Later, when I confronted Raphael, he denied everything. He appeared shocked and extremely upset by my allegations.

"Bella! Bella!" he cried, literally tearing at his hair. "*Si fermi, per favore*! Stop! How can you accuse me of such crimes?"

"*Mio bellissimo amore*," he kept repeating as if I would be charmed by what I'd naively labeled the language of love but was actually one of betrayal.

"Of course, you're upset," I said. "You're losing a great gig."

Or maybe I meant to say it. Maybe I called him a gigolo. Maybe not. I'd become what is referred to as an unreliable narrator. I was too devastated, too numb to understand much of anything. Just reacting. Determined to bury the pain, the betrayal as quickly, as efficiently, as completely as possible.

The following morning, we flew back to Denver.

Somewhere over the Atlantic, Ollie turned to me, removed his noise-canceling headphones, and said, "You do know the woman living with Raphael wasn't his sister, don't you?"

I stared at him blankly. Until that, too, sank in. Married? Which would also mean a daughter.

Of course.

"Sorry, C.L.," Ollie said before replacing his headphones.

He didn't sound sorry at all.

Twelve

H ere I was, two years after Raphael Accardi—who I never, ever thought of—orchestrating Bella Publishing's Hearts Afire conference celebrating twelve *fantabulous* years of romance!

And...at Castle by the Sea!

As Lord Lucan DeLaMer escorted Ollie and me on a private tour, I felt positively giddy. Finally, finally, I was *here* and conversing with a member of a family I felt invested in—if only through research for a disaster best forgotten containing a cartoon villain named Alaric the Beast and a childhood picture book currently on my bedside table in the Cavalier Suite located... somewhere in this magnificent warren.

Castle by the Sea!

Sir Lucan—"Do please call me Lucan"—was a gracious host. His accent conjured images of debating Plato in the original Greek, scurrying beneath gothic archways wearing a black academic gown and rowing on the River Thames as a member of some exclusive boat club, though physically, Lucan was built more like Old Man Pettigrew's blacksmith.

In the same way our host led us from room to ancient room, I had the strangest feeling *I* was being led. Having watched videos of Castle by the Sea about a thousand times, I attributed the feeling to the fact that so much was familiar—wall tapestries, crossed broadswords, suits of armor, priceless vases, and other curios, not to mention furniture one could point to and say, "This sideboard was made during the reign of the Virgin Queen;" "That salon sofa from when Britannia ruled the waves."

Ollie, who was expecting a text from FunTown Entertainment concerning a meeting about the stupidest project ever, barely glanced away from his phone screen.

When Lucan discovered my interest in Bannockburn, he lingered on the telling, much to my delight. "Midsummer's Eve, 1314, was the first skirmish," he said while standing before a suit of armor of the same period. "The following day, the slaughter." Upon adding, "And in a week, it will be June 23," I felt a sudden prickling in the back of my neck. I'd never connected the dates, not only between our pending conference and Bannockburn but with Camelot Faire. All three were associated with Midsummer's Eve.

"The old people referred to Midsummer's Eve as *"Oidhche Fhéil Eoin,"* Lucan continued, his gaze fixed on me. "Since my family links it to the tragedy of Bannockburn, I've always considered the day one of somber reflection. As you may know, my namesake, Lucan, rode out. Only his younger brother, who became the DeLaMer heir that terrible day, returned."

Mesmerized by my host and our surroundings, I wondered what it would be like to trace one's Irish-related lineage back to the time of Bad King John. To inhabit a place where past and present blended, where surely current Lucan sometimes wondered what century, what DeLaMer he was. Where family stories ended and reality began.

I am a medieval mistress, slippers whispering across rushes I'm constantly changing because, you know, hygiene, ordering servants and complaining because my particular DeLaMer has gone off hawking without me. Or I am lighting votive candles in our private chapel, beseeching God to safely return William, Alaric, or Lucan—the most common given names—from the latest uprising.

In the largest of the great halls—I'd lost count of how many— DeLaMar banners hung from walls and overhead rafters, all bearing the *sable bear rampant.* I had seen that bear on the surcoat of the knight

I'd long ago convinced myself didn't exist. And hanging above the drawbridge in the *Haunted Castles of Ireland* painting.

"Please tell me about the Knight and his Lady," I blurted. "I've been enamored of them since I was a little girl. Have you seen them, the ghosts?"

"Many times," Lucan said it so casually, reinforcing the feeling I'd stepped over some invisible line from *this* life to an entire other universe.

Ollie tore himself away from texting long enough to survey the oak-timbered hall. "I don't believe in any of that silliness." He frowned as if apparitions might be gazing down from a nearby minstrels' gallery simply to irritate him.

"What do they look like?" I asked, ignoring my partner. "Are they always the same ghosts? Do they try to communicate?"

"The Knight appears more focused on his Lady. Generally, she stands off to his side, watching him. A handsome couple they make."

Ollie rearranged his features in faux interest. "Creepy."

"Romantic," I countered. Perhaps Bella Publishing should commission a series of paranormal romances? Time travels? "Do they frighten you?"

"Following the first time, I experienced rather a shiver. But it always happens so naturally. They're just...there, as they've been for centuries. It's part of our family lore. Whenever I glimpse them, I say a prayer and wish them well. After all, they have as much right to enjoy Castle by the Sea as do we."

We passed from the great hall into a portrait gallery. "Then, there are the voices," continued Lucan, while we—at least I—surveyed centuries of DeLaMers. "Disembodied laughter, whispered voices, singing. Always the same melody. Perhaps a lullaby, rather plaintive."

I imagined my medieval matriarch seated at the head of a massive dining table, studying the faces of her husband and sons and relatives before they rode off to battle. Had she stifled a premonition of disaster, wept upon their departure, and after receiving word of their slaughter gone mad? Was she the one Lucan hears, forever wandering the castle singing crazy tunes?

Finally, Lucan guided us to the oldest part of the residence, which was at the bottom of a frighteningly narrow staircase opening onto the DeLaMer museum.

With an annoyed cluck, Lucan crossed to an arched stone opening above which was positioned a "Do Not Enter" sign. "Bloody docents never remember to keep this cordoned off," he muttered, repositioning two stanchions linked by a velvet rope across the entrance.

Then to us: "That passageway leads to the original castle, which is actually a ruin and dangerous to explore. Putting up the 'Do Not Enter' sign simply causes the curious to do the opposite. Hence, the barrier."

I peered inside the passageway. Its darkness, impenetrable as a black hole, drew me closer. I imagined it leading down to dank, fetid-smelling dungeons. Or an entire other world?

After Ollie complained the cell service was shit and we needed to wind this up, Lucan addressed me. "Perhaps later this afternoon, I might show you the view from the roof of our keep."

Anxious to learn what further secrets Castle by the Sea might reveal, I happily agreed.

∽

"I've been meaning to ask, have we met before?"

From our position on the castle parapet, Lucan and I gazed out at the expanse of water that had so captivated me in *Haunted Castles of Ireland*.

"I must have been one of those faces." I sensed my host was genuinely puzzled rather than being flirtatious. While our previous interactions had been via phone and email, he would have investigated Bella Publishing during rental negotiations for our Hearts Afire Conference. No way to miss images of yours truly.

"It's been nagging at me; why your face is so familiar."

Sensing my reluctance to pursue my faux celebrity status, Lucan directed my attention to our left. "Over here is our maze." Many feet below, a rectangular labyrinth had been created from meticulously trimmed and shaped yew trees. "Infamous or famous, depending on your point of view."

After I followed his pointing finger, he continued. "Family legend recounts people entering the maze and simply disappearing." He raised his arms and waggled his fingers. "Poof! Never to be heard from again."

I wondered whether Lucan had minored in Theatre at whatever fancy-pants university he'd attended. "It reminds me of the maze in *The Shining.*"

Note to self: Never explore the DeLaMer maze.

"I've glimpsed the Knight and his Lady there. A part of the maze, but not really. In their day, it would have been the bailey area. I like to think they choose to see only what pleases them."

"Yes," I breathed, immediately captivated. "Time must get jumbled in a place like this. Perhaps even for ghosts." I pressed against the battlement stones. Before us, the sea, more a moody grey than the cerulean of my painting; to our left, the maze, a sprawling pile of rubble, outbuildings, gardens, and pastureland; to our right, lawns fronting the castle entrance, currently teeming with workers erecting tents and booths for our conference.

Lucan pointed to the rubble. "There is where that passageway we earlier visited opens to. Those are the stones from our original keep. When it was known as Castle DeLaMer."

At those words, I experienced that peculiar, floaty feeling. *I have stood here, am standing here, will stand here. Or a place very like it. Not gazing out at a sea of water but a sea of rooftops.*

"...was much smaller and more of a working castle. Over the centuries, most of the stones have been repurposed to construct newer parts of our residence."

Lucan gestured to a pasture dotted with sheep and cattle. "Occasionally, we hold medieval reenactments there. Quite authentic. Sometimes, it's easy to forget the century in which we reside." He paused. "In a place this old, time has a way of bending in on itself or losing all meaning."

I imagined knights upon their caparisoned destriers breaking lances; chain mailed combatants hammering each other with war hammers and maces.

"I liken time to an endless ocean," Lucan continued, his manner reflective. "Where each moment, each event falls like a drop of rain upon its surface. There, each drop mingles with every other. No separation possible. All connected."

"I can see where living here would turn one's thoughts to the mystical."

Lucan confessed that his mother and grandmother had been aficionados of the occult, even holding seances. "The theory goes that Castle by the Sea is positioned along ley lines. Supposedly, currents of supernatural energy flow through them."

"I've heard of ley lines." This conversational detour was simultaneously fascinating and alarming since I would be sleeping—alone—in the Cavalier Suite.

"Our ancestors could access that particular energy," Lucan said. Sounds from the Hearts Afire's construction site drifted to us high on our perch, as did the screech of gulls circling the nearby beach. "Unfortunately, it's now a case of you see what you believe you'll see. And since modern man no longer believes..." He shrugged.

"I believe," I breathed.

Lucan's eyes bored into mine. "Aye, Ms. Lucy. I believe you do."

Since Bella Publishing was picking up the tab, our PR department had conducted a contest wherein winners enjoyed all-expenses-paid vacations to Hearts Afire. The resultant crowd was small but enthusiastic. Thanks to a combination of Lizzie Taylor-Wahlberg's leadership and the hard work of the castle and publishing staff, Hearts Afire had been flawlessly executed. No doubt tomorrow's closing ceremonies would be the same.

Strolling through the area, I spied Max Dockerty, clad in his usual black leathers and knee-deep in female fans. After purchasing a motorcycle shop, "Duke Rocker" had pretty much retired from his writing gig save for the occasional public appearance.

"Ms. Lucy." I turned away from our Bad Boy to the petite blonde wearing a hoodie sporting our slogan, "Love Makes the Words Go

Round." She smiled up at me. Her face was familiar, though I saw so many people...

"Seraphina!" I plastered on my professional smile, ignoring the inner flash of dread upon recognizing my Italian tour guide. Yes, Seraphina was a reminder of Raphael Accardi, but *he* didn't matter at all. I'd jettisoned that worthless carcass somewhere over the Atlantic.

After a quick hug and exchange of pleasantries, Seraphina said, "You once promised to introduce me to Duke Rocker." She cast a glance toward Max.

When I didn't immediately respond, she rushed on. "I watch your channels and follow every update and was beyond so excited when chosen to attend..." She shrugged her slim shoulders, managing to look elegant even in her hoodie. "It is fate, is it not?"

While Seraphina had helped orchestrate Raphael's betrayal, seeing her shining, eager face, I couldn't snub her. Besides, if I really didn't care—and I didn't—Raphael Accardi was a non-issue.

"I'll text Max to meet us at the gastro pub by the souvenir shop."

This I can do. Seraphina wouldn't be so gauche as to broach the subject. Though, really, she should have the good sense to at least appear embarrassed for her part in breaking my heart. Correction: not breaking it. Annoying it.

Minutes later, I found myself sitting across from the lovely Seraphina, wondering why I'd ordered a Jameson whiskey when I didn't even drink.

"I will never understand what happened between you and Raphael," Seraphina said, following a pause in our conversation. "Upon your leave-taking, Raphael was *devastato*. Brokenhearted."

My throat constricted. I didn't, wouldn't think about that...him. Raphael Accardi was less than a speed bump in my thirty-six years.

"How could Raphael be upset?" I asked, unable to hide my annoyance. How dare Seraphina play the innocent?

She frowned. "I do not understand."

"When you recommended him to Ollie. To squire me around. And...do other things. I'm sure I wasn't the only one. We call a man like Raphael Accardi a gigolo." I didn't add, "And a woman like you a madam."

Seraphina stared at me, her sea-glass green eyes round and puzzled.

"I never met Raphael before that day in Capri. Though we do now keep in touch. He yet speaks of you. He remains sad for the parting."

It was my turn to stare. "Raphael was not part of Premium Escort Tours? Like... an extra choice from your menu of services?" Seraphina frowned, still appearing confused. "You know, an added benefit...a friend...provided for tourists like me?"

Seraphina cried, "No, No, *Signorina!*" Reaching across the tabletop, she grabbed my hand. "That would be unprofessional. Illegal. We have for forty years been an impeccable business, I assure you. "

She appeared so honestly shocked I knew she wasn't dissembling. Trying to sort through her confession, I slumped back in my chair. Seraphina continued speaking while my mind replayed the scene in Ollie's suite. So adamant. So cocksure in his accusations. Yet, other than the credit card statements, which I'd barely glanced at, what proof had he produced?

No. Ollie would never be so deliberately cruel as to trick me.

Would he?

"I don't understand," I protested. "Raphael's married and has a child. I saw them. In his apartment."

"*Sorella!* His sister. She and her *bambina* live with Raphael. Why would you think otherwise?"

At that moment, Max Dockerty strolled through the door. Even in the dim light, I saw Seraphina blush and her eyes widen, our conversation immediately forgotten. In full Duke Rocker mode, Max strutted to our table. Before I could formally introduce them, he reached for Seraphina's hand and lifted it to his lips. "I wish I knew how to say beautiful in Italian," he murmured.

Oh, for fuck's sake.

Their gazes locked. I imagined cartoon hearts encircling their heads, bluebirds tweeting, turtle doves cooing.

Well!

I stood. "I'll leave you two to get better acquainted," I said, before leaning into Max and whispering in his ear, "I'll expect a thank you for introducing you to wife number four."

Later, in the Cavalier Suite, I wrestled with the revelation of Ollie's betrayal. No way to sugarcoat the truth: Oliver Harrison Scott had deliberately sabotaged Raphael and me. He had watched me bleed out in front of him. Glibly piling lie upon lie, his face never losing its faux sympathetic expression.

"Sorry, C.L.," he'd said, twisting the knife one last time upon revealing Raphael's "marriage."

Now, it would be Oliver Scott's turn to be sorry.

Thirteen

V eronique Vixen, aka me, wiggled my way along one of several hallways, mindful of my four-inch stilettos and extremely tight floor-length gown. I was already deliberately late for my meeting with FunTown execs, a meeting Ollie had been negotiating for months, after which Veronique/I would officially close our Hearts Afire conference.

No problem. This wouldn't take long.

FunTown, an up-and-coming media conglomerate, was interested in a series of Mr. Happy picture books Ollie was pushing to expand Bella Publishing's brand. His idea: turn Mr. Happy into the next *Diary of a Wimpy Kid* series or Dr. Seuss or *Where the Wild Things Are*, depending on his audience. "Mr. Happy is a joke," I'd explained, the product of a late-night giggle fest with Lizzie Taylor-Wahlberg detailing the names she'd bestowed upon hubby Brandon's most intimate body part.

"It's the concept they'll be buying," Ollie had countered every time I expressed reluctance to pursue a "concept" originating as a penis. "Franchises. Merch. Brand recognition is the bomb, C.L. Trust me."

"Here," my guide finally said, halting in front of an enormously tall pair of wooden doors open to a library nearly the size of Ute Creek's.

"There you are!" Ollie stood on one side of a long polished table while a trio of FunTown executives sat opposite. His extra wide, friendly smile signaled his irritation.

Scanning Ollie's outfit, I commented in a breathy voice, "Going full-blown hipster, are you?" Ollie flushed, expanding his grin until it resembled a clown mask. His skin-tight skinny jeans, purple and black optical illusion T-shirt topped by a multi-colored checked shirt, grey beanie, and ironic brown suede boots had been chosen to assure FunTown's management that a bachelor who hated kids was *the* perfect vessel for creating a children's series.

I turned my attention to the trio at the conference table. Striking a Marilyn-Monroe-singing-Happy-Birthday-to-JFK-pose, I cooed, "Good afternoon, gentlemen."

The execs sat up straighter. Two adjusted their ties. The third licked his lips. Of course, they'd be titillated. Veronique Vixen was pretty much the physical manifestation of all the delicious steaminess packed into her various imprints bearing names like *Lusty Lords and Ladies, Between Colonial Sheets, The Lords Bounty and Their Passions, Irish Lassies in Love.* I enjoyed playing Veronique. She was so over-the-top— bold, sensual, brimming with double entendres that when channeling her simply popped into my head. Physically, she was every bit as outrageous. Hair the color of Tweety Bird, curling and spiraling and cascading nearly to her overly padded butt and shimmering gold, excessively low-cut, sleeveless gown with strategically placed foam inserts so that boobs and butt were cartoonishly large.

"I hope you'll forgive little old me for being late!" A suggestive wink of false eyelashes that could double as curtains and a pursing of lips painted a deeper red than a British telephone box.

Side note: The few telephone boxes I'd spotted since arriving in Ireland were green or green and white.

"No problem!" the black-suited execs chorused.

I slunk into the room, my stilettos tap-tapping in time with my clinking bracelets. Between my gown and the profusion of jewelry, I probably mirrored the twinkling lights on a Christmas tree. A very expensive Christmas tree.

Another rictus grin from Ollie. He slid a glance at his assistant and current squeeze, Patricia St. Tara, who was frowning at the screen of her iPad Pro.

"Shall I sit here?" I asked, maneuvering carefully onto the edge of a Queen Anne chair nearer the center of the room. With all that butt padding, not to mention my extremely tight corset, it was impossible to get comfortable. "Ooh!" I said, which was as much a protest regarding my constricted lung capacity as any further mimicry of a fifties sex goddess. "I am so very, very *happy* to meet you all."

Crossing my legs, I hiked up my gown until it revealed a provocative glimpse of fishnet thigh-high stockings.

After which, I proceeded to demolish Ollie Scott's career.

∽

Mr. Happy's First Day at School.

Patricia St. Tara—name as fake as her Brazilian butt lift—is Bella Publishing's irritatingly snobbish head of "concepts" and a bunch of other buzzword titles. After Ollie claps his hands, signaling showtime, Patricia bends over her iPad Pro, severe black bob hiding her face. While Ollie narrates the many ways Mr. Happy will catapult FunTown into the 21st-century version of Disney, she obediently taps her keyboard.

A litany of firsts. *First Trip to the Dentist.* Tap. *Doctor...* Tap. *Movies...* All with related drawings that appear on the projector screen positioned in front of a wall of books. Ollie's accompanying sales pitch overflows with the latest meaningless jargon explaining why Mr. Happy will differ from every other children's series in the world.

Veronique Vixen twists a strand of canary-colored hair in the proximity of her formidable cleavage. Waiting and watching.

Ollie finishes this portion with *Mr. Happy's First Trip to the Beach.* "Imagine," he says. "A sun-drenched stretch of beach with laughing parents, Mr. Happy's little sister constructing a sandcastle, and Mr.

Happy's helping because he's the perfect role model for today's beginning readers. Cute while simultaneously impish…"

Impish? thinks Veronique Vixen, noting he'd dropped his hipster lingo.

"A nostalgic brand reminding parents and grandparents of simpler, more carefree days. Our research shows the public…"

Blah, blah, blah.

Veronique wets her lips with the tip of her tongue and caresses the sapphire and diamond necklace Ollie purchased in Milan, further drawing attention to her awe-inspiring attributes.

FunTown's suits are more focused on Veronique's fingers than the screen.

Tap.

Another series. *Mr. Happy Meets… Crossing Guard… Waitstaff… Policewoman… Mechanic… Barista…*

Veronique winks, purses her lips, flaps her fake eyelashes, and adjusts the delicate shoulder strap of her Art Deco purse, further calling attention to her cleavage. A distracted Ollie stumbles over his spiel while Patricia, intent on the presentation, robotically taps, pauses, taps.

FunTown's execs remain mesmerized.

While Ollie pauses in his spiel, awaiting a new image to appear, Veronique breathily interjects, "How about this idea for a series? Why not *Mr. Happy Fucks a Porn Star?*"

Patricia whips her head around, strands of her expensively cut bob slashing across her cheeks.

Ollie gasps.

The FunTown execs blink. Frown. Look puzzled. Horrified.

"Or *Mr. Happy Gets His First BJ?*"

"Clarabel!" Ollie cries. His face has turned as scarlet as Veronique's lips. Patricia fumbles with her computer, which has inexplicably frozen.

Veronique continues. "If we want to expand our demographic to the LGTBQ community, why not *Mr. Happy Gives Pizza Delivery Boy a Giant Tip?*"

"Is this some kind of a joke?" sputters First Exec.

Second Exec's gaze sweeps the room. "Are we being punked?"

"Are you drunk?" asks the third.

Veronique's mouth quirks. "You do know Mr. Happy is a penis, don't you?"

Stunned silence. Abruptly dropping the Veronique Vixen persona, I directly address Ollie. "I explained all that to you when you came up with this harebrained idea."

Ollie's gaze swivels between me and the execs. He tugs at his beanie. "Ha, ha. How naughty you're behaving, Veronique! Perhaps you'd better—"

"Not to mention possible trademark issues. Does the owner of Mr. Happy have a legal claim to the name? Could there be copyright problems? And since those drawings look nothing like the actual Mr. Happy, could he file a lawsuit disputing the image?"

Patricia stares at me. "How about putting Mr. Happy in a hat and sunglasses," she finally manages. "Would that work?"

"We're a family-friendly enterprise," fumes First Exec. "This is most inappropriate."

"Unprofessional," echoes Second Exec.

"Disgusting," agrees the third.

I stand. "Sorry to have wasted your time, gentlemen. Please note I repeatedly warned Mr. Scott about peddling porn to children, but he ignored me."

I wiggle my way toward the library door, silently applauding Veronique's Oscar-worthy performance.

A final twist around to view Ollie, his usually rubbery mug reduced to a gaping mouth and bugging eyes.

"Raphael Accardi," I say. For a moment, I am back in Rome, encircled by the arms of my beautiful lover, dreaming of a villa on the Amalfi coast, of plucking lemons so sweet we can devour them like apples, of swimming naked in a swimming pool guarded by statues of gods and goddesses. "I will never forgive you for destroying us."

Once outside the library, I lift Veronique's skirts so I can move like a regular human being.

Now, if I can find my way back to my suite.

Lost. Maundering about like some demented squirrel; totally turned around without any reliable points of reference.

Ollie's voice assaulting me from... somewhere.

After slipping off my heels and tossing them aside in order to navigate without breaking my neck, I'd plunged deeper into Castle by the Sea. So much easier if I'd been a ghost, able to pass through walls and wish myself wherever I wanted to go because I was totally disoriented. I'd not even spotted a familiar landmark to assure me I was headed in a recognizable direction—meaning toward an exit and away from Ollie.

"Clarabel! Stop! What the fuck is wrong with you?"

Finally, after descending a wicked set of stairs, I found myself in the DeLaMer museum. I remembered the "Do Not Enter" passageway in the adjoining room, which would lead to the outside, at least according to Lucan. From there, I could follow the noises of Hearts Afire's closing ceremonies, currently in progress.

I paused to orient myself. Everything around me was quiet; no yelling Ollie, no footsteps tripping down the vice.

Entering the adjoining room, I immediately spotted the warning sign and the stanchions off to the side. Fluorescent lights popped and buzzed like agitated wasps. Stepping to the passageway, I peered inside. Previously, the darkness had seemed as impenetrable as a moonless, starless night, but the opposite end appeared more the color of twilight. Further affirmation it led outside.

Tentatively, I entered. One step, two. Uneven stones digging into the soles of my feet. Reaching out, using the wall on my left as a guide, I edged deeper into the gloom. Enveloped suddenly by a cold as relentless as a Christmas blizzard. Goosebumps rose on my arms and rippled across my limbs. Though I couldn't see my breath, it surely hovered about me like a persistent suitor. Sweet baby Jesus, but the air was frigid enough to slice my lungs to ribbons.

"Bella!" The whisper was so faint it didn't immediately register.

"Bella...Bel."

I swung my head back toward the entrance, expecting to see a figure. Not Ollie, but someone who'd mistaken my name for that of my publishing company.

"Bel-la!" Like someone teasing.

How peculiar. Yet I was more perplexed than alarmed. The acoustics were so janky that outside sounds could have somehow been contorted. Hearing was a tricky thing; echoes could be disorienting.

Ears straining, I continued on until the cold receded, and the strange voice was replaced by a roar like that of a conch shell when you held it up to your ear. Or that of the Irish Sea itself.

The atmosphere thickened; the air smelled metallic, like a burning wire. Or as it did in the aftermath of a rainstorm? The way it had at Camelot Faire before I'd seen the knight who wasn't there?

The knight. I remembered then we'd deliberately chosen today's closing ceremonies to be held on Midsummer's Eve.

I experienced a frisson, though not of fear. Excitement? Anticipation?

"A handsome couple they make," Lucan DeLaMer had said.

The Knight and his Lady echoes in my head. *Her name is Bella,* I decide, *and they play hide-and-seek and other lovers' games, chasing each other until the knight catches her, wraps her in his arms, and demands she surrender a kiss. They both laugh, this Knight and his Lady, the laughter castle goers swear they hear. And what I heard—what I think I heard—was that an echo? Or simply a wish?*

A sudden sharp pain pierced my skull, come and gone almost too quickly to register. Leaving a feeling of being split? Out of sorts? Not disoriented exactly. Doggedly, I continued moving toward the exit, where the darkness had faded to the equivalent of pre-dawn.

I wondered whether Lizzie had planned a bonfire or some related celebration in addition to Veronique Vixen officially ending the conference. That would account for the lambent quality, like viewing flames through a haze.

Or Limbo, like the fog that had hidden my knight?

A loud crack, reminiscent of wood against wood, followed by shouting. Other unidentifiable noises.

I paused near the opening. So... I'd escaped Ollie and made my way... somewhere. Nothing to do but act my way through closing ceremonies, deal with the fallout from Mr. Happy, fire or buy out or sue my former friend and... I wasn't sure where I was headed from here.

~

"Oh, my!" I breathed, taking in the most remarkable sight. "This must be what they call raining men!"

I hadn't emerged onto Hearts Afire festivities, but an unfamiliar courtyard brimming with males in various stages of peculiar dress and engaged in athletic activities consisting of maiming each other with pole axes, staves, war hammers, and other weapons. The cracks I'd heard earlier were caused by wooden staves smashing together, though I also heard the ring of steel on steel.

How very odd.

Was this the area Lucan said was used for medieval re-enactments? But this area was enclosed, an actual bailey. Had I entered the wrong tunnel after all? I did know I'd never seen tourists or employees who looked anything like these guys attired in a mishmash of chain mail, pieces of armor, padded shirts, and ill-fitting pants. Maybe they'd been booked for a re-enactment at another castle and shown up here by mistake. Might this be the surprise Lizzie had alluded to over the last few days? An Irish version of the Rumbler Revue? Or, more precisely, the *prelude* to Lizzie's surprise since the current action was too chaotic and unchoreographed to be anything other than a practice.

Whatever.

Showtime!

Jiggling my shoulders in a half-shimmy, totally owning Veronique Vixen's sexy, sexy persona, I plunged—or rather carefully stepped—into the fray. Several men lounging near a stand of lances and other weapons noticed me first, freezing like human mannequins. *Hmmm.* Surely, before they'd agreed to perform, they'd watched videos of Veronique and been briefed on the whole Bella Publishing thing. Maybe they were concerned because they knew I wasn't supposed to appear before the big reveal.

I veered around several pairs of wrestlers rolling about on the distinctly unhygienic ground, raising my skirts and monitoring my stocking-clad feet as I did so. A rough-looking bunch with their beards, long hair, and weathered faces. They definitely spent way too much time outdoors without sunscreen.

I'll bet you don't get a lot of gigs.

Not that I would criticize my forever friend when she officially sprang her surprise.

I stepped closer to the action. In the far corner, a trio on horseback, each dressed in battle gear and wielding lances, took turns knocking a dummy with a shield suspended from a swinging pole. An actual quintain. Impressive!

Good thing I'd stuffed lots of euros in my purse. I could use them for tips.

All right, Veronique. Let's get this show on the road.

I smiled, waved, and blew kisses. Or Veronique Vixen did. Were those looks of alarm? Disbelief? I conducted a mental inventory of my costume—foam boobs and butt in place, wig securely fastened, though the no shoes bit was definitely out of place. *What?* They seemed to be specifically ogling my arms. Admiring the results of my targeted exercise regimen? Or puzzled because they looked too slender for my fake voluptuous body?

These gym rats must not be too bright.

Seeking someone who looked to be in charge and could answer my rapidly expanding list of questions, I scanned the courtyard. Several wrestlers paused in their grappling. An older man with flowing white hair and beard—an impressive stand-in for Santa Claus if Santa was a lot thinner and fiercer looking—demonstrated wicked moves with a pole axe. The men who'd been watching him nudged each other and pointed at me.

Soon, these...curious creatures...would be falling all over me in lustful admiration, but first, I needed to find—I saw him then, the man who *must* be their leader. An Alpha among Alphas, engaged in ferocious swordplay with a shorter, stockier opponent. Grunting and sweating and dancing around like some lumbering ballerina, graceful in his own way. Save for short leather boots and legs encased in some sort of leggings that did nothing to camouflage his massive thighs, he was otherwise naked. Even from this distance, I noted an overabundance of hair clinging to his chest in a most ungentlemanly way.

Monster Man. The perfect Veronique Vixen hero. And everything Clarabel Lucy despised.

Halting well out of reach of those slashing swords, which were obviously the real deal, I studied Hairy Beast. What was he thinking? What was the point, the theme, the routine of this free-for-all? What sort of professional training did he, any of them, have in dance, choreography, or anything other than bashing people's heads in? Unless swordplay would be part of their forthcoming act? Maybe they planned on executing various feats of strength accompanied by some Metalcore-style music.

Hairy Beast and his opponent, both panting like exhausted bulls, abruptly halted and swung their attention to me. Gazing coyly up at the Beast through my curtain of false eyelashes, I fixed him with a coquettish smile. In response, he raised a bulky arm to push back long strands of dark, wet hair and wipe his forehead, revealing more hair in places I didn't need to see. *Yuck!* It was one thing to write about sweating, heaving specimens, but in real life, it required all my acting skills to refrain from wrinkling my nose in disgust. In addition, the Beast's mustache made him look like a seventies porn star. But didn't porn stars manscape? Did they even have manscaping in the seventies? Whatever, this guy needed a whole body waxing.

Not sure Lizzie had thought this particular engagement through.

Easing forward, I extended my hand to the Beast. Slipping into my Marilyn Monroe voice, I introduced myself. "Veronique Vixen. So pleased to meet you."

The Beast stared at my hand as if it held a pile of toxic waste.

Something like a growl emerged from his mouth, followed by a string of words in a peculiar language. Irish Gaelic?

The courtyard stilled. Overhead, the sky, which had been the anodyne shade I'd come to associate with Ireland, darkened to a sullen grey. As of one mind, the other men left their posts to crowd behind the Beast, gabbling at each other while carrying way too many weapons.

"Hey, fellas!" I cooed, pretending this was all perfectly normal.

More of their odd language, though something about the inflections and rhythm was familiar. And then I recognized the cadence, the individual words—Anglo-Norman French. *Wow!* These guys were serious about authenticity—even if they weren't speaking the language properly the way I'd learned it. Which made the thread of their conversation difficult to follow.

Still impressive!

"Bravo!" I cried, clapping my hands and doing a little jump, rewinding back to my Shirley Temple days when I'd just received the *bestest* birthday present ever!

Including the Beast in my compliment, I addressed them in their tongue. "Aren't you adorable! And even speaking in your time period!" I fanned a hand in front of my face. "I'm simply overcome!" Murmuring among themselves, too low for me to understand. "Shall we converse in English?" I continued. "I want to hear all about what a show you'll be putting on for little old Veronique."

The Beast said something like "God's bones" or "God's balls!" which might be in keeping with his character but was undeniably rude.

"What's next?" I pressed. "Are you readying for your dance routine?"

Blinks. Frowns. Stares.

I felt like Jane Goodall upon first encountering chimpanzees in the wild.

"Will I be Queen of Love and Beauty, who will reward her valiant champion with a kiss?" Since they were ignoring my plea to speak *normally*, I'd reverted to Middle English, which I was more proficient in than Anglo-Norman French.

Santa moved closer to the Beast. If Beast was the leader, I sensed it was because Santa allowed it. His faded blue eyes inspected my face and form, undoubtedly measuring what he saw. Santa whispered something in the Beast's ear.

A barely perceptible nod of acknowledgment. "What are you doing here?" he demanded.

I was suddenly very aware of the Beast's sword, resting easily in his right hand, an extension of his limb. And that he too scrutinized every inch of me, gaze lingering on my bare arms. *Medieval ladies never exposed their limbs*, I remembered, with a sudden shiver.

"Who are you with?" the Beast pressed.

Focus.

"Hearts Afire, of course," I responded, straining to maintain my Veronique persona. "As you well know!"

The Beast glowered. "Are you from outside the pale?"

"I've already told you. Hearts Afire Conference. Bella Publishing's twelve-year celebration." If this was an actual dress rehearsal for my forthcoming surprise performance, it promised to be a bust. And if this *was* the performance booked strictly for me, where a bunch of employees and Hearts Afire fans would momentarily jump out of hiding to yell, "Surprise!" I'd rate it a D+. No climax, no script, meandering, pointless.

And the Beast? 1) Desperately in need of grooming. 2) Attitude problem. 3) Zero charisma. Grade: F-.

"Are you one of de Lacy's stragglers?" asked the Beast's sparring partner, a grizzled creature who'd mashed his long hair in some sort of a man bun, not as a fashion statement, but more so his vision wouldn't be impaired while hacking off limbs or strangling opponents.

"De Lacy?" I repeated, batting my false eyelashes. He must mean "Lucy," though they would only know me as Veronique Vixen, wouldn't they? "I don't know of whom you speak." Maybe I'd misheard. Translating from English to a pretty much dead language wasn't the easiest feat.

Lucan? De Lacy? "Are you talking about Lucan DeLaMer?"

Something like a squawk from the Beast.

"You're not really dancers, are you?" I asked, persona slipping along with my temper. I had no idea what was happening, but I needed to make a quick exit, blow off the rest of Hearts Afire, find my way back to the Cavalier Suite, pack my bags, and flee this nutso place.

A mist had slipped from the lowering clouds. Great, soon, my makeup would start running, and I'd have to pick my way back to the castle amid the muck.

Reaching into my purse, I pulled out a wad of euros. "A bit extra for your enjoyment, fellas. And the fun time had by all. Sorry, I have to depart, but—"

"Clarabel!"

I whirled around to see Ollie running toward me, frantically waving his arms.

The actors behind Monster Man watched his approach with a mixture of wonder and amusement. A few laughed. I had to admit that Ollie, in his hipster garb, looked ridiculous.

But then, so did we all.

Ollie skidded to a stop. "What?" he looked from me to the audience, eyes bulging in surprise. "Who are these people? Some sort of Irish gang?"

"Actors, as you must know since Lizzie would have had to get your permission to pay for this ridiculous charade." I turned back to the Beast with what I hoped was an ingratiating smile.

From his position several steps behind me, Ollie said, "They look dangerous."

"Is he some sort of jester, Alaric?" asked Man Bun, nodding in Ollie's direction. "He—they both—are dressed very odd, are they not?"

So, the Beast's name is Alaric.

"Mayhap they are some of the wild folk from beyond the pale," this Alaric character mused. "There could be anything in that land."

"Aye," said Man Bun. "Remember those tales of werewolves?"

WTF?

Ollie inched closer. "Are they speaking Irish? Sounds kinda French but not like any French I've heard, I can tell you that."

"Part of the act," I said shortly, not allowing our current situation to soften my dislike.

"Hey, is he the one who caused you to blow up Mr. Happy? Are you dating this buffoon? Is that what this is all about?"

"Don't be ridiculous," I hissed, returning my gaze to the sword in Alaric's hand. Brutal enough to lop off a man's head with one sweep of the arm? Something was really wrong here. These guys weren't like any entertainers I'd ever encountered. Maybe I'd stumbled upon a criminal enterprise that terrified its enemies using old-fashioned weapons.

Good thing I'd included pepper spray in my purse. My worries about running into the Irish mafia or holdovers from the Troubles who were plotting a kidnapping in order to create an international incident appear to have been justified.

I held out the wad of euros to Alaric. "Once again, thank you. And now, I fear, Veronique Vixen must depart."

Alaric scrutinized me before gingerly taking the notes in his ham-like fist. Several bills fell to the ground.

"Careful! Those're fifty euro banknotes." Ollie scurried forward, scooped up the bills, stuffed them in a back pocket, and attempted to snatch the remainder from Alaric. Man Bun stepped forward, snarled something, and smacked Ollie's hand away.

"Watch it, dude!"

While Alaric's expression remained neutral, the air of menace emanating from him was palpable.

"Back the hell off," I said out of the side of my mouth. Man Bun moved closer; one of the wrestlers approached from the opposite side.

"Hah!" Scooting backward, Ollie crouched in a martial arts stance. Did he seriously believe the hundreds of times he'd watched various *Karate Kid* movies and the Kung Fu classes he'd largely skipped during Ute Creek's Summer Youth Programs qualified him to face off against a human tank?

"Would you stop?" I snapped, totally breaking character. "You are seriously pissing them off."

"How much did you pay your boyfriend to fuck with me?"

Punch. Punch. Kick. Kick. Ollie stepped back and repeated the pose, the punches, the kicks.

As if taking the measure of some alien species Alaric watched him, while those in back craned their necks. Man Bun shifted his sword; the wrestler lowered into a half-crouch.

"I apologize for my...the jester... here," I said, keeping my focus on Alaric, who, with one word, could determine our fates. "Sunstroke, I think," gesturing to the woolly sky. "And now we really must—"

"Hah!" Ollie cried, apparently mistaking these barbarians' inaction for fear. "I'm onto you!" After executing another feeble kick in his impossibly tight jeans, he whirled around, displaying his back. A second whirl, a "Hah!" and a clumsy leap. Upon landing, he delivered a series of uppercuts into empty air but close enough to Alaric that he might consider Ollie a challenge.

"You're not gonna get away with your bullshit plot, you and C.L.!"

Alaric stepped forward and almost negligently cracked Ollie atop his beanie-clad skull with the pommel of his sword. Ollie crumpled to the ground like a dropped bird.

"Hey!" I yelled. You couldn't just go around using physical violence (except in Bella Publishing's romantic suspense line and half the movies coming out of Hollywood). "What the hell?"

Ollie sprawled motionless upon the earth. Losing interest, most of Alaric's cohorts returned to their previous activities, totally unconcerned that their leader might have just committed murder.

"You need to get a doctor," I called after them. "Does anybody here have any medical training?"

The Beast rotated his sword arm, his eyes never leaving mine. Was that some sort of implied threat?

"Never mind." I imagined whipping out my pepper spray and emptying it into Alaric's grimy, sweaty face. "I'll take care of him myself." Somewhere in that hipster garb was a pocket holding Ollie's phone. Not only would I dial 999 for an ambulance, I'd insist upon summoning the police.

With that, I spun on my heel. "If we were in America," I said, over my shoulder, "I'd slap a lawsuit on your nasty ass and make sure you and your fellow Neanderthals never work again."

I hadn't taken more than a handful of steps before Alaric grabbed my arm and jerked me back toward him. Unfortunately, his grasp included yards of wig hair. The ferocity of his movement threw me off balance. My wig was too securely fastened to completely give, but it shifted enough to continue my backward trajectory. In a vain attempt to break my fall, I reached for Alaric. Only to clutch empty air.

The last thing I remembered was a crack, like the crack of wood on wood, but it was the crack of the back of my head, slamming into the unforgiving earth.

Fourteen

Clarabel Lucy's Crossword Puzzle:

4 Across) Surname of white-haired Santa Claus knight:

Answer: Lackford

3 Down) Name of Lackford's wife, the regal one with the pouty lower lip and endlessly put-upon manner:

Answer: Jocelyn

1 Down) Surname of Hairy Beast, a throwback to seventies porn stars and irritatingly persistent presence at the bedside of my particular nightmare:

Answer: DeLaMer

After that, my imaginary crossword puzzle kinda dissolved. Name of residence? No idea, though I vaguely remembered being carried up at least one vice and into a large room. Which didn't make sense since it wasn't the sprawling Castle by the Sea of these past several days. But I might be hallucinating, I might be in a coma, I might be dreaming an extended dream, or I might be dead, in a bardo state and creating this world around me.

If the latter were true, however, I wouldn't have included the Incredible Hulk and these particular surroundings, nor would the conversations intruding upon my half-sleep be so mundane. Surly Stash couldn't get it through his head that I wasn't a spy for these de Lacy characters, though James Lackford gently disavowed him of that.

How long have I been out? An hour, a day? What if I really did die and am hovering between death and rebirth?

I wasn't at all terrified by that possibility since I still felt like me, seemed to be physically "me," and the surrounding world was normal enough in an abnormal way. Though, if I *had* cast off my physical form, wouldn't I have conjured a less pedestrian afterlife? One without Jocelyn, who I already knew—the way a woman knows such things—was in love with Sir Grumpy Pants rather than her elderly husband? Without her repeatedly shaking me awake to force down some odd-tasting concoction smelling of chamomile and dirty feet? Or the Beast nagging me in his teeth-grating, persistent, sarcastic rumble to impart details of my life?

Probably not dead, then. Maybe an extended dream? What if... What had Lucan DeLaMer said? Ley lines... centuries mixing and mingling...

Something very like a finger poked me hard near my collarbone.

"Are you awake, finally? We must be off for Trim Castle," said the Beast, "and if you canna sit a horse, you can be left to beg alongside the road, for all it matters."

I opened my eyes. While my head still hurt, it was more a dull throb. Some sort of black bar obstructed the vision in one eye, but that should disappear with my headache.

I didn't want to look at Alaric, and not simply because he was probably the most socially graceless person I'd ever met. *Concentrate. There's something else, something elusive, something important I need to shake free from the jumbled mess in my head.*

"Patience, Sir Alaric," said James Lackford, who stood beside him. "Remember, kindness breaks no bones."

Alaric growled. "'Tis not a matter of kindness. 'Tis a matter of treachery, as you well understand."

I was now fully awake, or maybe I was dead and thinking I was awake, or maybe I was still sleeping and thinking I was awake because if I really were awake, I would be smack in the middle of a medieval movie. Canopied bed with surprisingly soft pillows that smelled of rosemary and lavender when I shifted position; massive fireplace with flames casting the painted and tapestried walls in shimmering shadows; Sir James reminding me, with his flowing white hair and pale tunic, of a medieval Zeus rather than Santa Claus; Lady Jocelyn, dead ringer for the wicked queen in *Snow White*, save for the blonde hair coiled on either side of her head. And, of course, Alaric DeLaMer. Dressed in a hauberk, coif pushed back from his mass of dark hair, and all of it covered by a blue surcoat with a black bear. The quintessential knight. Readying for battle?

With me? I rather liked the idea of making an opponent angry enough to contemplate violence. Regardless, if Muscles for Brains thought to engage me in a battle of wits, even in my weakened state, I would annihilate him.

"So, you told me your name is Clarabel Lacy?" Alaric glowered down at me from his great height, bringing me back to the present.

"*Lucy!*"

"Lacy?" He repeated.

I shifted on my pillows to better glare at him, though we were so close I might have been a bit cross-eyed. "As I've said a million times, Lucy. L-u-c-y."

Lord Lackford placed a hand on Alaric's forearm in a placating manner. "You're awake now," he said, smiling down at me. "Are you hungry?"

Before I could answer, yes, I would love something other than Jocelyn's smelly concoction, Alaric butted in. "You called yourself by a different name in the bailey. Valenium Vixum?"

"You're mistaken." Wary of my tender head, I turned carefully to address Lord Lackford. "I would be very grateful for some food."

"Aye." Sir James gestured to his wife, who'd been monitoring my interrogation from her position by the fireplace. When Lady Jocelyn complied, I noticed she stood infinitesimally closer to Sir Grumpy Pants than her husband. Her gaze swung from me to my interrogator, then back again. She was very beautiful, though her glittering eyes reminded me of a reptile's.

"Alaric's guest is in need of sustenance," Lackford murmured to his wife. "Something substantial, but not so much to dis-ease her stomach since we will soon be traveling."

"This woman is not my guest," Alaric said through gritted teeth after Jocelyn departed. "She arrives uninvited, pretending she holds some sort of bills of exchange the like of which no one has ever seen; painted and costumed like some freakish mummer or a whore who crawled out of the second circle of hell. Or, more specifically, this place called Vail, Colorado, which no one has ever heard of. "

Wow, there was a lot to untangle, particularly since I couldn't translate some of the phraseology, and he really mangled the pronunciation of "Vail, Colorado." Obviously, I'd revealed more in my semi-conscious state than I'd intended. And while Alaric had referred to Veronique as a whore, being categorized as a fallen woman made me feel dangerously risqué. As a risqué woman, I would enjoy a) lying and b)driving Alaric DeLaMer nuts.

"You misheard me." I struggled up on the pillows, releasing more flowery scents—and noted one of my fake boobs was missing. "I am from Vail, Vail Castle. In Cornwall. At the very tippy tip of the kingdom. Land's End, we call it." It should be sufficiently isolated to allow me to invent an entire anthology of related fairy tales.

Alaric ran a frustrated hand through his hair, reinforcing his air of untidiness. "Cornwall is a long way from Ireland for an Englishwoman."

"Ireland is also a long way from home for an Englishman," I retorted. "Yet here you are."

Alaric's eyebrows shot up, and he jerked forward as if I'd goosed him with a cattle prod. Thinking he was about to hit me, I instinctively flinched.

Instead, from somewhere beside the bed, he retrieved my wig and held it up as if dangling a scalp.

With his free hand, he leaned over and tugged at my hair, which barely reached my shoulders. "What happened here? Do you have lice? Is that why you cut all your hair off?"

"You're disgusting!"

"Only women of poor repute wear wigs. Or those afflicted with baldness."

"Do I look bald to you?" I snapped, wondering what had happened to my wig cap. And imagining how ridiculous I must look with my disheveled hair and missing boob.

Sir James cleared his throat. "Mayhap your attention, Alaric, would be better served—"

"Did you and that jester perform some sort of act?" He jiggled the wig in front of my vision. "Is that why—"

Ollie? I'd forgotten all about him. "Where is my...jester? What happened to him?"

Alaric shrugged his massive shoulders. The flickering light from the fireplace and lanthorn caught the links on his mail and flickered across the bear on his chest. What was it? What revelation, what memory danced at the edge of my consciousness? What was right before me, nudging me to remember? My attention was caught by the pommel of Alaric's sword—the sword he'd used to crack Ollie's skull open.

"Is my partner dead?"

Alaric didn't respond, which was an answer in itself.

Why didn't I feel more? Because this was a dream, and I might be dead. Or...increasingly, I wondered whether Lucan DeLaMer's ghost stories, of people drifting in and out of centuries, had some validity. What if I wasn't dead or dreaming but had somehow been transported back to what... to the time of Bannockburn? Why not? Their attire appeared period-appropriate.

"So why were you disguising yourself?" Alaric persisted. "What are you hiding?"

"Has anybody ever told you you're a pest?"

Rather than directly respond, Alaric reached out and removed the black bar from my lashes. "Have you a spider in your eye?"

False eyelash. Not invented for centuries. "Part of my costume."

Alaric examined the lash, rubbing it between his fingers before tossing it over his shoulder.

"You might as well remove the other one," I said sarcastically.

He leaned forward, his fingertips hovering around my eye. "Just pull. Carefully, and—ow! Not my real lashes."

None too gently, he peeled off the second one and tossed it in the direction of its match.

We glared at each other. His anger certainly seemed out of proportion to our actual interaction. And why did he keep staring at my mouth? If this had been a Veronique Vixen approved novel, Alaric would already be struggling against an overwhelming attraction that would inevitably blaze into passion and, finally, soulmate-style, forever love. Stranger things had happened, were happening, so why not?

"Maybe I am a mummer." I raised my arms languidly above my head, realizing it wasn't only my head that felt bruised. Alaric's gaze traveled the length of my bare arms, though not in what could be described as a lustful fashion. "Maybe my partner, who, thanks to you, is DEAD, and I traveled from castle to castle performing all sorts of lovely plays. Mummers...actors change their appearance all the time."

"Is that why you stuffed your gown with spurious...curves?" He retrieved my fake boob from its placement near the wig and waved it in front of me. "And this...sponge... is it more of your costume?"

"What are you doing with that? Why were you putting your hands on me?"

"It was sticking up out of your gown. You, Clarabel Lacy," he said my name improperly, emphasizing the wrong syllables, "are a woman of many secrets."

"If I weren't so exhausted, I'd slap you silly." Hoping to end this ridiculous conversation, I turned my face away from him.

Whack!

"Do not ignore me," Alaric said, waving the fake boob in front of me.

"Did you just hit me with that sponge?"

"Unless you are going to tell me you have a prick between your legs, you're no mummer."

Oops! Forgot acting was a male profession.

"And what sort of mummer hails from a castle? Or wears a king's ransom of jewels upon her body?"

Yeah, that.

"Do not fear," said Lackford, reaching out to rest his gnarled hand atop mine. "We wrapped your rings, wrist pieces, all your jewelry for safekeeping and placed them in your pouch."

At that moment, a servant entered bearing a tray of food, which she placed on the chest beside the bed.

With a jerk of the head, Lackford pulled Alaric away to leave me in peace. Sir James wrapped an arm around the younger man's shoulders and, with their heads close together, engaged him in a monologue occasionally broken by Alaric's nod. After settling the tray in front of me, I studied my nemesis, outlined as he was by the roaring fire. Legs, thick as tree trunks, planted firmly apart. He seemed to have grown out of the earth, out of the castle stones, insinuating no power on heaven or earth could dislodge him. *Alaric DeLaMer.* The flames played across his mail, his surcoat with its *black bear rampant*, and his dark hair, painting highlights of red and amber.

My stomach abruptly dropped as if I'd been riding a tilt-a-whirl.

Turning away from James Lackford, Alaric twisted around to stare directly at me, his expression not glowering or angry, simply intense. Piercing. Devouring. I felt it then, the electric charge coursing between us. Air crackling, sparks flying. A transformer blows. Cities, entire nations plunge into darkness. Earth shifting. Fireworks erupting. Universes colliding.

No. Alaric DeLaMer and the Camelot Faire knight could not be one and the same.

Yet, the way Alaric stood. The way he stared. *How easily the mind plays tricks,* went the war in my head. *False memories. Mixing up past and present and forcing both to mesh together. Creating a coherent narrative out of chaos.*

Slumping back on the pillows, I closed my eyes, trying to logically explain it all away. Yet, regardless of what might or might not have happened at Camelot Faire, I appeared to have somehow been dropped into a time that hadn't existed for seven centuries. How to make sense of that?

"Please, just go away," I muttered to no one in particular. Did I assume such an utterance could return me to my "before" life?

If so, I was once again mistaken.

It took two days to reach our destination, Trim Castle, the largest Norman castle in Ireland. I remembered that from when I was contemplating sightseeing following Hearts Afire. And that it was a beautiful ruin surrounded by the River Boyne.

No longer a ruin, of that I was certain. And home to...well, soon I really would meet characters who'd changed the course of a kingdom, wouldn't I?

Alaric had left Castle DeLaMer in the hands of a small garrison while his household, Lord and Lady Lackford, their retinue, and I rode out in abominable weather upon a muddy mess that passed for a road. The gentle beauty I'd once marveled at from what was then Castle by the Sea's battlements had been replaced by an ocean of grey. As I rode, bundled in a woolen cloak, hood, and gloves doing a passable job of keeping me warm and dry, I wrestled with my predicament: I'd indeed traveled back in time. Initially, I'd experienced a certain euphoria. Somehow, I'd transgressed the boundaries, the limits of physics to be *here*. While our finest minds generally agreed on the impossibility of time travel, they couldn't even explain phenomena as ordinary as ball lightning, butterfly migrations, sky quakes, the construction of Egyptian pyramids, or even the lack of snakes in New Zealand.

Yet here I was.

I'd felt smug, special, privileged. Until we'd struck out for Trim Castle, and I realized I'd been deposited in a Gaelic hellscape.

Whatever gods resided here in Ireland had apparently decided Clarabel Lucy, creator of Hallmark-style-happily-ever-afters, was due a dose of brutal reality. While I dared not ask anyone around me, "Hey, what's the date?" I had an approximate idea. Edward Bruce, Robert the Bruce's brother and a name I'd already heard uttered many times with dread or disdain, would die in 1318, and the famines, which would kill millions, began in 1315 and tapered off after 1317. Most likely, I'd been transported to 1317. Which, to paraphrase the line from a popular 1960s song, was not a very good year.

Ever watchful knights in full battle garb and gear scanned the murk for the glint of a spear or mail or other signs of Edward Bruce, who'd recently appropriated the worthless title High King of Ireland. What the current famine hadn't destroyed, Bruce had, burning fields and villages and slaughtering their inhabitants, squandering the initial goodwill from natives who had prayed he and his fellow Scots would rid Ireland of their Norman oppressors.

Only to find their savior, bringing pretty promises and hope, had brought war and death instead.

The rankness of rotting earth, of boglands collapsed into stagnant lakes, the putrescence of corpses sprawled beside the roadway, and carcasses in surrounding pastures caused me to repeatedly turn my face into the fabric of my hood in a vain attempt to blunt the stench. Vague shapes gradually revealed themselves to be animals, bloated bellies with legs sticking out like toothpicks. Unmoving bundles of rags lining our pathway denoted the dead or those nearly so. As we passed, a few stirred enough to raise skeletal arms, too weak even to hold begging bowls, while their babes mewled like kittens. I'd never seen or imagined the like and was vaguely aware of the tears slipping down my cheeks, though those around me were entirely focused on our escorts, our watchdogs who would warn us at the first sign of the enemy. The other, the human devastation, must have been too commonplace to merit attention.

We continued on: sheep in a movable pen, surrounded by a fence of iron, inhaling the scent of fear which overrode even that of death and decay. The tension in my body exacerbated the pounding in my head, which had returned full force. Edward Bruce's destiny might not be to die near Trim Castle in the year 1317, but he might be readying an attack from a copse, behind hedgerows or burned-out buildings. Only the sight of Alaric's broad back among his fellow knights calmed me. Whoever Alaric DeLaMer was, however we might or might not be connected, he was my protector. They all were.

So, we rode. Disturbed, not by an ambitious Scotsman who would soon be brought down by his own careless ambition, but by the starved and starving who marked our route.

~

My first glimpse of *him*, the man some historians subsequently labeled "the greatest traitor," occurred when I was savoring an oddly flavored but delicious bite of salmon. That and similar delicacies, caught fresh from the nearby River Boyne, would have graced the menu of the 21st century's most expensive restaurants. I was even more appreciative following the pottage and bread we'd eaten the previous evening in the monastery granting us lodging.

I was seated in Trim Castle's great hall, a recently constructed marvel of oak-timbered roof, brightly plastered and painted walls and tapestries the like I'd only seen in museum photos. *"Here we have the Apocalypse tapestry...The lady with the unicorn..."*

When *he* burst into the great hall—Roger Mortimer, 3rd Baron Mortimer of Wigmore, 1st Earl of March and current King's Lieu-tenant of Ireland. The man who, along with England's queen, would lead a rebellion against Edward II ending in Edward's deposition and death, and meet his own fate upon Tyburn's gallows, where his naked corpse would remain for two days and nights afterward as a reminder to all who might contemplate similar treason.

Dead more than seven hundred years. As was everyone here. Such ran my morbid thoughts. I blinked and returned my attention to the baron. Bareheaded, with coal black hair and startling blue eyes. Of a good height, Mortimer carried himself with the grace and confidence of a natural leader, though I might have been projecting more charisma onto him than he merited because I knew his future.

A sudden hush. At the high table, Mortimer's wife, Joan, who'd been speaking with Jocelyn Goodknyght, abruptly halted to monitor her husband's approach. Minstrels ceased their playing. There it was again, that fear rippling through the hall, at least among its non-combatants. In these perilous times, all news threatened to be grave.

I will summarize here Roger Mortimer's portentous news, which soon enough made the rounds. Walter and Hugh de Lacy, who were, oddly enough, related by marriage to Mortimer, had killed one of Mortimer's most loyal knights, Hugh de Croft. De Croft had carried letters bearing the royal seal to the de Lacy brothers, ordering them to appear at Trim Castle in order to submit to Mortimer in his capacity as Lord Lieutenant of Ireland. Giving them one last chance before Mortimer and an army, even now encamped on the plain beyond the castle, hunted them down. The brothers' reply was to murder Hugh de Croft. In the past, the de Lacys had vacillated between loyalty to King

Edward and to the Scots, even deserting Mortimer in a previous battle. This final treasonous act effectively signed Walter and Hugh de Lacys' death warrants.

So, here was the origin of Alaric DeLaMer's antipathy toward me. Though in what world Veronique Vixen could be conspiring with the likes of the de Lacys seemed a dunderheaded fantasy.

From the press of knights who'd followed Roger Mortimer to a secluded corner, I picked out Alaric. Studying him from this distance, I had to admit he wasn't homely but rather possessed of a brooding, even appealing vibe. Over the past several days, I'd mulled over the connection, non-connection between him and the Camelot Faire knight. Why hadn't I immediately recognized this Alaric? I tried to think back to that day, to compare then and now, but it was all a jumbled mess. Once again, my so-called photographic memory had failed me.

Another question to ponder: Why had I named my antagonist in *Robin of the Rood* Alaric the Beast? Was that some sort of premonition?

As if sensing my perusal, Alaric raised his eyes to me. Immediately, I looked down at my trencher. The salmon, succulent only moments before, now sat heavy in my stomach.

There was so much noise and tension crackling through the hall that my head throbbed. Everything was just so overwhelming. Finally, I slipped out, thinking to return to the small chamber I shared with several others in Trim's three-storied keep. The courtyard was wrapped in a winding sheet of fog and smoke from the fires within and without the castle, for the surrounding area was a mass of tents. Roger Mortimer's army. Shivering, I pulled my cloak closer. Despite the activity in the great hall, the bailey remained largely empty. Head down, I passed Trim's well, barrels and buckets sprawled like drunk-ards; a pair of grooms leading saddled horses to Trim's stables. The lonely clip-clop of the horses' hooves added to the low hum of distress that had become my constant companion—my personal tinnitus of the soul. Ever lurking just below the surface of my consciousness until I stopped and really listened. There it was, the truth creeping forward, forcing my attention no matter how I vowed to ignore it.

I was homeless, rootless, barely understanding the language, ignorant of the most basic routines and customs, and surrounded by suspicious strangers. A blind woman stumbling toward the abyss. Ceaselessly, I'd worried about my predicament until the pounding in my head was worse than the aftereffects of Alaric DeLaMer's brutality.

Plan. I need a plan. A workable plan. A plan to survive until I can figure out a way to get the hell out of here.

Instinctively, my hands strayed to my Art Deco purse, the chain of which I'd threaded through and secured around the girdle I'd been provided, along with a cote hardie and some passable undergarments. If it was stolen, I would be totally lost. My plan had gotten this far: break up my jewels and sell them piece by piece to moneylenders or pawnbrokers who surely plied their trade in Dublin. Alaric had said my jewelry was worth a king's ransom—

"A word, Clarabel Lucy."

I spun around. Speak of the devil. Alaric DeLaMer materialized out of this miserable, incessant mist to stride toward me.

"What do you want?" That omnipresent thrum was immediately drowned out by annoyance. Was he going to accuse me of conspiring with the de Lacys to kill Hugh de Croft?

Alaric halted before me, legs spread apart in that familiar arrogant stance.

"Your husband's name, Clarabel Lucy?"

I gazed up at him, noting the increased pace of my heart, obviously caused by irritation. "Really? You're about to ride off to war, and you concern yourself with my husband's name?"

"I had no chance during our journey, but now I seek answers."

In anticipation of this moment, I'd already concocted an entire autobiography, but I sighed heavily to signal my annoyance. "William. William Shakespeare."

Alaric rolled the name around in his mouth as if testing an exotic food. "Why have I not heard of him?"

"Because you're an illiterate oaf?" I silently countered, though he really couldn't know anything about a man who wouldn't be born for centuries. I waved a negligent hand. "He pays a scutage so he'll not have to fight."

"Who is your husband's liege?"

Now, things could get dicey. Titles were held by a handful of families, and if I gave an actual name, he could easily investigate. I glared up at him. "His Grace, our king, of course."

Alaric's eyebrows drew together in a frown. He shifted his stance.

"And you are in Ireland because?"

"My husband is here. In Dublin."

"William Shakespeare, baron of Vail?" He scanned my face. I didn't need a mirror to know I was a disheveled mess. Five minutes in this miserable weather and drops of water clung to my eyelashes and cheeks—not at all like the scented mists with which my esthetician had once spritzed my skin in order to add "that extra glow."

"Precisely."

"Why Dublin?" he asked, adopting the manner of a police interrogator grilling a serial killer.

"Why not?" I retorted, though my internal computer was spitting out all related research, which wasn't much. Nearly wiped out by fire in 1304, a famine a few years later, preceding this one...

"Who would willingly hie themselves to that cursed town? And with Edward Bruce recently burning its outskirts, not to mention this nonsense with the de Lacys, what manner of husband would allow his wife to roam about as she pleased?" Alaric paused, and I swear, his eyes burned with malevolence. "Unless you truly are a spy for the Scots, Clarabel Lucy?"

I couldn't suppress a laugh. "You never give up, do you? Perhaps my husband, like you, is unpleasant, and I prefer to have as little to do with him as possible."

Alaric suddenly grabbed me by the wrist and pulled me closer. *Is this where you're going to kiss me?* I worried because he was always staring at my mouth, and that could only mean one thing. I'd outlined so many identical scenes, my brain immediately went haywire. Should I slap him? Would he gut me with the dagger at his belt? Or would he ravage me so thoroughly I'd be left breathless, barely able to stand from the delicious weakness in my limbs...

Alaric slid his free hand down to my purse and twisted open the clasp, retrieving its contents.

"Hey, what are you doing?" I tried to snatch the items, which he held above his head as if denying a treat to an over-excitable dog.

Beyond us, lights from the great hall struggled through the fog, as did the murmurs from its inhabitants. Scrape of invisible footsteps, a muffled curse, the splash of a bucket being dropped in the nearby well, the rhythmic squeak of its rewinding.

"I've been pondering the items in your pouch, and I have further questions."

Knowing it would irritate him, I fluttered my eyelashes. "You've been thinking about little old me? I'm flattered."

"Not you, your jewelry."

"Have you been imagining how lovely my earrings would look on you? How nicely my necklace would contrast with your chest hair?"

Alaric stared at me blankly before clearing his throat and repeating, "Questions."

He unwrapped two pieces of jewelry—my Milanese necklace and a personalized cuff bracelet I'd had engraved in textura script with the motto, *Dieu et mon droit/ "God and my right."*

"I think you've been misnamed, Alaric DeLaMer. Alaric the Beast better suits you." It felt strange saying that aloud as if the thorn-in-the-flesh from *Robin in the Rood* was an actual human being who would come to a deservedly hideous end.

Alaric snorted. "I've been called worse." After holding up the necklace, he arched an eyebrow. "Sapphires, Clarabel Lucy? Do you fear poison?"

Rather than arguing about the magical property of gemstones, I said, "What I fear is you rummaging in my personal possessions."

Alaric ran a thumb over the diamonds and sapphires, which were set in platinum, a metal unknown in this age. "I've not seen the cuts of these stones before. Or such an intricate setting."

"All my jewelry is from Venice," I responded, hoping that sounded sufficiently exotic to forestall further questioning.

Alaric raised an eyebrow. "Sir William Shakespeare must be a very wealthy husband." He curled the necklace in his palm. "Which makes your lack of servants, your roaming around on your own—unless you count your jester, which I would not—all the more puzzling."

"Things are done differently where I come from."

"Apparently so." Alaric returned the necklace to its length of brocaded silk and focused his attention on my cuff bracelet.

While I doubted my tormentor had ever seen an actual bracelet before, he appeared more interested in the inscription, shifting it about, seeking optimum light.

As if the dolt could read.

Which, surprisingly, he could.

After repeating the phrase, "*Dieu et mon droit,*" he commented, "The battle cry of Richard Coeur-de-Lion."

It had also been one of Edward III's mottos, but since future King Edward was currently preschool age, I couldn't ridicule Alaric for being only partially correct and order him, like some obnoxious game show contestant, off the stage.

"Another piece from the Venetians?" he mocked.

I held out my hand. "Are we done here?"

After further minute inspection, holding up each ring, my earrings, and a second bracelet, Alaric returned all my pieces without further comment. Only to retrieve a slim tube in a delicate pink color trimmed in gold. *"Perfect for the discreet female,"* the ad had promised.

My pepper spray!

During our conversation, the courtyard had been shaken awake. Footsteps and voices from the great hall, nearing. A trio of swans, which had been drifting in the moat surrounding Trim's keep, honked and flapped their wings, protesting our intrusion.

"What is this, Clarabel Lucy?" Alaric asked, extending the tube. His thick fingers overlapped plastic indentations that were designed *"to discreetly fit in the palm of your hand."* "Some sort of magic stick?"

My mind was blank; my gaze laser-focused on the cylinder.

"Put that back. You've no right—"

"Is this also from Venice? Or Stonehenge, mayhap, which was transported from Ireland to England via Merlin's wizardry? Entertain me with a fantastical tale about your magic stick, Clarabel Lucy."

"Werewolves," I choked. "I carry it in case I meet a pack of were-wolves... beyond the pale."

Alaric grunted. I was mesmerized by his index finger resting on the button, which, according to the salesman at Dick's Sporting Goods, emitted a "maximum strength" stream via an "advanced delivery system with long-range protection up to twelve feet." Minus the flip-top safety cap I'd removed because if I was attacked by the Irish mafia, I'd be too terrified to remember to pop the cap and die crying, "Wait! Wait! I've almost got it!" while they beat me senseless with their shil-lelaghs.

"Give me that." I gentled my voice as one would when seeking to tame a skittish beast. Or an idiot with pepper spray.

"Another of your secrets, Clarabel Lucy?"

Viewing with horror Alaric's index finger pressing ever so gently on the trigger...

"Don't touch that!" I screamed.

Just as Alaric released a stream of spray into my face.

Part Eight

ALARIC AND CLARABEL

1317–19

Fifteen

ALARIC

In early July, we rode out to destroy the de Lacys. The terrain was largely flat, which allowed easy travel and lowered the risk of ambush. Snaking throughout was the River Boyne, which provided much-needed sustenance since Edward Bruce's forces had laid waste to any meadows and tilled fields that had survived this god-cursed weather.

As we rode, my thoughts repeatedly returned to the last time Lucan had read *Topographia Hibernica* before Wendsbury's fire. I'd been grown then, but I'd still been captivated listening to my brother translating from Latin in his slow, careful fashion. Foolishly believing Ireland was indeed a magical land. I envisioned its countryside rich in pastures and meadows, carpets of woods and copious bogs, all blessed by gentle rains and a climate milder than our own. A place where hawks of all persuasions and eagles, numerous as our starlings, circled the skies while poisonous reptiles, including snakes, were rejected by the land itself. A Promised Land flowing with milk and honey, though —according to Gerald of Wales—the bees were frightened off by yew trees, which were poisonous and bitter.

To which Lucan, who had actually visited Castle DeLaMer, raised his head and said, "Always those heathens and their damnable trees."

Causing Beatrice, his fussy but adoring wife, to cover the ears of one toddler who nestled upon her lap while frowning a warning in the direction of a second.

Perhaps such memories explained why I so hated Ireland. When everything else was stripped away, it reminded me of Lucan, the DeLaMer who should have lived.

Our initial campaign against Edward Bruce and his followers had begun soon after Bannockburn. Where once I'd been an indifferent fighter, now conflict allowed me to release what I marked as rage, though I was never good at plumbing my emotions. When I was focused on besting my enemy, the jumble of thoughts denying me sleep, the succubus nightly tormenting my bed, the demons I could not otherwise outrun simply dropped away. I found solace in my newfound belief that fate, rather than a Divine plan, decreed whether I prevailed or joined my brother. All the prayers and supplications added not a jot to the length of our days. Realizing such matters were determined by a random casting of the runes made me careless of my safety. It also made me a more ferocious warrior.

These thoughts and others I kept to myself.

Each night, after we bedded down and I crawled into a tent with several others, I resurrected my nightly ritual.

Hating it.

Dreading it.

Powerless to alter it.

My first memory of a morning, my first thought when I laid me down to rest. After which, I thumbed through a string of random contemplations the way I thumbed my paternoster beads. Or, I would roam the great hall, stables, or battlements, passing like a specter among those who slept and others who, like me, attended to midnight tasks. Since I seldom drifted off before lauds, I was perpetually sleep-starved. As I had been for nearly two years.

Katrin. Nestled against her with only a counterpane covering us, for it was the height of an English summer. Enjoying the warmth of our bodies where they touched, her back to my chest, our legs slotting easily into each other.

A stir and sleepy mumble. Slipping my hand down my wife's naked flesh to her rounded stomach, thanking God for the emerging life that had banished the darkness enveloping me since Lucan's death and my father's broken heart on the heels of it.

Moving aside the fragrant mass of hair concealing the nape of Katrin's neck, pressing my lips to her. "Good morrow, wife."

Another murmur before she'd turned over to smile her sleepy smile up at me. A traitor's smile, it turned out to be. Why had she not told me? Why had I not noticed? Hadn't I experienced enough death to recognize when it stared back at me?

This night, the next bead I thumbed bore the annoying countenance of one Clarabel Lucy. A rude creature and not at all attractive. Too pricklish. And her speech—a garble of so many different languages and dialects and peculiar phrases, as if she were attempting to compose a tart out of the ingredients for a mutton stew. Both could be classified as food, and both were edible, but beyond that, they had little in common. Sometimes, I had to stare at her mouth, hoping the shape of her lips might give me a clue to the sounds emanating from it.

Still, she spouted her nonsense with such passionate certitude, I could scarce hide my amusement. And while I'd been disavowed of any connection to the de Lacys early on, I enjoyed watching her face flush and her expressions change with each whirling of that quicksilver mind. This much was obvious. Clarabel Lucy was hiding something...

Nearby, my squire shifted, and James Lackford groaned in his sleep. The *parfit* knight off the battlefield and a lion on—though the lion's roar became more muted upon each engagement. *I hope you do not love her,* I thought for the thousandth time. While I had never responded to Jocelyn Goodknyght's advances, I suspected others had. And should Sir James know, I prayed he was indifferent to his wife's infidelities. That he, at least, dreamed peaceful dreams.

But because I did not, my thumb and index finger remained on the Clarabel Lucy bead. Remembering the aftermath of loosing that poisoned spray, I smiled in the darkness. Lucy had shrieked and hopped about to my great puzzlement until I too felt the backflow from its burn. Half-carrying her squawking form to Trim's well, I'd repeatedly doused her head in bucket after bucket of water. After which, I tore a strip from her chemise, wet it, and bathed her eyes.

Ah, the cursing. Or I'd assumed 'twas cursing because I couldn't understand the half of it.

Finally, Clarabel Lucy had stood before me, her mantle discarded in the fracas, the rest of her clothes soaked clear through, her hair plastered round her face, glaring at me through half-slitted eyes.

"I believe your spray *will* protect you from any werewolves who cross your path," I said.

Hands fisted, trembling with a combination of cold and rage, she sputtered some nonsense about fucking the horse on which I rode.

It was then I did a most unforgivable thing. I laughed. "You look ridiculous," I blurted. "Like a drowned stable cat."

Her face scrunched even more, and then, wonder of wonders, Clarabel Lucy's countenance transformed from anger to mirthful, and she joined me, both of us laughing until we were out of breath with merriment.

It felt good. Not only because I cannot recall the last time I'd found anything even moderately amusing but because Clarabel Lucy possessed the sort of laugh I could listen to forever.

Aye, it was far better to fall asleep to the echoes of that peculiar woman's laughter than the way I usually did.

To the screams of my Katrin before her body slammed against the cobblestones.

~

The end was simple enough. The victory ours. Roger Mortimer flew the dragon banner, signaling the suspension of the codes of chivalry. No quarter or mercy would be given to Walter and Hugh de Lacy or anyone who sheltered them.

War seems to pass in the blink of an eye while lasting an eternity, so I have no idea how long we fought, only that we were successful, returning the de Lacys' previous betrayals tenfold with *their* corpses spread across the peat bogs and fields, with the stench of *their* putre-fying flesh perversely pleasing to my nostrils. Roger Mortimer, Lord Lieutenant of Ireland, had well learned the lessons of Bannockburn. As had we all. We were a brutal, disciplined fighting force that would annihilate anyone who thought to gainsay either Roger Mortimer or our King Edward.

Now, all of County Meath was under English control. Furthermore, we sensed it, the shift in fortunes. That Edward Bruce and his dreams of an Irish kingship had gone up in smoke with the countryside he'd put to the torch. And with the smashing of the de Lacys.

Roger Mortimer was finally reaping the rewards of power following a decade of faithful service to our king. 'Twas time now for our commander, with us beside him, to subdue the rest of Ireland.

Sixteen

CLARABEL

We rode through the sprawling suburb of Oxmantown, which would bleed into Dublin proper. Our trip from Trim Castle had been uneventful, accompanied as we were by Lord Mortimer, who had returned from his battlefield victory long enough to welcome his daughter Alice into the world, hug his other nine children, and strike out for Dublin to preside over Ireland's Parliament.

Lady Jocelyn and her husband, who owned a town house in the city, also traveled with us. All too often, I sensed Jocelyn's eyes boring into my back, probably because she was upset that Alaric had ridden beside me throughout. If she only knew he was doing it because I'd ordered him to leave me alone.

"Where do you reside in Dublin?" asked Alaric. Despite my vow to ignore him, I'd found myself repeatedly sneaking glances his way throughout. There was something undeniably sexy about a man in uniform—particularly the medieval version. Alaric exuded confidence and strength, and knowing how thoroughly he'd helped crush the de Lacy brothers, well, Bella Publishing could have written an entire series of romances around such a man.

Too bad the real Alaric DeLaMer was such a butthead.

"I no longer have a residence in Dublin," I said airily, pretending great interest in Oxmantown's most prominent landmark, St Mary's Abbey, a sprawl of buildings off to our right.

"And what happened to your residence?" Alaric swiveled his head to study me, one eyebrow raised in his usual smirky way. As if he didn't believe me. Which he didn't. We both knew I was lying. Which was part of the fun.

"It burned down, like so much of the rest when the Scots threatened Dublin earlier this year. Most unfortunate. Thatched roof. I plan to lease a town house."

I enjoyed sparring with Alaric. Despite his dour appearance, he had a quick wit, and sometimes, the way he looked at me, well, if this had been the twenty-first century, he would have come out and said, "We both know you're full of shit."

I imagined Alaric DeLaMer as a metrosexual flying in and out from the coasts, facilitating a brainstorming session for a new imprint or eyeing himself in a full-length mirror and asking whether his skinny jeans made his ass look big.

"What is so amusing, Clarabel Lucy?" he asked.

Shaking my head, I pretended interest in the scattered crowd lining both sides of the road. While I must return to my former life, I was enjoying this part of my "adventure."

"Tell me about your husband. If you no longer have a local residence, from where will he be traveling for your reunion?"

"Lord Shakespeare is not really allowed to travel," I said, dismissing Alaric's question with an airy wave.

"Is your husband infirm?"

"It's just that—"

"I understand. He is very old and nearly blind, which was the only reason he agreed to marry you."

Where once I would have bristled like a disgruntled hedgehog at Alaric's insult, I'd realized it was his clumsy way of teasing.

"Quite the contrary." I refrained from adding "smarty pants." "My husband is only two years old. You know how it is with arranged marriages."

"But you told me." Alaric puffed out his cheeks. "Do you even have a husband?"

I sighed dramatically. "Even you must understand one cannot consummate marriage with a toddler."

"Ah, and by the time your spouse is old enough to legally perform his marital duties, you will probably be dead of old age, so why worry?" True enough. In this age, I—both of us—were past our prime.

"Aye. Though I think my toddler husband's conversation is more pleasing to my ear than some." I twisted in the saddle to face him full-on. "Men can be such a pain in the arse, don't you think?"

I was rewarded with a fleeting smile and a shake of the head. We rode in silence for a bit, passing through an area of small but well-kept cottages laid out in tidy squares, perhaps indicating the handiwork of an overly conscientious city planner.

"Did I ever mention I have been to Cornwall?" Alaric asked.

Uh-oh. Now, he would call me on more of my fabrications.

"We have mines there. Joseph of Arimathea, who was a tin trader, visited one of them. At his side was Jesus, then a young man, who provided succor to the miners laboring there."

History's first union organizer? Okay, I wasn't the only one who stretched the truth. "Odd I never heard of you or your mines," I responded, lifting my chin. "Then again, Cornwall is a very large place."

Alaric snorted. "What a spinner of tales you are."

Pretending offense, I glared at him. "Do you know what I wish, Alaric DeLaMer?"

"What, Clarabel Lucy?"

"That I still had my magic stick so I could spray you until you quit pestering me!"

Alaric grinned. "I'll not forget the look on your face afterward."

"You could have permanently blinded me," I said, unable to suppress a laugh, which he soon joined. "You, Alaric DeLaMer, are a scoundrel. A scoundrel and a *beast*."

"Merely speaking the truth." His gaze met mine. "One of us has to."

We smiled at each other, we sharers of a private joke, and my breath caught in my throat, obviously irritated by the dirt stirred by our horses' hooves.

Our banter was interrupted by Lady Jocelyn, who maneuvered her palfrey between us and smiled as if she too were amused. Addressing me, she said, "Once we arrive in Dublin, it would please me to help you settle in."

"How kind," I said, my gaze drifting to Alaric. He had schooled his expression to neutral, but I, because of that woman thing, knew Alaric returned Jocelyn's desire full measure.

And did not care at all.

There's an old tale involving Death, that if you knew where He resided, you'd never go there. Looking back, that's how I feel about the day I met Naga the Alchemist. I could not know then he would destroy my life, and Alaric's too, in the end.

Following our arrival, Lady Jocelyn had guided me to a ramshackle town house in the city center, across the lane from the Lackfords' own. In order to pay for renovations and staff, I had to start selling my jewels. Jocelyn obligingly provided the name and directions to a local moneylender. While my head was filled with related plans, they were not enough to drown that omnipresent hum of distress: *How do I return to my century? I must. I must.*

The city of Dublin, that part within the walls, was little more than a square mile across. With Christ Church Cathedral in its heart to act as my guide, I set out, flipping up my hood to protect against the mist seeping like an open wound from the sky.

Matteo the Moneylender was located at the end of a lane near one of Dublin's public water fountains. Because I had turned my nose into my hood to lessen the stench exacerbated by the mist, I did not see Naga the Alchemist leaning in the doorway of the Elixir of Life Apothecary Shop. When he greeted me with, "Lady, good day, give you our Lord," I jumped.

"I did not mean to startle you!" Naga's smile was amiable, though looking back, I would more label it "sly." And later, when pondering the circumstances of our first meeting, I wondered whether Naga the Alchemist had been waiting for me.

Probably.

No doubt.

After exchanging pleasantries, Naga peppered me with questions in between hawking potions efficacious for stomach ills, coughs, heart palpitations, and "to rid your new residence of the rodents therein."

While he nattered on, I found myself staring, the way you do at something out of harmony with its surroundings—or other members of its species. With his snow-white—or white-blond hair—odd amber eyes and androgynous face and body, I couldn't decide whether Naga the Alchemist was beautiful or repulsive.

"I've a multitude of available services," said Naga. "'Twould be my pleasure to assist you with all your needs."

Gesturing to the sign painted with three gold balls hanging above Matteo's shop, I said, "I really must be going."

"Let me accompany you. I know everyone worth knowing and a few besides."

With his sonorous voice, Naga would have made an excellent podcaster of the macabre. *"Here is another dark and disturbing tale..." "My experience with a psychopath began..."*

"I am an expert on jewelry," he continued, ignoring my hesitation. "I will procure you the best price."

While following him, I noticed the dragon stitched on the back of his robe with strategic openings that allowed him to spread it like a dragon's wings. Laughably theatrical, though an alchemist probably needed to cultivate a flamboyant persona in order to distract from the fact that changing base metals to gold was as likely as me walking across the Irish Sea.

Matteo the Moneylender wasn't nearly as impressed by my jewelry as Naga, who gushed over my Milanese necklace.

"I am not sure." Matteo studied my display with suspicion. "I've never seen anything remotely comparable to these cuts. Nor the metal."

Of course not. They won't be invented for centuries.

"Where did you acquire these?"

"China," I said, remembering Marco Polo and the Silk Road.

"I've seen similar during my travels," Naga said airily. "They are of the finest quality."

Unless Naga the Alchemist was a time traveler, he most certainly had not. Which meant he was a fabulist. From then on, I privately referred to him as Naga the Charlatan.

Another of my mistakes.

Naga was instrumental in negotiating the sale of a black opal Art Deco ring I'd purchased because it reminded me of Scott and Zelda and *The Great Gatsby*. I left Matteo's with a comfortably full purse.

"Now," Naga said, steering me into his shop. "I've something 'twill rid your residence of those rats we earlier discussed."

The "something" turned out to be arsenic, which he carefully measured out and handed me in a stoppered jar. "Much more effective than cats or rat catchers," he said, accepting a silver penny in payment. "Lady Lackford often purchases arsenic."

I didn't remember mentioning Jocelyn to him, though I might have.

Watch yourself. Helpful Naga might appear, but I likened him to a jackal in search of his next meal. If the opportunity arose, I did not doubt he would trade information, anything about me for his own purposes.

The longer I lingered in Naga's presence, the more off-kilter I found myself. It was his face, I decided, which was impossible to categorize. One moment, it appeared feminine; the next, his features shifted, and he was a comely lad with a preternaturally unlined face. I imagined him donning a human mask or injecting himself with botox centuries before it was invented.

"Where is your home, Lady Lucy?" Naga asked, absently rearranging the various jars, tools, and dried herbs on his worktable. "'Tis not Ireland or England."

I considered launching into my spiel about Land's End and Vail, Colorado, but Naga would see through my fantasy-weaving. "How should I use the arsenic?" I asked instead.

After he explained and I readied to leave, he said, "If you ever decide to sell your necklace…I have great respect for Milanese jewelers. So many quaint shops there."

I hadn't mentioned the origin of my necklace. Had I? Maybe. But even if I had, Milan was an ancient city famous for its trade. Such a comment would not raise suspicion.

But Naga was not done. "What do you know of alchemy?" he asked.

I shrugged. "Thomas Aquinas was an alchemist." Many intellectuals, lords, and monarchs were interested in alchemy. Edward III would even hire his own royal alchemist when seeking to fund his campaigns at the beginning of the Hundred Years War. But since Edward III was currently five-year-old Edward of Windsor and most likely playing marbles, jacks, and king of the castle, I did not elaborate.

"To transmute one substance to another—once one finds the key, riches, immortality, nothing is impossible, is it?" Naga made a sweeping gesture, causing the wings of his robe to swish like a bird puffing its feathers.

Though I knew better than to risk further exposure, I nearly asked, "What about time travel? If you can spin riches and live forever, can you bend time?"

"How old do you think I am, Lady Lucy?"

Who are you? What are you?

An oppressive silence settled between us. A sickly yellow miasma, as if the sun were trapped within, drifted through the shop's opening.

"No idea."

"I have spells and potions." Dropping his voice to a seductive level, he said, "As an alchemist, I am privy to many secrets."

I imagined Naga slicing me open and studying my entrails in order to divine the future.

"Because you're not from here, I shall reveal something 'twould be prudent to remember."

Do not be fooled. Naga is Dottie Lucy-Flack in another costume.

"Your jewelry tells its own tale, if one has ears to listen."

Knowing he expected me to ask, "What do you mean?" I bade him good day, clutched my arsenic close, and exited the shop.

"The Feast of the Assumption of the Blessed Virgin," Naga said, continuing our conversation through the opening. "Midsummer's Eve is optimum, but since that is past, consider mid-August." He shrugged theatrically. "These things take time, do they not?"

"What are you talking about?" I asked, losing my temper. Why couldn't I have left innuendoes, drama, and b.s. back in my future?

"As Mother Mary ascended into heaven, 'tis a day for the initiated to traverse other realms." Naga raised his arms, causing his dragon wings to expand. "Would *you* like to traverse other realms?"

"Thank you for the arsenic." Deliberately turning my back, I picked my way along the lane, my pattens repeatedly sinking in the mud.

"Do wear a sprig of holly when you embark upon your journey," Naga called after me. "The points on its leaves will keep you safe."

$\sim$

The following afternoon, I was surprised by a visit from Jocelyn. Since we lived right across a narrow lane from each other, it wasn't much of a visit, more like a handful of steps.

"Please help celebrate Sir James' birthday this even," she said, following the usual pleasantries. "He would most enjoy your company."

I nearly asked whether their good friend Alaric DeLaMer was also invited, but why should I care about a man who'd not bothered to show his ridiculous face even once following our return from Trim Castle?

Jocelyn continued. "These are sad times for both my lord husband and Sir Alaric. Bannockburn, you know."

I was surprised since, by my calculation, the anniversary of Bannockburn was a month ago.

"Since that tragedy, my husband and Sir Alaric have paid for more Masses than I can count."

I was simultaneously annoyed Jocelyn kept mentioning Alaric—and eager for her to continue.

"They've haunted St. Patrick's Cathedral with their Masses for the Dead, one after the other. For certes, 'tis necessary, but one's birthday should be a time of gladness. One cannot live forever in the past."

Since I was literally living in the past, I made no comment other than to accept Jocelyn's invitation and quickly usher her out.

After pausing in the kitchen to converse with my newly hired cook, I retired to the privacy of my bedroom, located off a hall behind the kitchen.

Why had Jocelyn Goodknyght invited me to Sir James' birthday? Did it have something to do with Alaric? Did she think the contrast between me and her own fine self would remind Alaric of how much he loved her? Was she toying with her husband, Alaric, all of us? If nothing else, this would give me an opportunity to observe the pair, to see whether Alaric might betray his true feelings. But what exactly *were* his true feelings? While I'd never witnessed Alaric being anything but polite, Trim Castle gossip maintained they'd been paramours. Did Alaric love Jocelyn so desperately that he must forever guard his feelings lest they boil to the surface, or had they merely enjoyed a fling? Had my writer's imagination plotted an eighty-thousand-word romance when it barely merited a sentence?

"You're pretty damned despicable." I addressed an invisible Alaric while loosing my girdle and placing it atop the brightly painted chest at the foot of my bed. "Would it have killed you to visit one lousy time? Can you really be that busy?" Yes, the Irish Parliament was in session, but Dublin Castle was within easy walking distance.

Flopping down on my quite lovely bed, I stared up past the poles holding my curtains to the ceiling. Had I been able to choose any architectural design in my other world, I'd probably have manufactured something similar, only with the requisite modern conveniences. While renovations were ongoing and the upper story where servants slept was low-ceilinged and warren-like, my room was spacious and dramatically masculine with rough-hewn ceiling beams and floor planks so wide I marveled at the size of the trees producing them. I liked the contrast with my delicate wall tapestries and the embroidered samite cloths draping my bed.

What I did not like was maneuvering my way through a world where I must purchase arsenic from charlatans to eliminate rats; where frequent baths were achieved only with great inconvenience; where children were hanged upon gibbets for petty crimes; where animal waste was so greatly prized it was deposited in public dung-heaps.

And where the Four Horsemen of the Apocalypse were not the subject of some arcane Bible verse but our daily reality.

~

"Clarabel Lucy," Alaric DeLaMer's gaze homed in on me seated on a bench in the Lackford's solar. "Without your husband again?"

I huffed and rolled my eyes, hoping I'd not betrayed my happiness at seeing my nemesis. Not happiness. Non-annoyance.

Alaric lingered in the doorway, seeming to take up its entire space. I'd forgotten how enormous he was. And hairy, though his careless coiffure and beard were kind of growing on me. Not literally, thank god.

"You came!" Lady Jocelyn leaped from her chair near a fireplace huge enough to swallow a Volkswagen and hurried to him. Sir James called a greeting from his spot near the blazing fire. "Come join me, friend. Warm off the even's chill."

Instead, Alaric sauntered in my direction. I braced myself for another round of cross-verbal-swords-with-Clarabel-Lucy.

While my bench, which contained a cushion so thin it made prolonged sitting uncomfortable, was large enough for two, I wasn't about to surrender my space.

Alaric halted in front of me. I ignored him to examine the embroidery on my sleeve. Alaric nudged my knee. A lifetime of court etiquette, and he behaved like one of Bella Publishing's *Knights of the Road* bad boys?

I glared up at him. "What do you want?"

"A place to rest my bones," he said. "Will you move, or must I set myself upon your lap?"

"Beast!" I breathed, scooting so far to the edge I risked falling off.

Once seated, Alaric positioned himself so his knees grazed mine. Hardly surprising, given his bulk and the limited space. "Tell me, Clarabel Lucy. Have you been wreaking havoc on the town and its defenseless inhabitants?" His easy manner intimated we saw each other all the time rather than…never.

I angled my knees away. "How can I when I've been so busy making my residence—which is right across the way, in case you didn't know—habitable?" Not quite the truth. Weather permitting, I enjoyed exploring Dublin. Usually, I disguised myself in male clothing because men had more freedom of movement and didn't have to deal with escorts telling them, "Don't do this," "Don't go there."

"I do know where you reside," Alaric countered.

Unless he'd purchased an invisibility potion from Naga the Charlatan, I doubted that. "Have you been spying on me?"

"Do you need watching?"

"We've made something special for both you and my lord husband." Jocelyn had miraculously materialized beside my tormentor. Reaching out to grasp both his hands, she cried, "Dear Alaric!"

Hold on there! Flirting right in front of your husband?

"How are you faring? Remember the merry celebrations we've shared over the years? I do so miss them."

I glanced behind them to Sir James, who appeared completely content—and clueless—nestled in a high-backed chair surrounded by a raft of pillows and with his legs propped on a makeshift footrest.

Poor man. Poor, deluded old man.

Alaric withdrew his hands while acknowledging Jocelyn's words with a curt nod.

Are you so overcome with passion you can scarce manage a head movement?

After ordering a maid to bring our treat, Jocelyn dimpled at Alaric. "I've not forgotten your favorite dessert. Despite the scarcities, I pray you'll be pleased with the result."

Could you be more obvious? Dear God, someone put me out of my misery.

Rather than respond, Alaric slipped free from her grasp and crossed to the fireplace area, where he poured two drinks from a jug of wine atop a folding table. A flash of annoyance marred Jocelyn's lovely features.

"Apologies for my thoughtlessness," she said, trailing after him. When she reached for the goblets, Alaric shook his head and muttered something unintelligible.

"How fares your husband?" Alaric asked after returning to my side and handing me the wine. "Has he shed his swaddling bands yet?"

"He's fine, thank you for asking."

Alaric snorted.

After he settled beside me once again, I found myself eying him over the rim of my goblet and recalling the first time I'd seen him, all sweaty and musclebound and practically naked in Castle DeLaMer's bailey. *But that wasn't the first time. Remember when he bowed his knee before you? When he raised his head and your eyes met, and the Earth tilted upon its axis?*

Why is this bench so small?

I was sure I could feel Alaric's body heat through his clothes, which speaking of, the buttons running down the front of his cotehardie pulled too tight across his chest. Whoever had once described Alaric as a fop needed glasses, which thankfully had already been invented.

"Do I unnerve you, Clarabel Lucy?" Alaric leaned toward me until our shoulders touched. "Are you going to whip out another of your magic sticks and render me immobile?"

"That was you, dunderhead," I muttered, refusing to shift away.

Fortunately, at that moment, the maid returned with a tray of sweets. After Jocelyn cut her husband a slice of his birthday treat, sambocade, which resembled cheesecake, she crossed to us.

"Spiced wine custard. Your favorite."

Jocelyn also handed me a bowl. The custard contained way too many cloves and enough cinnamon to gag a normal human. After one shuddering bite, I gave Alaric the rest.

Afterward, Jocelyn bustled about, scolding Sir James for sneaking a third slice of sambocade, ordering Mary to remove the remains of our repast and a second servant to light the wall torches and freshen the fire. Sir James and Alaric conversed, he from his chair and Alaric beside me. I enjoyed observing their easy manner, the pleasing rumble of their voices while discussing Sir James' latest ailments, parliamentary doings, and whether Roger Mortimer would launch another campaign before summer's end.

Absently, I watched my tormentor's hands dance as he talked. Despite their brutish appearance, they were oddly graceful. Sometimes, they rested, loosely curled, upon Alaric's thighs; sometimes, he ran them through his hair, though why bother since it immediately returned to its former *deshabille*; sometimes, he jabbed them in the air to illustrate yet another incomprehensible martial arts maneuver. When his hands clenched and relaxed, I imagined them wielding his sword the way they had upon our first meeting.

I was so lost in contemplation I didn't immediately realize that Jocelyn had removed some sort of fiddle—I recognized it as a citole— from a chest and handed it to her husband.

"Join me." Jocelyn beckoned to Alaric, who immediately abandoned me to stand beside her while Sir James caressed the citole's strings.

Reminding me this was how people entertained themselves before electricity.

What a pretty sight Alaric and Jocelyn made, he the dark knight and she the delicate-as-a-lily lady in her pearl and gold crespine and flowing cotehardie. The scene left me unsettled and yearning for something similar. Yet another feeling I ignored.

"Let us start with *Western Wind*," Jocelyn said to Sir James, who obligingly thrummed a background melody.

"*Western wind, when will thou blow?*" Jocelyn began in a clear, lovely voice.

Alaric joined in.

"The small rain down can rain.
Christ, if my love were in my arms,
And I in my bed again."

Their voices blended seamlessly together. Though I was loathe to admit it, they were quite talented. Hardly surprising. Once darkness descended and conversation and game boards lost their charm, what better way to pass an evening?

Alaric and Lady Jocelyn continued with what was obviously a familiar repertoire. Sometimes, Sir James joined in, his voice quavering on the higher notes. After a song detailing the pains of unrequited love, Jocelyn addressed me. "Since you appear ignorant of our choices, please select one of your favorites and entertain us." Behind her smile, Jocelyn's hatred vibrated like a tuning fork. Particularly when Alaric left Sir James' side to return to our bench.

"Aye, Clarabel Lucy," he teased. "Gift us with your voice."

If Alaric thought to unnerve me with his nearness, he would be disappointed. Or that I'd be undone by shyness. I was Dottie Lucy-Flack's daughter, after all.

I mentally ran through a catalog of songs until settling on the perfect choice.

"*Down in the valley,*" I began. I didn't bother translating from modern English. Dublin was a port city with multiple languages the norm, never mind the hodgepodge of French, Latin, and Middle English spoken by most of the nobility. Another language would not be considered odd.

Even with my eyes closed, I sensed the intensity of Alaric's gaze. Who could not be moved by such a beautiful melody? I conjured my father and all the times we'd snuggled while he sang; awakening to the whisper of his voice long after he'd died and me not knowing.

"*Roses love sunshine,*
Violets love dew..."

My voice faltered. Maurice had loved roses. The soft brush of Sir James' fingers across the citole strings anchored me, returning me to the moment.

"*If you don't love me, love whom you please,*" I continued, this time in Anglo-Norman.

"*Put your arms round me, give my heart ease.*"

I imagined Daddy, no longer earthbound, watching just beyond the firelight. Free to follow me across the street or across the centuries.

I opened my eyes. Alaric was close enough that I could reach out and touch his chest or run my fingers along the curve of his cheek through his hair. At this moment, I wouldn't mind, particularly with the way his gaze remained riveted to mine.

"*Build me a castle, forty feet high*
So I can see her as she rides by..."

By the time I finished, I felt as though I were drifting like a bird riding a wind stream, untethered and free to flit among elusive worlds if I really, really believed. I remembered Naga's enigmatic words. If I could transport myself into my future on the Feast of the Assumption, would I? Tonight, the idea held no appeal.

"A lovely piece," said Sir James, putting aside his citole. "Melancholy but lovely."

If Jocelyn commented, I didn't hear it. I was too caught up in the nearness of Alaric, in the way he'd cocked his head, studying me. "*Give my heart ease*," he finally murmured as if tasting the rightness of the phrase.

I could only nod.

Seventeen

꧑

ALARIC

"God's nails! What is she thinking?"

Clarabel Lucy poking her nose about Dublin like some merchant inspecting goods at Scarborough Fair, when she was obviously a woman pretending to be a man and fooling no one. Jesus wept; what male went about wriggling his arse in tunic and hose, flinging his arms about, and making other gestures that not even a mummer, performing a female part, would mimic? The worst of it was she must believe herself invisible because she went out without a servant or escort. If Clarabel Lucy did have a husband—a dubious assumption— he should lock her in a donjon for safekeeping.

I'd first spotted Bel following a visit to James Lackford. Sir James had been feeling poorly and unable to attend Parliament, so I often slipped away to spend time with him. Upon leaving, I'd spotted Bel half a lane ahead. Well, I'd not initially known it was her, but my attention had immediately been snagged—like seeing a gaggle of geese dancing a carol. And after I'd identified her, my initial reaction had been to confront her about her idiocy.

"Do you have some demented need to become other people?" I would ask.

"First, that ridiculous Veronica Valenium, and now some tradesman the like of which mankind has never before seen?"

But knowing Bel, she'd glower and push out her lower lip like a naughty child before spewing some fabulism. The moment I walked away, she'd contrive some other ridiculous costume and behavior. I'd no choice but to follow her. Not all the time, but when I could not shake my concern for her or when Parliament was particularly stultifying. Which was basically each and every hour of every day. Its major business consisted of declaring the remaining de Lacys' felons and outlaws, confiscating their property, and banishing them from Ireland. Since English and Irish law were one and the same, and there was no one to speak up on behalf of the traitors, we lords simply nodded our agreement and counted the days until the session's end. Then, we would don our armor and sweep the south to cross swords with some rebels. Until that blessed day, Clarabel Lucy made for an interesting distraction, particularly since her reactions to her explorations made no sense and caused me endless speculation. What could possibly be going on in her febrile brain?

If Bel was truly a resident of Dublin, she would be familiar with its layout. While Dublin was the size of a middling English town, she acted like every lane and alley, church, and shop was a novelty. Sometimes, I wondered whether her memory flickered like a candle's flame in a draft. Or perhaps in the place she came from—whatever she chose to call her holding on any particular day—such sights were novelties.

Generally, Bel set out after midday meal, though her habits were known only to herself, without rhyme or reason or weather or, apparently, household duties. She spent hours quayside watching fishermen unloading their catches from the River Liffey, even following the carts bound for Fishamble Street, as if she'd never witnessed a fish market. Mass at St. Patrick's Cathedral before visiting the many smaller churches, aping the most pious pilgrim. Chatting with leather-workers, coopers, turners, and blacksmiths, even questioning tanners, apparently oblivious to the stench of their trade, which, in any civilized society, would have been located outside city walls.

It was inevitable that Bel would find her way to Dublin Castle, where Parliament was being held.

A pity she chose this particular afternoon.

Once again, I'd been shadowing her; once again, she'd been oblivious. Apparently, Bel believed herself to exist inside an enormous soap bubble fashioned from a child's blow tube where nothing or no one could touch her. After surrendering my weapon as was custom, I followed her into King's Hall and watched from a discreet distance as she wandered about. Since Dublin was the administrative center of the Pale, business was being conducted even now by my lord Mortimer upon his dais, as well as merchants in smaller groups scattered throughout. It amused me that Bel pretended interest, which she, with her uncertain grasp of the language and being a woman besides, could never hope to understand.

Upon noticing a pair of mercers pointing at her, I swore. Jesus, her vulnerability made me want to tear my hair.

"Clarabel Lucy!" I barked, striding up behind her.

Bel jumped, emitted a startled yelp, and spun around. "You're mistaken," she said, making a half-hearted attempt to deepen her voice. "I am but a clerk looking for the exchequer's office."

Despite myself, I laughed. She was just so entertainingly absurd.

Her shoulders sagged, and in her normal voice, she asked, "What are you doing here?"

"Keeping you free of trouble. By the rood, 'tis miracle you've not been accosted—or worse."

"How did you recognize me?"

"Do you think me daft, Bel?" I asked, slipping into the nickname I'd been calling her in my head since our first ridiculous encounter. "You look naught like a man, even in that nonsensical garb."

Bel had forgotten to flip up her hood, though she did wear a bycocket, which did little to hide the strange rainbow of shades that comprised her hair coloring. "Highlights," she'd once called them. Whatever that meant. Reaching out, I tucked a strand of hair behind her ear before tugging her hood forward to shade her obviously feminine features. "Why are you so enamored of foolish costumes? First Vallenium Victorum and now this."

Bel lifted her chin in that stubborn way she had, which generally signified she was about to exercise her sharp tongue or launch into another of her tales.

"Dublin is fascinating. And now that I've hired all the necessary help and my residence is looking quite lovely…"

Before she could continue, we were interrupted by several knights who burst through King's Hall's massive open doors.

"Make way!" one shouted.

Onlookers parted; conversation ceased. Sensing trouble, I automatically reached for my dagger and mourned its loss.

Trouble it turned out to be. Here is the short of it: a pirate named Thomas Dun had been employed by Robert Bruce to ferry Bruce's soldiers across the Irish Sea in order to plump up his younger brother's army. Responding to King Edward's call for Dun's capture, these knights, now approaching Roger Mortimer, seated on an elevated throne beneath a baldachin, were here to provide proof of Thomas Dun's demise.

I was tall enough to see the unfolding scene. After bowing before Mortimer the lead knight, who carried a large basket, slowly, dramatically lifted the lid to reveal a dark cloth covering some unrecognizable object.

Judging from the size, approximate shape… Ah, we could be a brutish lot, couldn't we?

"What's happening?" Bel asked, unable to see around me.

Removing the covered object, the knight tossed it at Roger Mortimer's feet.

Thump. A commonplace sound that turned my blood to ice.

Leaning forward, Mortimer carefully unwrapped the package and raised the severed head of Thomas Dun.

Gasps. Murmuring. A woman's scream so near it pierced my ears, leaving me momentarily paralyzed before I wrapped my arm around Bel and swept her away from King's Hall.

Such is the way of things in Ireland, I kept thinking. Although we'd safely exited the cluster of buildings that comprised Dublin Castle, I was surprised by the continued racing of my heart and the sick feeling that had settled in my stomach.

"I'll accompany you home," I managed. My head pounded like a battle drum. *Boom! Boom!* Why would the sight of a severed head so unnerve me? I'd seen far worse. Because it was unexpected, out of place among ordinary people, ordinary activities?

No. Something else.

That thump... that scream... What had those sounds hearkened back to? What images lurked in my memory? I was all too familiar with them, though they crept out of their lairs at night, not now... not now... when the day was fading, when clouds hovered like smoke above the chimney tops threatening yet more rain but not dark. I was upright, moving through the streets with Bel's grip upon my sleeve.

I must have escorted Bel in the proper direction. I'm not sure whether she spoke to me. If so, I responded by rote. *Thomas Dun's head. Thomas Dun, the Pirate.* But I was remembering another death under similar ordinary circumstances, when the world was one way and in the next, past, present, future destroyed in the time it took to...thump...

I didn't want to remember, not here, not now...

Yet I was lost in it.

King Edward had been kind. He'd not questioned Katrin's fall from the battlements as anything but an accident. I knew better. The act had been deliberate. Suicide. And if thus publicly ruled, all her property would have been forfeited. Katrin would have been buried outside consecrated graveyards with a stake through her heart. Most likely at a crossroads, where her confused ghost, not understanding which direction to travel, would be forever stuck. King Edward's pretense had saved our family from disgrace and Katrin, I hoped, from eternal damnation because all the proper prayers were allowed to be said and Extreme Unction given.

"Alaric!"

From Bel's tone, she'd repeatedly called my name. I shook my head. For the space of a heartbeat, I'd not recognized her.

We had reached her town house. "Is something wrong?" she asked. "Is there something you haven't told me?"

Pulling myself out of the past, I frowned down at her. What was I doing here? How had Katrin bled over from her usual place into the daylight hours?

"What happened back there?" Bel asked, her expression tight with concern. "Is Dublin in danger?"

"Do not go out without an escort," I said, ignoring her question. "And dress properly. Do not even think to gainsay me on this."

After making sure Bel was safely inside, I made my way back to Dublin Castle's barracks and readied myself for what horrors the night would inevitably bring.

~

Katrin perched on my shoulder the way gargoyles perch on the exteriors of a thousand different churches. When my thoughts wandered in different directions, as they were increasingly wont to do, I, remembering my punishment, dragged them back.

Always.

No matter the passing of time, no matter whatever events—or people—distracted me, I knew I must forever serve my penance.

Because all the rationalizations, explanations, or absolutions granted me by a dozen confessors could not explain away the reality: my Katrin, my kind, sweet Katrin, who gazed at me from huge dark eyes, eyes that could fill with tears one moment and shine with happiness the next, had killed herself—along with our child—rather than endure another moment as my wife.

What had I done? Like revenants rising from the grave, the possibilities tormented me. Ever mindful of Katrin's naivete, I'd striven to be tender and caring. Had I crushed her fragile temperament by mocking her when I'd meant to tease? Dismissed her observations because she was so much younger? Grown impatient and short-tempered when she merely sought my approval? Been selfish in my lovemaking?

How did I fail you, Katrin?

I'd been in the bailey, near the mews, conversing with our falconer when I heard it, a scream like one of my peregrines magnified a thousand times. Looking up to the battlements, I saw her fall.

Thump... Scream...

Were your arms outstretched as though you were flying? Did you drop like one of my hawks after spotting its prey? Had your limbs been flailing as if seeking purchase in mid-air?

I played the scene each way so many times I had no clear idea of the truth.

Still, it all came down to this: I, Alaric DeLaMer, had driven my wife to suicide.

Which was why I must stay away from Clarabel Lucy.

Eighteen

CLARABEL

I didn't see Alaric again until Fair Green, Dublin's largest annual fair. Located just outside the city's west wall, it lasted more than a fortnight, with goods arriving from as far away as the Holy Land.

I had been strolling among endless stalls of merchandise, a surprise considering the ongoing famine. The monetary system, as I had it figured, was simple but clever with pennies, half pennies, and farthings doubled or cut into fours, as needs may be. I'd already purchased beeswax candles, hair ribbons, and even some sugar from North Africa, which was costly by fourteenth-century standards. Mindful of Alaric's admonition about going out alone, I was accompanied by my maid, Elle. While her official duty was to carry all my purchases in a basket, I had to repeatedly reprimand her for wandering off. She was particularly fascinated with the antics of trained monkeys and bears, which we, in future times, would label animal cruelty.

I spotted Naga the Charlatan standing in front of his stall with its pots, jars, and various medicinal plants bundled and hanging overhead. Reminding me again of his cryptic remarks regarding the Feast of the Assumption. (As if I hadn't spent subsequent nights creating and discarding plans zapping me back to the 21st century.) Hoping for some insight into local folk tales or a scrap of information that clicked, I'd questioned most everyone about alternative meanings to the Feast of the Assumption. Mysterious disappearances? The medieval version of time slips? *"Aye, I saw her in the field one moment, and the next, she's walking alongside me." "Donna stand in Castle DeLaMer's bailey before vespers, or you'll ne'er be seen again."*

Nope. The Feast of the Assumption basically consisted of blessing the summer harvest, attending Mass, and, at least during bountiful times, feasting.

What had Naga meant? Had he simply been playing with me? Burnishing his alchemical credentials, hoping to suck me in? I debated further questioning him but decided I'd rather beat myself over the head with a smithy's hammer.

Still, I found myself drifting toward his booth. Between hawking his potions and powders, Naga regaled a small group of fairgoers with fabulist histories of Ancient Rome and Britain, throwing in a description of Charlemagne's golden armor, "which you can witness should you visit my humble shop." While Naga's magnificent voice, punctuated by the opening and closing of his dragon's wings, could mesmerize a corpse, I was more struck by his gaze, ever-watchful, ever-calculating. Reading his audience in order to better exploit their weaknesses.

Despite knowing better, I moved to where I could discreetly continue my perusal. What was I thinking? That Naga would magically drop my escape key into his tall tales?

"Lady Lucy!" Naga called.

Reluctantly, I approached the alchemist's stall. "Did that arsenic powder solve your rodent problem?" he asked.

"Aye." I forced myself to gaze directly into his eyes as if their depths would reveal my answers. To break the pseudo-spell Naga so effortlessly cast, I asked whether he could recommend something for nervous stomachs. James Lackford's indigestion appeared to be worsening, and despite Jocelyn's outward solicitousness, I suspected she dropped her act behind closed doors.

"Basil and barley helps balance the humors." After handing over the indigestion powder, Naga murmured, "Time is of the essence. Come visit."

A cock of the head and the alchemist suddenly looked achingly young, even innocent. As if the figure stitched on his back should have been an angel.

That unexpected glimpse of possible vulnerability threw me off. *Another lost soul? An eccentric façade to hide the wounds beneath?* But Naga the Alchemist was ever the hustler. He and I were speaking two different languages, discussing two different matters—I focused on escape, and he conning me with vagaries ultimately designed to divest me of my money. Or, more probably, my Milanese necklace.

My armor of enmity firmly back in place, I stepped away. Only to run into a stone wall in the form of Alaric DeLaMer.

"Clarabel Lucy!" Alaric frowned down on me. "I am pleased to see you dressed today as the appropriate sex."

He didn't appear pleased. He appeared his usual glowering self.

Gesturing to Elle, who was cheering on a nearby pair of jugglers, he added, "And accompanied by your maid! Dare I pray you actually heeded my recent suggestion?"

I hope I managed a proper frown in return, though in truth, since arriving at the fair, I might have been searching for him. "You know I never pay attention to anything you say."

Alaric laughed. Actually laughed.

"I like it when you laugh," I blurted. *Crap!* Now, he might get the impression I didn't hate him. Though I had to admit I was the teensiest bit relieved to see him in good spirits following our last peculiar encounter.

Reality check: Weren't all our encounters peculiar?

After we fell in step together, Alaric informed me he was here because Fair Green sold the latest in armor and weapons. "Only the finest when we face the Scots. Which will be soon, God willing."

"And here I thought you were stalking me again. How disappointing!"

It was also disappointing that a silly stroll could make me feel so...

light. As though this was a lovely day and a lovely moment in my life. One, looking back from the vantage point of years, I would savor and mourn for its fleeting novelty.

We drifted to Cook Street, where ovens were set up to bake and sell fresh snacks. Alaric purchased two minced meat pies for us and later waited patiently while I bought soft cheeses and early ripened pears for Sir James and bars of Castile soap for myself.

Happy, I thought. *This I could do forever.*

Unfortunately, forever lasted until we ran into Lady Jocelyn inspecting bolts of brocaded silk at a mercer's stall.

When I inquired about her husband's health, she answered without taking her eyes off Alaric, "As well as can be expected, given his age."

Annoyed at her blatant ogling of *my* companion, I removed my cheeses and pears and Naga's remedy from Elle's basket and thrust them in Jocelyn's face, specifically referencing the indigestion powder as a reminder of her wifely duties.

Don't care. Don't care.

While Jocelyn continued flirting and Alaric stared at her like some dopey dog, I found myself staring at *him.*

Today, Alaric was hatless, his tunic a plain though brilliant blue—a color I'd noticed Anglo-Normans favored while the Irish preferred a more colorful array, particularly saffron. His only piece of jewelry was the brooch pinning his cloak. And the signet ring on his pinkie finger, which he seemed to wear or not for no discernible reason.

I conceded Alaric's pornstache nicely framed his mouth, as his close-cropped beard did his jawline. I must be getting used to that broody look because the overall effect wasn't sexy, exactly, but it wasn't unpleasant. *What color are your eyes? Brown or gunmetal grey?* Had I been describing Alaric in a romance, I shouldn't have mentioned anything to do with guns, though cannons would be kind of introduced in another decade, and we at Bella Publishing never fretted over anachronisms. I could have written Alaric was the spitting image of Jason Momoa or Justin Bieber, and no one would question it. Well, maybe my Robin of the Rood would be more Bieber-like...

"Bel!" Alaric was shaking my arm. "Why do you have that strange look on your face?"

I blinked. "Sorry. Just woolgathering." Was that even an expression they'd understand? I smiled up at Alaric, which earned me a frown from both him and the beautiful Jocelyn.

"Are we done here?" I asked, aware of my rudeness and not caring. I had no idea why Jocelyn was glaring at me with the intensity of a laser beam. Good thing they hadn't been invented...

It was only later, after we were several stalls away when it hit me. The reason Jocelyn might have been angry.

Was it because Alaric had called me Bel?

Over the next fortnight, I spent most evenings relaxing in Lord and Lady Lackford's private chamber. I pretended not to be worried about Sir James, who sometimes jerked in his chair the way my stepfather had when pierced with sudden pain. While we talked and he snacked on squares of sambocade, I surreptitiously scrutinized him. Did his hands appear more red and swollen? Was that another lesion on the back of his hand, on his cheek? (And didn't his pallor appear grayer, or conversely, healthier?) Was his breathing unusually labored? I felt that same sense of dread as when I'd sat beside Maurice's bed during his death watch. *Stay away!* I would order myself at the finish of supper, when the hours yawned until bedtime, and I felt the pull of that household across the way. Inevitably, I'd take my usual place on a bench in the Lackford's solar and pretend I wasn't storing up memories for when Sir James' great chair was empty, and all we had was the echo of his voice and his laughter and his storytelling.

My obsession had nothing to do with Alaric DeLaMer, who, following the closing of each day's Parliament, also appeared. Rather than share my bench, he sat on the floor near a fireplace that was either cold or lit, depending on the weather. With his knees bent to his chest and his arms looped about them, making a place to rest his chin, he watched Sir James as he told his tales.

Alaric's and my gazes sometimes met, and I fancied us co-conspirators, both of us cherishing history in the form of a grand old man in his twilight recounting tales of the crusades—the Baron's War, the Battle of Evesham, and the conquest of Wales.

Still, as with Maurice, I deluded myself.

His illness doesn't have to be fatal.

Medieval potions can be as effective as modern medicines.

But there is no cure for old age, not in that century or ours.

Judging from Jocelyn's poorly stifled yawns, she'd heard Sir James' anecdotes many times before. As had Alaric, though, for him, it must be like replaying a favorite song that never grows old. Coupled with that unspoken fear: *"Will this be the last time I see you?"*

Because in three days, Roger Mortimer would ride out with Alaric and his men as part of the Lord Lieutenant's force. Whether the campaign lasted two weeks or two months, I knew Alaric worried Sir James would not be here to greet him upon his return.

Soon after Alaric's departure, the Feast of the Assumption would arrive. I would be the one, God willing, who'd never see Sir James... anyone...again. My plan was to ride to Castle DeLaMer, where I hoped to duplicate the conditions that had transported me here so I might return to the 21st century.

No wonder these hours were bittersweet.

"Is it true Kind Edward is the handsomest man in the kingdom?" I asked, eager to distance myself from my melancholy and to hear first-hand what chroniclers were even now penning about the reign of Edward Caernarvon.

"Not at all." Jocelyn looked up from the stretched cloth of the embroidery hoop into which she'd been industriously poking a wicked-looking needle. "There are others far comelier."

Her gaze, as it so often did, drifted to Alaric.

"And Queen Isabella?" I pressed, irritated by Jocelyn's blatant infatuation. "Is she as beautiful as they say?"

Not until centuries later would Isabella be called the she-wolf of France. For now, England's queen was considered pious, devoted, and loyal to her husband. After it all crumbled, she still asked to be buried in her wedding outfit along with Edward's heart. So what might be the entire truth regarding a king, his consort, and a marcher lord? Had

Isabella and Roger Mortimer even been lovers, or had that been the speculation of later scholars?

"I'm told I look like her," Jocelyn said, smoothing a hand over her hoop and readjusting the remainder of the tapestry that spilled out across her lap onto the floor.

The faintest flicker across Alaric's face. From Sir James as he plumped and rearranged his pillows: "She is more than a decade younger, *ma femme*."

A glimpse into the inner life of a marriage? Though Sir James' insinuation was correct. Here, a woman in her thirties was a shriveled husk. As the poet Robert Herrick would someday write about gathering rosebuds because time is flying: *And this same flower that smiles today/ Tomorrow will be dying.*

Time was indeed flying. And Alaric—all of us—had known our share of dying.

But you'll live for many years, I thought, silently addressing him. *And I'll not be here to witness your end. I'll look back on this—and you—as a paragraph in a novel penned long ago. I'll shrug and say, "Did I write that? Silly me, I can scarce remember."*

Sir James' storytelling seemed to have tired him out. His breathing alternated between gentle puffs and snuffling. Jocelyn appeared intent on stabbing the cloth in her hoop to death. Alaric and I shared a comfortable silence.

I don't want to leave.

Despite Alaric's careless barbering habits, I had to admit he was handsome. Okay, not handsome but presentable in a rough-hewn-man-who'd-just-returned from-a-six-month-wilderness-trek sort of way.

I don't want to leave...you.

"Your turn now, Clarabel Lucy," Alaric challenged me. "Entertain me with one of your fabulisms."

In the light from the fireplace flames, his hair was the color of sunset deepening into night; his body, even in its scrunched position, powerful enough to keep real or imagined monsters at bay.

I could gaze at you forever.

"I'm waiting," Alaric prodded, his voice taking on that annoying teasing tone that I, God help me, secretly enjoyed.

We stared at each other. A current, identical to the one at Camelot Faire, zapped between us. Silence, until I regained control of my silliness.

"Must I?" I groused, pretending irritation.

"Aye, you must."

I ran through a hundred possibilities before it came to me—the perfect narrative for Alaric and me.

"Once upon a time," I begin, savoring the introduction of a phrase that will someday open countless similar stories. I launch into my version of Beauty and the Beast—selfish siblings, a dimwitted merchant and father, who owing to his stupidity, places kind-hearted daughter Beauty in danger. After stumbling across a seemingly empty palace filled with luxuries beyond the merchant's ken, he spends the night scheming to claim the riches for himself. The following morning, the merchant wanders out to a garden where he plucks a rose to take to his Beauty.

A hideous beast immediately appears.

Alaric watches me with interest. While the story of Beauty and the Beast is thousands of years old, I don't recall a medieval iteration.

"The Beast is enormous," I say. Measuring my mythical anti-hero, I stretch an arm above my head. "With limbs like stone pillars. And hairy. And so untidy, as if he never quite learned to properly dress himself." Here, the side of Alaric's mouth lifts in a half-smirk. "He glowers at women, even when they are charming and, dare I say, irresistible. And when the Beast does deign to speak, he snarls like a bear."

"He simply can't abide empty chatter," Alaric counters.

"Even the Beast's subjects agree he is ill-mannered and probably in need of a...spanking."

"Really, Bella? How old is this beast?"

"Well," I retort, "if he was punished by having his head chopped off, that would end the story, wouldn't it?"

It takes a moment to realize that Alaric had called me "Bella" and that the nickname emerged naturally from his lips. Such a curious sensation, I feel, one impossible to label. *Bella...Bel... Come out and play.* My teasing mood evaporates. I want only to retreat to ponder the meaning behind that casual slip of the tongue.

"Continue," Alaric prods, seemingly oblivious to his blunder.

I clear my throat and proceed, shrugging off those alien emotions, another carelessly uttered nickname. "The Beast demands Beauty be sent to him so he can execute her because her father picked a flower in her name and, therefore, deserves death. The Beast is like that. Most unreasonable, with the vilest temper."

"The Beast has reason to be vile," Alaric murmurs. "Beauty is the most irritating woman he's ever encountered."

"Before their first meeting, the Beast is nervous and jumpy. For while the Beast is puffed up and so fierce children flee at the sight of him, he is actually afraid of...hobgoblins, which proliferate like toadstools in his kingdom. Beauty, who is, naturally, beautiful and walks with the grace of a—"

"Rampaging elephant—"

"...hind, daintily trips into the garden where the Beast awaits. The Beast doesn't hear her because he has hearing problems. Due to all the hair growing out of his ears."

Alaric turns his head away, not quickly enough to hide his smile.

Why have I not noticed how arresting your countenance? I can't be drawn to such hypermasculinity. Yet, here with all this talk of knightly adventures, here where you are perfectly suited to your environment, I find you... I don't know what I find you...

Alaric turns back to me, his expression once more faintly sardonic.

"Oh, and it's nighttime. When Beauty calls his name in a voice more melodious than a choir of angels, the Beast is so startled he turns and, because he is half-blind in addition to being hard of hearing and having the world's worst reflexes, sprays her with his magic hobgoblin spray."

"Which she richly deserves!" Alaric says, not even bothering to hide his grin.

"No," I say, "and quit interrupting. Since Beauty is obviously not a hobgoblin, she remains very much alive and well."

"A pity."

After that, I recount other adventures involving magic rings and mirrors, enchanted furniture, a bit of shapeshifting, and finally, treachery, which results in the Beast's death.

"But Beauty, despite the Beast's abominable manners and slapdash personal hygiene, has fallen in love with him. She rushes to his side, sobbing and crying, 'I love you!' Her tears bring the Beast back to life, but not as a horrible monster. No, with her kiss and confession, the Beast has been magically transformed into the handsome prince of Beauty's dreams."

I am so caught up in this emotional ending I find myself swallowing back tears. Ridiculously, I am overwhelmed with so many feelings I can't make sense of them.

What is wrong? Why am I reacting like this?

How can I think to leave you?

Hopefully, nothing will happen. With you gone, perhaps the guards at Castle DeLaMer won't even allow me entrance...

In the flickering light, Alaric and I stare at each other.

"Who would have thought it?" I finally whisper, unable to finish with the requisite, "They live happily ever after." The words are stuck, refusing to pass through the lump in my throat. I am undone by a rush of emotion, fighting back threatening sobs.

Alaric's gaze remains locked to mine. I am mesmerized, drowning in this moment, in the physical rightness of him.

A log in the fireplace crumbles, shooting sparks up the chimney; Sir James awakens with a snort and jerking of limbs; Jocelyn huffs loudly and mumbles something indecipherable, reminding Alaric and me we're not alone.

I don't have to go. Tell me you want me to stay. As if Alaric had some inkling of my secret plan.

"Time to put my lord husband to bed," Jocelyn says, abruptly rising. She tosses her tapestry on the bench so forcefully it skitters off, tumbling into the shadows, moves the half-eaten sambocade from the table beside Sir James and shakes him awake.

Alaric shifts position and stretches. "Clarabel Lucy, spinner of tales," he says.

Shattering the spell.

~

Soon after, I said my goodbyes, my mind roiling over Alaric's behavior. It was always push-pull with him. Somewhere, I'd read that men in relationships were like rubber bands, their emotions stretching and constricting, one minute open and vulnerable, the next dismissive. How would I know? Beyond penning or plotting romance novels, I was a novice regarding matters of the heart. (Not that I was having a romantic—any relationship—with Alaric.) My affair with Raphael Accardi had been the equivalent of opening a Bella Publishing novel at the page where the lovers have overcome all odds and are free to indulge their passion happily ever after. Raphael's and my courtship had been perfect...until it wasn't. There'd been no dénouement. It had been severed neatly, cleanly the way a sword severs a limb. I could track its arc—infatuation, lust, exhilaration, betrayal, bitterness, and then pretty much packing everything away like discarded mementos in a spinster's hope chest. But with Alaric?

"Fool!" I whispered. Standing in the middle of the deserted lane between the Lackfords' home and mine, I felt like an animal caught outside during a blizzard, hunched over and praying simply to *endure*. *We aren't HEA lovers. We're dysfunctional stereotypes in* Games People Play.

Not that it mattered. When Alaric returned from his campaign, I would be gone—hopefully—and that would be that.

"Bel."

I spun around. I hadn't heard the Lackfords' door open and close.

Hand to heart, I cried, "You scared me!"

"Aye, because you have a way of *never* paying attention."

Before I could make a sarcastic reply, Alaric grabbed me by the wrist and pulled me close enough that I fancied I could feel the stir of his breath upon my face when I gazed up at him.

"What are you doing?

"Promise me something, Bel."

That nickname again. Uttering it like a caress. Because my brain was wired from a lifetime of reading and writing romance novels to describe things in such terms.

My prickly armor vanished, replaced by the peculiar racing of my heart. "What?"

Bars of light leaked between the wooden shutters in my residence.

Above us, in the Lackford's chamber, a shadow passed across the buttery square before shutters slammed closed, leaving just enough light to decipher Alaric's expression.

"Promise you'll do nothing foolish when I'm away."

How could I make such a promise? But, if I was successful and Alaric returned to find me gone? For the first time, I wondered whether my disappearance would upset or worry him. Unless "Promise you won't do anything foolish" was the medieval equivalent of a sales-clerk wishing you a nice day.

Surprisingly, Alaric drew me to his chest. Surprisingly, I allowed him. My face pressed into the fabric of his tunic, which smelled faintly of wood ash from laundry soap.

"Promise me, Bel. I canna have you gallivanting about when I'm gone. Though 'tis easy to pretend otherwise, we are the outsiders here."

His embrace tightened until I imagined myself passing through flesh and bone the way a specter passes through walls so we might meld together. Alaric wasn't afraid. Alaric faced his dragons in what-ever form and slayed them. I needed a dose of that courage.

"I promise." Had Alaric just decided my future for me?

We stayed pressed together until the lights in the lane were snuffed out, and we were shapeless forms in the gloom. I could not make myself step away. Alaric felt comforting, safe. *Safe.* There was a word. When was the last time I'd experienced that? Not since I was a little girl. Not since—

"I will hold you to your word." Alaric abruptly released me and walked away.

Until *he* was the shapeless form melding with the dark.

Nineteen

On the Feast of the Assumption, I exited Dublin via Thomas Street, averting my eyes from the human misery lining this ancient road. If I dwelt on individual faces, I would be immobilized. Later, this disaster would be referred to as "The Great Famine." Across Europe, millions, both human and animal, would perish. Poverty. Starvation. Disease. War.

Mindful of Alaric's fussiness concerning traveling alone, I attached myself to a group of merchants. Throughout the hour ride, I weighed the pros and cons of "home." Pros: *sunshine, mountains, friends, the Duchess, modern technology, books, toilets, hot water, and showers.* Cons: *Alaric.*

Once I neared Castle DeLaMer, I reined in the mare I'd named Blixette and stared up at the portcullis. I'd not seen Alaric's home since the afternoon I'd stumbled into the bailey. Spotting movement on the battlements, I thought suddenly of the Knight and his Lady. Despite the highly suspect renderings in *Haunted Castles of Ireland,* were they already part of Castle DeLaMer? I should ask Alaric.

"Promise me you won't do anything foolish."

I knew as I think I'd known from the moment Alaric uttered that sentence, I wouldn't even attempt to implement my nebulous "plan."

I'd been going through the motions, pretending I was undecided when—

"Clarabel! C.L.!"

The voice was so familiar it did not immediately register as out of place. And impossible. *He* was dead.

I swiveled in my saddle. Like something out of *The Walking Dead,* one of the scattered bundles lurched toward me.

"Ollie?"

"C.L.!" A choked cry, and Ollie Scott fell against my stirruped leg, clawing at me with filthy hands. "I've been so fuckin' terrified! It's been awful, awful!"

My former friend smelled as terrible as he looked. Over what little remained of his original clothing, his rags fell back to reveal skeletal limbs.

"What are you doing here?" I asked inanely. "Aren't you supposed to be dead? Alaric said so." But he hadn't really. I'd inferred it from his silence.

"Dead? I'd've been better off." Ollie clung to my leg like a frightened child.

I immediately felt bad I'd given Ollie Scot so little thought these past weeks. Despite his betrayal, I probably should have mourned him a teensy bit.

"Some of those brutes threw me in a dungeon or something. Filthy. Rats. Slimy walls. You can't begin to... And then they interrogated me like I was some sort of spy..."

Because I'd learned to mistrust everything Ollie said, I asked, "How could they interrogate you when you can't speak their language?"

"French. Remember all those years in Paris, which seem like a dream now I'm here in this fuckin' crazy version of *The Matrix.*" He made horrible hacking noises that were probably sobs.

Reminding myself I was a compassionate person, I forced myself to allow Ollie to remain pressed against my leg.

"Didn't you try to find the door, the passageway and reverse engineer yourself back to the future? Do something to improve your condition?"

"D'you think they'd let the likes of me into their courtyard? Other than tossing us scraps from their tables, we're left outside to rot. And sleep in the mud. I had my shoes stolen and my watch and... It's been unspeakable. You can't imagine."

Yeah, I pretty much could. Surprising how a man who possessed endless ingenuity when it came to making money couldn't figure out how to maneuver in a decidedly less complicated society.

"We'll get you something to eat," I said after he'd calmed down. "I have a town house in Dublin. I'll take you there."

More hacking noises. After Ollie finally composed himself, he gazed up at me through a tangle of greasy hair. "We need to figure out how to get back to Colorado."

"What's this 'we' stuff?" I nearly blurted. While I could muster sympathy for his plight, I'd neither forgotten nor forgiven his treachery. After getting him settled and making sure he could survive, I had no intention of allowing Oliver Scott back into my life.

"I've replayed it over and over again, trying to remember how this happened," he babbled.

"You'll feel better," I said, "once we're home."

Ollie stared up at me. His tears had left streaks down his dirty face. "Umm. My legs are really, really weak, C.L.," he whined. "D'you mind if I ride and you walk?"

The same nightmare. Night after night. Chasing Alaric along a passage that warped into an endless maze. Forever lost with no way out, no way to find him.

I found myself twisting my hands like a madwoman while pacing my chamber, my slippers creating patterns atop the tapestries I'd ordered laid on my wooden floor. Even though I knew better, I *knew* Alaric had been killed on a campaign.

I knew.

I found myself imagining the DeLaMer family history, spooling back centuries, imagined the facts of my Alaric's life being carefully inked upon parchment where I might peruse them.

Imagined myself asking current Lucan DeLaMer during our tour of Castle by the Sea:

"May I see your family history?"

Lucan leads me to a family vault where he withdraws a thick leather-bound volume. I open it to the proper page, scanning the lines until I see it.

There: the date of Alaric's death. Reduced to marks on a piece of vellum.

The very idea made me shudder.

If you knew where Death resided, you'd never go there.

Stop!

This was foolishness. My psyche remained hostage to a past with a father who had been long dead while I'd gone about my childhood believing otherwise.

I was plagued by such a restlessness, a sensation of my world being wrongly tilted. It came down to this: without even the prospect of seeing Alaric, my days had been leached of their promise. Despite being a "modern woman," my happiness had come to revolve around one man. A man who had never, before these past several weeks, inhabited the same universe as my romantic fantasies.

Save for Camelot Faire?

Why did all the things I'd once found so unappealing now draw me to him? Why did I continually dwell on the sensation of Alaric's big hands around my waist during our last meeting; my response to being pressed against his massive chest, wrapped in strong, comforting arms; the heat of him even through layers of clothing?

It wasn't that I was in love with Alaric DeLaMer or anything. It was just more, well, with him gone, I felt half-formed, half-alive.

Suck it up! You're here for a reason other than an inappropriate crush. Figure it out.

My detour from the twenty-first century must involve something important. To that end, the phrase "easing the suffering of others" kept intruding. I might have been a writer of frivolities, but I had centuries of knowledge in my fertile brain, just waiting to be tapped.

Still...of what practical use was a person who could name the parts of a castle but not construct one? Format a manuscript but was unable to start a fire without matches? Fillet a fish—with a proper knife purchased from Williams Sonoma—but actually catch one without a rod and reel? Wax eloquent on events leading to the Magna Carta but was incapable of cutting my nails before fingernail clippers were invented? I'd learned to sing and tap dance, slap on makeup and different costumes, and pretend I was Veronique Vixen or Sally Merryweather or Tiffy Chapeau-Whitehouse while giving dramatic readings, but if it hadn't been for my jewelry, I would have been sprawled right alongside Ollie on the roadway outside Castle by the Sea.

Maybe I could teach children. Education was an important ingredient in obtaining a better life. But the youngsters begging in the streets or huddled near city gates needed food, and in a world where everyone lived from harvest to harvest, a knowledge of husbandry—which I did not have—was more important than proficiency in math or reading.

Then, it came to me. The answer had been lurking in my subconscious since Fair Green when Alaric had purchased those minced meat pies from one of those movable ovens.

Yes. This I could do.

~

"I want to go with you," Ollie said, barging into my room. He craned his neck to see where I kept the purse from which I'd retrieved an earring.

Note to self: Change hiding place.

I cast my former friend a baleful glance. During the month he'd lived with me, Ollie had recovered nicely. Translation: he was driving me nuts with his whining. He also spent lots of my money gambling, whoring, and getting drunk at each and every inn located on Winetavern Street, after which he'd spin ridiculous plans for reverse time travel. He bossed my staff around, yelling in a French few could even begin to grasp, causing Elle and another chambermaid to come to me in tears. *Sexual harassment, anyone?* Oh, and he'd kitted himself out with an expensive wardrobe. Which kinda made me laugh. Despite the fact that Ollie's quiff had long grown out and

his meticulous skin regimen had been left behind on the marble coun-
tertop in the bathroom of his suite at Castle by the Sea, he'd taken on the
look of a metrosexual/hipster trapped in a bad costume drama.

"I don't need an escort." I was doubly annoyed because I hadn't
informed Ollie of my outing, which meant he'd been eavesdropping
again.

"While you're at your moneylender, I'll just pop in next door to
visit Naga." When I humphed, Ollie said, "You're always going on
about my drinking, but I've been gathering necessary info. Reconnais-
sance. That freak knows lots of things."

"Yeah, like how to part you from *my* money."

"You can be such an ass, C.L. I've talked to him about, 'you know.'
I'm pretty sure he can help us."

Later, after visiting Matteo and trading an earring for a satisfyingly
heavy purse, I endeavored to sneak past The Elixir of Life, where Ollie
and Naga had their heads together.

Unfortunately, Ollie spotted me. "C.L., get in here!"

Cringing at the use of a nickname I'd repeatedly ordered him to
quit using, I reluctantly entered. From behind his jumbled worktable,
Naga greeted me with his usual lifting of the corners of his mouth, like
an over-botoxed movie star.

"Did you know Naga is immortal?" Ollie asked, mugging in a way I
hadn't seen since our reunion.

"Just stop it! You sound insane."

"I think he can help us with our *problem*," Ollie waggled his
eyebrows meaningfully—as if they could identify the exact nature of
our *problem*.

"Speak for yourself, Ollie."

Observing our interaction, Naga ran his long, delicate, perfectly
manicured fingers the length of a nearby stone pestle.

Ollie turned back to the alchemist. "Can you like bend time?"

"Time," repeated Naga. He seemed to perfectly understand Ollie's
execrable French. "An illusion. Faces in the clouds that aren't really
there."

Right. Naga the Charlatan fed you back what you wanted to hear.

175

No doubt he was already reeling Ollie in with some fanciful—and expensive—way to transcend the laws of physics.

Naga spoke directly to me. "Would you like to see my laboratory?" He gestured to a wooden door located between his overloaded shelves.

"Yep!" Ollie cried, clapping his hands.

"No," I said and left, stalking back to my residence. Ollie was the perfect example of "Loose lips sink ships." He needed to shut up rather than go around blabbing about things that could get us into trouble. Good thing England wouldn't burn witches for a couple of centuries. It was also a good thing most people dismissed Ollie's Pidgin French as gibberish. But Naga? What was going on in that calculating brain of his?

Ollie and I *were* proof unexplainable events happened.

The Earth *was* filled with wondrous things.

It was also filled with charlatans. But charlatans could be dangerous.

Ollie really needed to stay away from Naga the Alchemist.

As did I.

These things I knew: that the Little Ice Age had begun, which meant decades of erratic weather. That next year's harvest would be more successful, though since Europe was overpopulated, Mother Nature would continue winnowing her herd. That tuberculosis, pneumonia, and bronchitis—none of them referred to by such names—would further decimate the population. I knew that in Ulster, a hundred or so miles to the north and where Edward the Bruce was holed up, conditions were even more dire. Because the province was completely rural and lacking the commerce associated with cities, residents had been reduced to cannibalism, including the exhumation of corpses, with all that ghoulish act intimated. That their plight was a fitting punishment, a chronicler later wrote, because some Ulstermen, when traveling our way, had eaten meat during Lent.

I knew this was the time the fairy tale *Hansel and Gretel* made its first appearance.

Because I was purchasing grain, I knew that, despite price controls, costs had skyrocketed. That the grain had to be dried out in jars, further diminishing its nutrition, and that Dubliners complained four pennies worth of coarse bread was not enough to fill a belly for even one day.

All this I knew. As I commandeered the necessary ovens and paid to have loaf after loaf of bread baked. After which, I helped distribute the loaves.

Even though I knew my project would only marginally ease suffering, I was proud of my contribution.

Thus, the weeks passed. Quickly. Quietly.

And without missing Alaric.

Hardly at all.

When Lord Lackford's health allowed, I accompanied him to St Bartholomew's, a hospital he'd recently founded. With his physical deterioration, Sir James' thoughts had naturally turned to his personal Judgment Day. Caring for the less fortunate was an accepted way to balance one's sins against one's good deeds in order to gain a swifter entrance into heaven.

"It is better to pray with works than with words," he sometimes said, quoting Innocent III, one of the thirteenth century's bossier popes.

This was the first martial campaign in which Sir James had not participated. So, while he never complained, he often appeared restless or distracted, staring off into the distance, lips drawn, one hand resting against his stomach, which seemed to be the locus of his illness. Hoping to brighten his waking hours, I visited him as often as I could when Jocelyn was gone, and I'd finished my duties.

Not allowing myself to contemplate the winding down of my friend's days.

Not allowing myself to compare this present to those last months with my stepfather.

Reminding myself that this was simply the ouroboros, which none could escape.

And which I must learn to accept.

~

"He's a good man," Sir James said, apropos of nothing. We were seated in the Lackford's back yard, which possessed a lovely menagerie of flowers, herbs, and spices all arranged in pots so that, depending on the weather, they could be moved inside.

I turned to Sir James in confusion.

"I was there when it happened, you know. Alaric's wife, when she died."

Immediately, I sat up straighter, my senses alert. I had long been curious about Alaric's marriage but hadn't dared ask anyone directly for fear they'd counter with, "Why do you care?" While at Trim Castle, I'd heard one of Jocelyn's maids comment that his wife had died of a murrain, which, because murrain is an umbrella term for animal-related diseases, had caused me to wonder aloud whether Alaric DeLaMer had married a cow.

Another caustic remark I regretted.

"Alaric and his Lady Katrin were at one of their Shropshire holdings. We were nearby, for I also have a residence in the area. Recently, we'd received the joyous news that Alaric's Katrin was with child. Lady Jocelyn was eager to personally congratulate them both."

I wanted to ask a hundred questions about Alaric's wife—was she pretty, kind, bitchy? Had Katrin and he also been childhood sweethearts? How long had they been married? Were they desperately in love, or had the alliance been a contentious one?

Instead, fearful of distracting Sir James from his tale, I remained silent.

"Lady Jocelyn had become quite fond of Katrin, even though she was much younger and had always been retiring. Shy and lovely, I always thought. Reminded me of a roe, with those huge eyes. " Sir James paused before continuing, his voice husky. "My wife had ridden ahead of our party in order to be the first to congratulate them."

Sir James' gaze was fastened above the roofline of the stables edging his property. I wondered whether he was mourning his lack of children, a strong male son to inherit his sprawling estates—or caught up in the memory of yet another tragedy.

"By the time the rest of us arrived, it had already happened."

"What do you mean, 'it'?" I pressed.

"Everyone in chaos, surrounding the body while my lady wife rushed to us, undone. Crying, 'She jumped, she jumped!'"

I gasped. A suicide? But how? Had Katrin plunged from a castle battlement? Why would a pregnant woman kill herself? Had she gone mad?

Sir James ran a gnarled hand over his face. "Which wasn't the truth, and I was distressed that anyone would utter such calumny. 'Tis difficult to feign happiness, especially for someone as guileless as Lady Katrin. And in her condition..." He shrugged. "Such things are just not done. Somehow, she must have accidentally fallen from the roof of the keep. Alaric said it was a favorite place for them, which added to his distress."

"Horrible," I managed, closing my eyes. No wonder Alaric was morose. It was a miracle he could function at all.

"By the time I reached Sir Alaric, he was cradling her body and—"

"Husband!"

I jumped and turned to see Jocelyn striding toward us. Though the day was warm, she carried a blanket over one arm. "I searched everywhere for you. You must na catch a chill."

Sir James ducked his head in either politeness or surrender. I sensed a tension between them but dismissed it because I'd grown to really hate Jocelyn Goodknyght—even while hating myself for hating her.

"Your husband and I, we..." I rose, needing to get away to contemplate this new, dreadful information.

I could not shake the tragedy of Alaric DeLaMer and his Lady Katrin. In my former life, I would have pitched it as an epic romance, one that would keep readers up all night, weeping over the unfairness of it all while simultaneously being swept away with the nobility of suffering for love.

I was more eager than ever for Alaric's return and fantasized about running into his arms. "I'm so sorry," I would whisper.

As if words that must have already been uttered ten thousand times could miraculously erase his heartache.

Because a part of me remained that little girl who rewrote the endings of fairy tales in order to grant the prince and his princess their happily ever after.

Twenty

F eeling melancholy for the silliest of reasons, missing Colorado autumns, so crisp and tart and tangy—like biting into a Granny Smith apple.

Missing...

Nope, another betrayal.

Don't think about it.

Mercifully, this last week had been notable for its absence of cumulonimbus clouds. But even on the brightest of days, the sky was softer here in County Dublin, as if seen through a filter. Not the perpetual haze of pollution that hung over the city itself, but a gentleness, a blurring about the edges, which, at another time, I might have argued, possessed its own charm.

I wasn't in the mood to find anything charming.

Along with other guests, Ollie and I exited Newgate to stroll in the direction of Fair Green, where the Feast of St Michael, or Michaelmas, as the Church called it, was being celebrated. Long before Christianity arrived in Ireland, pagans had considered these hours when day and night were in balance—twelve hours of sunlight, twelve hours of darkness—to be sacred. Sir James had also informed me that today was an official celebration of thanksgiving for a bountiful harvest.

"You should have seen it in years past," he'd said, his expression softened with memory. "Enormous cornucopias atop tablecloths white as summer clouds and overflowing with cabbages and onions, apples bigger than my fist, and so many other fruits and vegetables I could not name them all. And, *naturellement*, the hazelnuts, hazelnuts everywhere. A symbol of God's bounty."

"—end of September." Ollie was saying *something*. I dragged myself back to the present. "Which means we've been gone three months. Like *forever*. We've gotta get home. I don't even wanna think what's happening at Bella Publishing."

I glanced at my former partner. In his finely woven forest green surcoat belted with a jeweled girdle and topped by a miniver-trimmed mantle, Ollie looked like a hipster trying out a new fashion trend.

"This place is like living in a... not a third-world country, an eighty-sixth world country." He wrinkled his nose and sniffed as if smelling something offensive.

"Keep your voice down." I nodded toward Elle and a second maid, who walked close enough to overhear. "And for your information, I find much of our current...landscape charming." I *was* adjusting better to my new life, particularly since I'd started my bread project. Knowing I was helping alleviate hunger, even in the smallest way, filled me not only with a sense of purpose but gratitude. Usually. Not today. Today, I was spoiling for a fight, and Oliver Harrison Scott might provide an appropriate substitute.

"These people don't even have coffee, for God's sake."

While we still inhabited the same household, I interacted with Ollie as little as possible. Already, I regretted allowing him to accompany me. "If you're going to whine, do it somewhere else."

We veered toward the long tables that had been set up and, behind them, pavilions from which food was being readied.

"Never was a fan of the four-leggeds," Ollie said, detouring around a pile of manure. And now look." His jeweled rings caught the sun as he gestured toward the fluffs of sheep and cattle scattered across the flat terrain. "They're everywhere!" Followed by an overly dramatic sigh. "You know what I really miss, besides, you know, everything?

Colorado's falls. Especially the aspen. Think how beautiful Vail Valley is right now."

Though I wouldn't give him the satisfaction of agreeing, I did miss our state's pure, sharp air; its brilliant skies and dazzling sunshine; its great slabs of snow-covered mountains and tumbling streams. And yes, our aspens, golden leaves trembling from the winds that presaged the bleakness of winter.

"Bet you didn't know Ireland also has aspens?" I said to further annoy Ollie.

"Don't wanna hear about their goddamned trees," he snapped.

"They're considered evil because Christ's cross was carved from one. Ever after, they shudder with the memory, which is why their leaves shake."

"Do I look like I give a fuck?" Ollie schooled his face in that expression that hid any real emotion—happiness, amusement, anger, confusion—and adjusted the liripipe that was wrapped around his neck like some sort of ironic scarf. "Trees are trees. They're here for shade and firewood and for dropping seeds or pods or acorns to create other annoying little trees that shed their leaves, so they make a terrible mess to clean up. They're not sacred or magical or gateways to the underworld like these morons say."

Overhead, to the west, a pair of hawks circled, signaling the presence of a hawking party, and I thought of Alaric. All the while I'd worried and fretted over his safety, he'd already erased me from his memory banks.

I hope I never see you again.

And apparently, I wouldn't.

Alaric had been gone more than six weeks. You'd think after his return, he'd at least stop by to see how I was doing. *"Promise me, Bel,"* he'd said, pretending he actually cared.

You need to go to confession, Alaric DeLaMer, cuz you're a big fat liar.

Following a parade of other colorfully dressed guests, Ollie and I neared the makeshift tables—crossed by a dais reserved for those of the highest rank. I spotted the Lackfords—Jocelyn with one arm looped around her husband's back while patiently raising a goblet to his lips. Even from this distance, Sir James looked more haggard than ever. Behind them stood the one and only Roger Mortimer, conversing with several others, including a portly man in bishop's robes. (Immediately, I noticed Alaric didn't number among the group. Not that I cared.)

Where are you?

Before being seated, Ollie and I washed our hands in bowls of rose-water, after which servants dried them with linen towels. Pages went among the tables where guests were beginning to sit, pouring wine while jesters provided amusement, including bawdy songs and jokes—I so did not understand the medieval sense of humor—and juggling.

Ollie murmured something about scoring with a "bonny lass" (really?) and sauntered toward a pair of young women, their unbound hair signifying their unmarried state. A group of riders trailed past, dismounting near a stand of trees beyond the festivities. The returning hawking party. In the lead, a rider astride a bay stallion bearing a white blaze upon its face.

I recognized Alaric's horse, *Mort Rouge*. And Alaric.

Suddenly, unaccountably, I felt on the verge of heatstroke. The day immediately transformed into something incandescent and over-flowing with promise.

Because Alaric DeLaMer had intruded once again into my world?

"*Poor little fool*," a teenaged Ricky Nelson had once sung or would sing centuries into the future.

How well I could relate.

"Bel Lucy. Or will you be answering to Veronium Venice today?"

I stiffened at the sound of *his* voice, shutting out Ollie, who had been shunned by those bonny lasses and was currently complaining about ridiculous customs thwarting a healthy man's needs.

What is wrong with me? Reminder to self: I don't even like you anymore.

Schooling my features, I swiveled away from Ollie, whose mouth had gaped in horror upon recognizing the man behind us.

"Alaric DeLaMer." Viewing him for the first time in forever, my brain short-circuited. He seemed to have grown about a foot, as enormous as Andre the Giant in *Princess Bride,* so I was looking up...and up...until finally viewing his face.

Alaric didn't grant me a full smile, though the left side of his mouth lifted. Amused by my transparent attempt at insouciance? Or had he seen through my act to the emotions roiling beneath?

We stared at each other.

I wanted to say, *"I missed you. I dreamed of you. I'm so relieved you're here and safe. Why did you stay away so long?"*

"Did you keep your promise, Bel, or have you been up to your usual mischief?"

The laugh lines around Alaric's eyes were lighter than the surrounding skin, attesting to long days in the saddle and, might I observe, without the protection of sunglasses. His hair, ruffled from his recent ride, was untidy in the way that might make a woman long to run her fingers through it in order to, well, feel it.

A squeak, followed by a "Fuck no!" behind me, broke the spell. Ollie. Then, I remembered. The only time he and Alaric had met was in Castle DeLMer's bailey, right before Alaric knocked him out.

Alaric craned his neck to better view a half-crouching Ollie, who alternately glared at him and swiveled his head, seeking an escape route.

"Did you bring your husband this time, Bel?"

"Does he look like a toddler?" I retorted, annoyed he'd mention my imaginary spouse.

Alaric shifted closer until we nearly brushed shoulders. Ollie shuffled backward, licking his lips and tugging nervously at his jewel-encrusted girdle.

Alaric scanned him from boots to chaperon. "You don't look much like a jester."

As usual, it took Ollie several moments to translate. When he did, he muttered, "Asshole," in English. Then louder: "I am a..." before stuttering to a stop since he, no more than I, knew what title should be bestowed upon him.

"Tell us a joke," Alaric taunted, reaching out to tug Ollie's liripipe. "Or perhaps kicking your feet around like a dying horse was meant to amuse us."

I choked back a laugh. Ollie glared, even as he jerked away, causing his chaperon to tilt low over his forehead.

"You could have killed me," Ollie gushed in a mixture of gibberish and French. "If we lived in a civilized place and time, I'd have you arrested and thrown in prison for..." he waved his arm vaguely. "Decades."

Alaric narrowed his eyes and cocked his head at Ollie, though I'm not sure he understood more than a handful of words. At that moment, a trumpet sounded from the high table. Dublin's archbishop, Alexander de Bykenore, stood to recite the grace.

"Come, *ma Bel*," Alaric said, turning away from Ollie in obvious dismissal. "Let us find a place where you might irritate me for the rest of the festivities."

He held out an arm to me. Ignoring Ollie, who huffed like an offended schoolgirl, I laid my arm atop his.

Ma Bel? While Alaric led us to some open seats, with a scowling Ollie trailing after, I experienced a wave of shyness. While I had a lifetime of practice maintaining a calm exterior, inside, I was Icarus, realizing I had flown too close to the sun and was now tumbling to my doom. Unable to catch myself. To change the trajectory of my fall.

I'd never felt anything close to this emotion before, not even with my *innamorato*. My love life had been a wasteland, populated by millions of words that were as meaningless as my belief I could write a bestseller based on a thousand-year-old book and a dead language.

Now, here I was. Such a poor wordsmith, I was unable to even put a name to my emotions.

Whatever my emotions might be.

~

The music was lively, in the style future centuries would label "Irish traditional." Before the head table, a storyteller regaled guests with a poem that appeared to have numerous mentions of "Sir Tristrem." It was hard to hear from this distance, particularly over the music, even if I'd been paying attention. Which I wasn't.

Alaric sat across from me, bareheaded, hair still tousled, his

186

surcoat, like that of his liege, Roger Mortimer, matching the bluest blue of Colorado skies.

Which I no longer felt nostalgic for.

The wine was surprisingly good; the more I drank, the more often I snuck glances at my no-longer-nemesis. Sometimes, I found Alaric doing the same, which caused me to immediately fix my attention on the trencher at my fingertips; the large silver platter brimming with fish from the River Poddle and Dublin Bay; the undeniably lovely smile of the *demoiselle* seated to Alaric's left, who seemed far too intent on engaging him in conversation.

No surprise. A widower with lands, position, and a respected family name was quite a catch.

Question: Why wasn't Alaric seated at the dais with others of his status? Because he wanted to be closer to me, of course, he did!

Alaric sliced a piece of salmon from the platter, placed it on his partner's trencher, and was rewarded with another of those simpering smiles.

Brazen. Gold digger. Hussy.

I hope she realized he was merely being polite. Like passing mustard and ketchup at a hamburger joint.

What is wrong with me?

Alaric DeLaMer's marital status or interactions with other women were a matter of indifference. Since our last meeting, he'd not miraculously morphed into *Sexiest Man Alive, 1317 Edition*. Still, I longed to tell him about my bread project, imagining his pleased smile and his words of praise. I wanted to tell him about the hours I'd spent listening to Lord Lackford's war stories and end with, "What was your campaign like? I want to hear everything."

If we'd not met today, would you have ignored me forever?

Sensing Alaric watching me, I turned away so only my profile was visible and blinked back threatening tears. Why was I so emotional? At the dais, Jocelyn's attention had wandered from her husband to me. I managed a watery smile, which she did not return, probably because the distance between us was too great to reveal my unhappiness. A relief, really. I didn't want anyone to witness my inappropriate burst of sentimentality.

Still, I felt a sudden piercing longing for...something...

"How quiet you are this day," Alaric said across the table, causing me to return my attention to him. "Are you ill?"

Unable to reciprocate his teasing tone, I managed a shake of the head. I felt shy and awkward, as I'd not since receiving my first writing award, which Dottie had snarked, "Must be some mistake."

Having Alaric close, unable to touch him, to revert to innocuous bantering when I wanted to discuss... important *somethings*...was its own torture. I rubbed my temple against a threatening headache.

I wish I hadn't attended.

I wish I didn't have all these conflicting emotions about you.

I wish...

More music, more poetry, more drinking. Soon, Archbishop Bykenore would signal the end of feasting with a closing prayer. After that, dancing. Since Alaric now appeared to be captivated by his barely pubescent female companion and had completely forgotten about me, I'd default to my strength. Disciplining thoughts that currently bounced around like manic ping pong balls to focus on something other than Alaric DeLaMer, who was certainly not all that. If I bumped into him in Vail's town square, I wouldn't look at him twice. Well, that wasn't exactly true. He would stand out quite unflatteringly among the manscaped and exfoliated males with their trendy clothing and weekly hair trims.

From behind, hands settled upon my shoulders. "Hey, C.L., missed me?" Ollie, smelling strongly of wine, leaned close as if meaning to whisper in my ear.

"What do you want?" I was not in the mood for Oliver Harrison Scott.

"D'you know cockfights are legal here? Apparently, they're kinda even considered like the sport of kings."

I shrugged off his hands. "Don't care."

"There's a game going on right now. Near the Franciscan Friary." He waved his arm in the direction of a cluster of buildings. "Gonna watch."

"Have fun." I was annoyed he'd interrupted my musings, which had been important, though I'd lost their thread.

"Gambling's involved," Ollie continued. "Just a few friendly wagers. Would you mind—"

Suffer his presence or give him a few coins? I chose the latter.

After Ollie scurried away, I poked at the stale bread of my trencher with my knife, my attention wandering back to Alaric and his Lady Diapers.

That smile. How fake. How phony. I hate you.

I imagined crossing out each line of the list I would someday scrawl in my make-believe journal describing Alaric: 1) Handsome. 2) Sexy. 3) Magnetic. 4) Interesting. 5) Interested.

Deliberately shutting out my tormentor, I observed the parade of pages bearing food and drink exiting the pavilions near the high table. Smoke from makeshift kitchens swayed above the pavilion roofs like kites in an uncertain breeze.

What mistake had spiraled me back in time to this accursed place? I was certain of one thing: it wasn't to find *la grande passion*.

I wish I were a professor, a mathematician, a Goethe, a Stephen Hawkings, or a da Vinci. Then, I could dispense knowledge, glorious knowledge, to those around me. Or that I'd learned useful skills like plumbing, welding, or nursing. Even if I'd been trained as a mechanic, I could adapt my expertise to invent something like, I don't know, a comfortable carriage with springs. Instead, all I was good for was to hand out bread.

One of the minstrels stopped near Alaric and Lady Diapers.

"Dearest sight of my heart," he sang. "*Blah, blah*, I have chosen you, *blah ditty, blah, blah, blah*."

Apparently, decent romantic lyrics had yet to be invented.

Which gave me an idea.

There was something, one little thing I *could* do.

My gaze fastened to Alaric. He'd twisted his shoulder away from his toddler girlfriend to focus again on me. A lift of the eyebrows, signaling, "Your move!" The minstrel had moved on to pester others with his awkward rhymes. While I, lucky me, possessed a repertoire of magnificent poetry at my mental fingertips.

Straightening my spine, I raised my chin and staring, directly at Alaric, began:

"They are not long, the weeping and the laughter,
Love and desire and hate:
I think they have no portion in us after
We pass the gate."

I admit this was about dazzling Alaric with words, even if they weren't my own. But such exquisite perfection!

"They are not long, the days of wine and roses:
Out of a misty dream
Our path emerges for a while, then closes
Within a dream."

Since there was no one here to accuse me of copyright infringement or plagiarism, I didn't need to announce that 'Vitae Summa Brevis' had been penned by a tragic nineteenth-century poet who had died at the age of thirty-two. The important thing was the sentiment. Didn't we all at some point mourn the fleeting nature of our own days of wine and roses, as ephemeral as whispers in a forest?

Okay, well, not the reaction I expected. Actually, lack of reaction, with Alaric's expression remaining neutral. Had my translation to Middle English dimmed the power of Ernest Dowson's masterpiece?

Then I caught it, the emotion flitting across his face, come and gone too quickly to label.

"I've known that before." Alaric's eyes were fixed on me; his right fist clenched around the stem of his goblet so tightly his knuckles showed white. "When a path emerges from a misty dream only to close again." Said so softly, so intently, as if meant for my ears alone.

I barely managed a nod. His words and his entire manner unsettled me. Alaric was a pure Alpha male. Untidy, uncouth, violent, blunt, and sarcastic without an ounce of tenderness or sensitivity.

"To be forever lost." Alaric's gaze drifted away from mine like the smoke above the kitchen pavilions. What tragedies weighed heavily enough to cause this rock of a man to lose his way? The death of his wife? The slaughter of his older brother? The lingering horrors of battle?

I swallowed hard, as if that could dislodge the lump in my throat, the trembling of my hands, the lightness in my chest.

I could no longer deny that I, too, was lost.

Lost and in love with Alaric DeLaMer.

The shadows on the green were long, those of the carolers—hands clasped together in a circle—bumping against the darkness that had arrived on the heels of a retreating sun.

While Jocelyn was one of those dancing, her husband remained at the dais. Face tired and drawn, Sir James stared fixedly into his goblet. Earlier, concerned for his health, I'd approached him.

"Would you like me to fetch some of your men to take you home?" I'd asked, noticing he'd barely touched his food.

"How kind you are," Lackford had said, favoring me with a piercingly sweet smile. Easy to glimpse the shy young man he'd once been, if not the scourge of the Scots. I reached out to stroke the gnarled hand resting atop the linen tablecloth.

"I can find one of your squires. Or your physician is nearby." I'd spotted him conversing with Roger Mortimer and Archbishop Bykenore.

"I prefer to remain here," Lackford had said. "Fresh air seems to keep the...unpleasantness at bay."

"Picturesque, I'll give 'em that," said Ollie, interrupting my musings. He'd returned from his earlier adventure to slump beside me, flush from winning "a bag of coins." He nodded toward the dancers. "One minute, those morons are screaming for two gamecocks to peck each other's eyes out, and the next, they look like something out of a friggin' fairy tale."

A harp, flute, and fiddle provided the music, accompanied by the tabor sketching out a rhythm. While the tune didn't exactly have one tapping one's feet, it suited the carolers, whose dance moves basically consisted of moving clockwise and counter-clockwise...and repeat. In the center of the circle, some woman sang some song whose lyrics I couldn't decipher. At regular intervals, the rest of the dancers joined in the chorus. Though that was pretty much it, the scene was lovely.

Ollie hummed something that may have been a Bruce Springsteen song. Out of everything we'd left behind in the past/future, I missed the variety of music the most.

"Have you ever wondered 'what makes me knock your fruit juice loose' means?" he asked.

"What are you babbling about?" I asked, but without heat. I'd had enough wine to temper my animosity.

"'Uptown Funk.' Bruno Mars."

Ollie stood, facing me, and made some weird jerky movements with his neck and shoulders while leaning close and wiggling his butt in the air. His version of dancing?

"Stop. You look like you've just been tazed."

Ollie held out his hand, pulling me to my feet. "C'mon, C.L. Dance with me."

He slid a hand around my waist. "Let's show these losers how things are done in the 21st century. Remember when we used to practice the box step?"

"Sixth grade. Mrs. Grubner's first mixed dance class." It hit me then. In all this kingdom, in all this world, Ollie Scott was the only one who shared my memories. "Maybe I should throw in a heel step or shuffle ball change."

Ollie smirked. "No tap shoes." He placed my left arm on his shoulder, his right on mine, positioned our free arms, fingers intertwined, and maneuvered us into a reasonable facsimile of Mrs. Grubner's instructions.

We executed an awkward series of box steps, marginally keeping time with the music. Over my shoulder, I spotted a group of fire twirlers. Brandishing batons—if batons belched fire from both ends— they performed a synchronized routine of graceful arcs, circles, dips, and overhead spins. Looking like enormous fireflies flitting about the dark.

It was beautiful, and I shifted our position to better view them, automatically following Ollie's lead. Some of the twirlers contorted their bodies while manipulating the flames, which left thin trails of smoke in their wake, like souls departing the body. I thought once more of James Lackford and hoped he was enjoying the show. Or had been safely put to rest.

"You!" Ollie hissed, stuttering to a halt, his eyes enormous and fixed on a point behind me.

"Do you think it amusing, jester," said that familiar voice, "to maul a respectable woman?"

I turned to face Alaric, limned by the firelight. "Go find some balls to juggle," he said, pushing Ollie aside. "Bel and I have a respectable dance to enjoy."

With that, Alaric took me in his arms, an act I found disturbingly sexy. That feeling of heatstroke returned. Ignoring propriety, I pressed my cheek against his tunic, inhaling the scent of bay leaves and bilberry from his makeshift deodorant and the musk and cloves from his Castile soap.

"Tell me something, Bel." Alaric's voice was low and husky. "You're not actually wed, are you?"

I was so caught up in the perfection of the moment that I could only stare dumbly up at him.

"Bel," he reminded. "Marriage. You're not, aye?"

"No, I've never been, actually."

Alaric pulled me so close I would have had trouble breathing if I weren't already breathless.

"Good."

Music drifted across the green; fire twirlers cast their flames like nets upon the dark. What I wanted, truly wanted, was to forego banal conversation. For Alaric to woo me and seduce me. To drown in the essence that was Alaric DeLaMer.

So, this is how it feels to be forever lost.

"What sort of dance is this?" he asked, resting his chin atop my head. Since my hair had not yet grown long enough to successfully mimic current fashion, I covered it with the thinnest of veils.

"It's quite popular in that country I told you about," I managed. "That strange, very far away place."

"Colorado?" he asked, his inflection on the wrong syllables.

When I nodded against his chest, he murmured into my ear. "They are very bold in that kingdom."

We were chest to chest and thigh to thigh. "Do you feel it?" I wanted to ask. The tectonic shifting of plates between us. So exhilarating and terrifying that a part of me wanted to flee...back to the 21st century, where I could forget about this hopeless passion. Setting aside the rather obvious problem that we were living in a century that no longer existed beyond a handful of dusty pages and poorly attended lectures, fourteenth-century England-Ireland decreed I was no fit partner for Alaric DeLaMer.

"Kiss me, Alaric," I whispered. Here, in the shadows where no one could see and which in the ruthless glare of tomorrow would be easier to deny.

He bent his head, but before our lips met, we were interrupted by shouts. Followed by a scream? Someone sobbing? Figures around us, running in the direction of the high table.

Even though our moment had been shattered, we remained too drunk on each other to do anything other than draw apart, our fingers still laced together, our gazes locked. Alaric was the first to move. Pulling me after him, we followed the retreating shapes. Around us, the dancers had scattered; the fire twirlers faded into the background until they were no more than the lingerings of a Hollywood Comes to the Valley fireworks extravaganza.

A crowd had gathered near the dais where James Lackford had been seated. Someone wailed—a mournful sound, the way hounds did when missing their master. I distinguished Jocelyn's voice from the cacophony, calmly issuing orders.

"What is it?" I asked, though I very well knew. What had Sir James seen when staring into the contents of his goblet? Had he already sensed that, with the darkness, Death would come for him?

"I warned her to leave him in peace," Alaric muttered. His fingers in mine were like ice; he exhaled his breath with a shuddering sigh.

We reached the high table, illumined by torches. Bystanders were clustered in a circle, eyes cast downward.

James Lackford would be lying there. The lack of related activity—

Archbishop Bykenore having taken charge rather than the Lackford physician—told us all we needed to know.

After making the sign of the cross, Bykenore recited something in Latin. With the first lines of the first prayer of the sacrament of Extreme Unction, everyone dropped to their knees and bowed their heads.

All except Jocelyn Goodknyght, who stood beside the Archbishop, staring, not down at her dead husband, but stone-faced into the night.

Twenty-One

ALARIC

Aye, death comes to us all. Sometimes, it arrives on stealthy feet and annihilates us in a heartbeat; sometimes, it allows us a long string of days before beckoning with a crook of the finger. I was blessed to have known James Lackford from the time I'd been a page in Roger Mortimer the elder's household. I petitioned God and all the saints to allow Sir James immediate entrance to heaven, reminding them he'd suffered enough in these last months to bypass purgatory. Sir James was a proud man and misliked acknowledging weakness, but few of us who reach old age escape the diseases that crawl inside and take up residence there. I'd seen what my friend hid from most on his bad days—the vomiting, cramping of the bowels; the times when his grip was so weak he could not make a fist, let alone lift a sword. When Sir James lounged, he could generally manage his symptoms, but I oft had to support him when he stood, complaining of lightheadedness or that his heart beat so rapidly he could not catch his breath. Even during our cozy nights of conversation, I'd mapped the subtle signs of his discomfort.

Privately, I expressed my sorrow to Lady Jocelyn, dressed in her widow's weeds and layers of veils. Mourning fashion suited her, and she played her role as skillfully as any mummer. Many remarked on Jocelyn's stoicism, as well as her solicitousness toward Sir James throughout his final days, but I saw it differently. Following our return from Trim Castle, Sir James had often started to speak about "my lady wife" before shaking his head and cutting off further confession. I assumed he was troubled by Jocelyn's infidelities or his lack of an heir. Now, I would never know.

Jocelyn honored her husband with all the pomp and circumstance demanded of a great lord and which he'd dictated in his final will. After we celebrated the usual Masses, I was part of a miles-long procession to a family holding within an arrow's shot of Castle DeLaMer, where my friend would be buried. Sir James' effigy portrayed him in his prime, a handsome figure and proud, though I couldn't erase my last image of him curled on the ground, legs drawn to his stomach.

That night had strangled any lingering vestiges of my love for Jocelyn. I'd witnessed no authentic sorrow on her face, not even when Sir James had been wrapped up and carried away while we, his fellow soldiers, wept. She'd played a part the way she always did.

Besides, I'd given my heart to another. That same night when I'd embraced Bel and we'd danced in the dark, I'd surrendered. I realized I'd been a coward. Or worse, a ghoul, for I'd crawled into the grave with Katrin, where I'd fed upon my guilt. No longer. I was here, I was alive, and Bel could be in my arms any time I wished. 'Twas true Clarabel Lucy was prickly, irritating, and the most peculiar creature I'd ever met. But more, she reminded me of *Topographia Hibernica,* where Gerald of Wales recounts so many fantastical tales you can search the width and breadth of this cursed island and never do more than glimpse the *possibility* of any wonders. Until...there it is at your fingertips, the rarest of jewels, just as Gerald promised. So, you catch your breath and think, *'Tis indeed a magical place.*

As Bel was magic.

Bel's and my days of wine and roses might not be long, but I intended to savor every moment.

Clarabel

When my escort and I neared Castle DeLaMer, my heart thrummed as frantically as a hummingbird's wings, not from excitement so much as fear. No, more terror that I would immediately be whisked back to the 21st century. Rather than a modest keep, I'd be greeted by the sprawling version of the castle's current iteration. Not Alaric and his knights, but grounds bustling with suits and Hearts Afire guests with "Love Makes the Words Go Round" T-shirts and tote bags. Had this all been an extended dream from which I would awake to find myself facing a trio of FunTown executives during a presentation of *Mr. Happy's First Day at the Beach?*

Please, God, no!

I wanted this so very badly I feared it would be denied me.

Interesting how one's heart's desire could change in a moment.

During the hour-long journey, I'd puzzled over the *why* of the note Alaric had sent. In addition to the whole different script and language thing, Alaric's handwriting was atrocious. I'd only been able to decipher his name and that by its position on the page. Recognizing Man Bun from my initial ignominious entrance to the fourteenth century as one of my escorts, I'd tried to engage him in friendly conversation. Man Bun's response was more monosyllabic than friendly, though I gathered Alaric wasn't angry at me. Nor had he fallen off his horse and broken a leg or anything. Still... a letter out of nowhere and oh, so properly signed with his family crest pressed into red wax constituted a summons.

Why?

By the time we neared Castle DeLaMer's drawbridge, I'd worked myself into a ridiculous state. Passing under the portcullis, I imagined it slamming down, separating *this* world from the other. Bella Publishing heroines often suffered panic attacks before getting pep talks from their sassy sidekicks, though I couldn't imagine Man Bun turning in his saddle to demand that I "Chillax, girlfriend!" If the stone archway, the edge of the bailey suddenly vanished, I would suffer alone.

I prayed. I closed my eyes. Opened them when the clip-clop from our horses' hooves changed from stone to earth.

Alaric stood in the middle of the bailey, monitoring my approach with an expression telegraphing I was the one person in the universe he most desired to see. I'd not observed that look on his face before, nor on the face of any man—at least when they gazed at me.

Something inside me melted—a lifetime of defenses, of walling up hurts with pretended indifference or hiding them away in the darkest corners of my psyche. *Please, please let this be real! Don't let it all vanish in the space of a heartbeat.*

Alaric reached my side without any sort of supernatural mishap. Holding my stirrup for me to dismount, he murmured, *"Ma beauté!"* and embraced me, quick and hard.

"I can't believe this is happening." My emotions swung like a demented pendulum. One moment, I felt disoriented as if sliding into a fever; the next, my senses were laser-focused—with my brain scanning and recording moments to recall when this was just a memory.

Alaric took me up on the battlements, where the wind blew off the sea. As it had when I stood with his future relative. "There," contemporary Lucan had said, pointing out Castle DeLaMer's ruins and its Venus flytrap of a maze.

Past and present, one atop the other, a palimpsest scraped and redrawn. I tried to act normal, to stay in the moment, *Right here, right now.*

Alaric smiled down at me. "I feared you'd not come." He brushed aside a strand of hair that had been freed by the breeze. He didn't look afraid. He looked more like...a man in love.

Note to readers: As if I'd ever actually seen a man in love except in the movies. And that was as fake as Bella Publishing's entire list.

"I missed you so. I knew you must be grieving and longed to comfort you. For as much as I mourn Sir James, I knew it must be worse for you."

Alaric kissed me. Our first kiss. Though his body blocked the wind, his lips were cold. I suddenly thought of the Knight and his Lady. Did householders glance up to the battlements at this exact spot and fancy they saw them? If we returned at sunset, was that when the Knight and his Lady came out to play?

"Will you stay with me, Bel?" Alaric asked, pulling me back to the present. "We are leaving soon on campaign, and I've had enough of waiting."

I drew back, searching his face, knowing what he was asking.

"We might dine alone in my chamber. And afterward..."

I reached up to brush my lips to his. "I am hungry, but not for food."

~

At the entrance to Alaric's solar, I did the dumbest thing. I giggled. When Alaric looked offended, I said, "Remember when I woke up in your bed, and you accused me of being a spy, and I thought you were the rudest beast ever?"

Alaric's expression softened. "Veronique Velenium?"

"Veronique Vixen," I corrected.

"I'd never witnessed the like. I'd no idea what you were up to." He shook his head. "What *were* you up to, Bella?"

"Don't you like voluptuous women?" I asked, fluttering my no-longer-false-eyelashes.

Alaric arched a brow. "No woman, save perhaps one having escaped from a lecherous monk's fever dream, ever looked like that." He paused. "Or would want to."

"I was a vision," I said, slipping into my Marilyn Monroe voice.

"You were absurd."

"And you," I said, slipping my arms around his neck, "were insufferable."

Our laughter echoed in the cavernous room. Was that what Lucan DeLaMer would someday hear and attribute to ghosts? The past captured within Castle by the Sea's age-old walls?

"I might have been in disguise that day."

"Running from your toddler husband?"

Sobering, I pressed closer to him. Against Alaric's chest, I murmured, "More like running from a life that didn't suit me."

~

Castle DeLaMer's solar had been thoroughly cleaned and lain with new rushes smelling of lavender. Alaric's bed frame was draped with the deepest blue velvet interspersed with the family coat of arms.

Lacing his fingers through mine, Alaric drew me to his bed. "I ordered feather mattresses, just for your pleasure."

Overcome by his thoughtfulness, I only managed to squeeze his hand. A part of me yet remained fearful. Not of laying with the man I would love into eternity, but because in Castle DeLaMer, time twisted in upon itself or wandered off like a naughty child.

Enough. For someone always in her head, endlessly creating other worlds, I'd been granted my heart's desire. It was my choice whether to live in the present or wallow in fears that would ever remain as ephemeral as smoke. *The future doesn't exist.* Except my situation proved that it kind of did. Still, what did it matter that this room would someday be a pile of rubble? Right now, we had a beautiful, *solid* bed, four walls to shield and protect us, the warmth from a fireplace to ward off the October chill, and my larger-than-life Alaric, gazing down on me, his beautiful dark eyes made infinitely darker from desire. How could our coupling not create a ripple across the universe? And when death took us, we would dip our fingers into the timeline of all that is, was, and will be, and retrieving this moment, turn to each other and say, *"Remember this? Remember when we began?"*

I splayed my fingers across Alaric's chest, certain I could feel his heart, both our hearts, through our clothing, beating fast, somehow meeting, blending, and becoming one. I buried my fingers in the thickness of his hair, hair I'd so often mocked, that I so dearly loved, as I loved everything about Alaric. He breathed my name against his lips.

"Is this love?" I whispered. "I've not felt it before."

"Nor have I." Alaric lifted my hand to his lips and brushed them across each individual knuckle. "I used to overflow with pretty sentiments. When I was young, and they meant nothing." He paused. "Or when I mistook lust and the need for conquest as love. Or perhaps love can take many forms, and each is true in its time."

I thought of Raphael Accardi and marveled that I'd been so devastated when Raphael had been a schoolgirl's crush. But if I lost Alaric... that could never happen. *Never.*

Alaric loosed the brooch that held my mantle closed. Once free, he tossed it on the bed, followed by my gauzy veil. After removing the hair combs and throwing them atop the mantle, he ran his fingers through my hair.

"I like this better than that mess you wore atop your head when you first rambled into the bailey. All those curls going every which way."

"You didn't find them irresistibly sexy?"

"I feared you'd been struck by lightning. After I realized 'twas a wig, I wondered why anyone would choose that as a substitute for hair."

"Would you stop?" I said, pretending annoyance. "This is supposed to be a solemn moment. Now, help me out of these clothes. "

Undressing in the Middle Ages without servants was no simple matter. My cotehardie was a tightly fitted gown with lots of buttons and lacing. By the time Alaric had wrested me free, we were both laughing, though I wondered about his past conquests. Had their clothes simply melted away, or had Alaric done something similar? I couldn't imagine him so light-hearted with Jocelyn Goodknyght. And after me, there would be no one else. For either of us.

Finally, I'd been divested of all save my chemise and hose, which were fastened above the knee by garters. I watched with hungry eyes as Alaric shed his cotehardie to expose his chest, so muscular and thick, with just enough hair. He was so perfect; this was so perfect. I could have wept for the gift that had been granted us.

"Hold me," I whispered. With only the thinnest of linen separating us, I felt that familiar current, the charged atmosphere the way it was before a thunderstorm. With Alaric's arms encompassing me, my ear pressed against his chest so I could feel the echo of his heart; I *knew* the stars and planets, all the heavens, had precisely aligned themselves in order to deposit me here.

With a man centuries dead, and I who am not yet born.

Alaric, now naked save for his braies, kissed me and spread me upon the counterpane. He pushed my chemise up past my stomach, his movements gentle yet persistent.

"Let me get this off you without tearing your sleeves."

As if I cared.

Our first coupling was fast and desperate—lips and hands, all our limbs tangled as we danced our dance. The solar was quiet save for an occasional crumbling log from the fireplace, our gasps, moans, and endearments. The scrape of his beard against my skin; the sureness with which his calloused fingers found their way to all the spots that most pleasured me; the scent of musk and cloves, the taste of it when I ran my mouth and tongue over the hills and planes of his body. Yet all of that felt distant, even as I was simultaneously overwhelmed with the pleasure of it. As if I'd risen from my body to stand by our bed, observing two discrete figures through frosted glass.

The second time was slow and sweet, with Alaric murmuring things like "so fine, my Bella," and more I couldn't catch since I always had to translate from Anglo-Norman to English, and my brain was currently on holiday. I felt unmoored, drifting away like a feather on an air current until Alaric yanked me back with a bite or kiss or caress or the shifting of his body that pinpointed yet another spot of pleasure.

When Alaric settled himself inside me, he gazed at me with those deep, dark eyes, and I wondered how a man could ever love a woman so much, a woman who did not deserve it—a woman who yet loved him as much in return. How had we come this far, two people who didn't even like each other, two people who lived centuries apart and yet had somehow found each other?

All those years, whether during quiet moments, alone or in a crowd, when I'd experienced that restlessness, that wishing I were somewhere else. All that time spent yearning for a nameless something just beyond my grasp, wondering if it was money or pleasure or a book or fame when it was all here—this man who looked at me with such adoration. Marking all my flaws and inadequacies and saying, "I accept them."

Had it been necessary to transport me to another time and place to find my beloved?

~

"Do you have ghosts?" I asked later.

Alaric frowned. "Why would you ask such a question?"

"The castle is old," I countered.

Alaric made the sign of the cross, a reminder he was fully a man of time. But then he tapped his forehead. "The only ghosts I've known reside behind my eyes."

Long ago, I'd heard something similar, I was sure of it, but the memory lurked out of reach.

Snuggling deep into the mattress, I rested against Alaric's chest. His breathing was deep and regular, signaling he was close to drifting off. I didn't want to waste one moment of our time together. Besides, what if we fell asleep and woke up to well...nothing.

"Why do you love me?" I asked.

I felt Alaric's shrug. "You know that in my old age, I've become a man of few words."

"The heart has its reasons," I said, parroting a famous quote. "Of which reason knows nothing."

"Let us enjoy our days of wine of roses," Alaric countered, running his palm over the curve of my hips, not possessively, for I was already owned but because he seemed as hungry to remain anchored to me as I was to him.

Our days certainly weren't long—four in total. Cocooned inside Alaric's solar, we made love, of course, but we laughed and told each other stories, some serious, more fanciful. Before the fireplace in our matching chairs, he retrieved a copy of *Topographia Hibernica* from a chest, pulled me onto his lap in his big chair, and read to me. With the fireplace flames caressing his features, I drank in his changing expressions, listened to his flawless translation from Latin, and experienced my own sense of awe that I had ever dismissed him as a barbarian.

When my beloved left on yet another campaign, I was what I described as "quietly devastated." Every moment away from Alaric would be torture.

Knowing he would return to me was enough.

It had to be.

Twenty-Two

〜

Winter rains had arrived. Dreary, brutal days. While regularly reminding myself there was bread to be baked and distributed and a hospital to be monitored, I spent long stretches of time curled inside my bed with its curtains closed, missing Alaric and mourning Sir James. On one of my infrequent trips out, I was followed by a skinny mutt—dogs were uncommon in Dublin for reasons I refused to think about—and took him home. He reminded me of John Wayne's dog in *Hondo,* so I called him Sam.

My canine companion was way more enjoyable than Ollie, who I tried to avoid. When we did meet, he had a one-track mind.

"Who's Count St Germain?" he cornered me to ask. It was one of the few pleasant afternoons in recent weeks, so I was tossing Sam sticks in the back yard.

I frowned. "European nobleman. Claimed to have found the philosopher's stone, which made him immortal. Charlatan, whose death is well documented. Why?"

"Naga the Alchemist said he knows all his secrets, including time travel."

I snorted. Sam trotted up to me, tail wagging, and dropped the stick at my feet. "Impossible. St Germain pops up in the mid eighteen hundreds—"

"Not if he's immortal."

"Stop it. Naga didn't say any such thing. You don't understand the language well enough to do anything beyond order a jack of wine or ask a servant if she'd like to—"

"You don't know everything, Clarabel. You're so wrapped up in that broody knight of yours you don't see what's going on beneath your nose."

"Which is?"

Ollie shook his head. "What if Naga's legit? What if he *is* some kinda magician? What if he could help us get back to where we belong?"

"I belong here," I said, turning my back on him. I tossed Sam's stick and ignored Ollie until he stomped away.

All Hallows' Eve: I'd forgotten. Not at all the light-hearted trick-or-treating ritual I'd known when we'd carried a costumed Blix onto the Duchess's front porch and passed out candy bars to a parade of pirates, cowboys, witches, princesses, ghosts and vampires, cartoon characters, and whatever superhero was popular that particular year.

Here, All Hallows' Eve was serious business. A perilous period when the dead more easily mingled with the living, when vigils were kept, fasting mandated, and protective crosses placed above front doors. When the bells of St. Patrick's Cathedral relentlessly tolled a funeral knell and criers, swathed in black, walked Dublin's streets ringing hand bells, exhorting passersby to pray for the already departed so they might more swiftly escape purgatory.

Though it didn't take All Hallows' Eve for the dead or nearly so to walk among us. They were in the surrounding farmlands, beyond city gates, spilling out of Dublin's almshouses and upon cathedral closes, crumpled in garbage-strewn alleys and along riverbanks. One morning, my maids opened our front door to a corpse sprawled like a gruesome welcome mat.

Mitigating such suffering—if only marginally—drove me to Matteo the Moneylender with my Tiffany bracelet. Not only did we need to increase bread production, I needed to better monitor those poor souls ensconced in St. Bartholomew's Hospital. I could not trust Lady Jocelyn to honor her husband's obligation. In fact, I'd seen little of Jocelyn Goodknyght since Sir James' funeral, though servants gossiped she split her time between here and the Lackford manor near Castle DeLaMer.

Whatever.

After emerging from Matteo's carrying a comfortable purse, I hesitated in front of the Elixir of Life Apothecary Shop. Ollie seemed to have disappeared along with a second Art Deco ring, and I just knew Naga, with his crazy promises, had something to do with both.

"Lady Lucy, Good afternoon to you," Naga called from his usual place behind his worktable. Almost as though he'd been waiting for me.

Stepping inside, I dispensed with pleasantries. "Has Ollie been here?"

Dipping his head, Naga observed me out of those disturbing eyes.

"What did you do, promise him that if he drank one of your potions, he would be whisked forward several hundred years?"

"Know ye what today is?"

I suppressed the urge to roll my eyes. "All Hallows' Eve."

"Aye, but it was erected on the bones of Samhain, a more ancient celebration. Samhain himself is called the Lord of Darkness. Each year, Samhain gathers the souls of the dead, which, as punishment for their sins, have been consigned to the bodies of animals."

"And your point is?" While such traditions might be fascinating, like watching the trailer to a horror movie without having to be frightened by the actual film, I had a purse full of coins, I was lacking an escort, and the afternoon was getting on toward a night when unsavory characters, dressed in animal costumes, would prowl the streets.

Naga absently fiddled with a nearby mortar and pestle. "Tonight, the lines between this world and the other blur, and the doorway to the other world will open, allowing supernatural creatures and the souls of the dead to step into our world. And we into theirs."

"Are you telling me Ollie is dead?" I asked sarcastically.

"I am saying if one knows how, there is a way to traverse all manner of worlds."

I personally knew the truth of that. But Naga the Charlatan had nothing to serve up but twaddle. I turned to go.

Naga stopped me with a commanding voice. "During certain hours on certain days on certain times of the year, there be little more than a hair's width between dimensions." He waved a hand gently before his face as if brushing aside a cobweb. "The trick is being able to find the door to that other dimension. That hair's width."

I believed that. I just didn't believe him.

"Perhaps your friend was here," Naga continued, fingertips skimming the lip of the mortar. "And mayhap I gave him the means to find that door."

"You're a fraud!"

"Nevertheless, if your friend does not return to your residence and you find evidence for the truth of my assertions, please remember I am here to be of service."

After I exited the shop, Naga called after me. "To help you uncover your own door."

November was called the "blood month," an ominous turn of phrase that rolled off the tongue in a thrillingly macabre fashion, though it simply meant farmers killed and salted their livestock throughout November in order to store enough meat to survive until spring.

By the first week of Blood Month, I knew Ollie would not be back; by mid-month, Roger Mortimer had moved his government to Cork. We received news of Mortimer's sorties from travelers arriving from the south. Frustrated with the lack of *instant* communication, I threw myself into expanding services at St. Bartholomew's and purchasing more ovens and grain to feed more people. Everywhere I went, Sam trotted beside me. His presence was surprisingly comforting. Though Sam was more interested in filling his belly than in being my protector, I enjoyed talking to him and laughing at his antics.

With the arrival of Christmas and Alaric's continued absence, my thoughts drifted to Ute Creek. The Yule Log would be hidden somewhere on Roja Mountain, and after being uncovered, our town hall would be opened for food, wassail, and gifts. We always gussied up the Duchess, opened her to the public, and arranged a visit from Santa—aka Old Man Pettigrew—who passed out sacksful of presents. Those things I missed. Not that Dublin didn't have its own celebrations.

The Masses were extra meaningful here inside the soaring edifice of St. Patrick's. The fact that *everyone* believed and the rituals were taken so seriously enhanced the season's mystical quality. One of the most interesting rituals involved priests interpreting signs of nature via specific biblical texts. From St. Patrick's pulpit, Archbishop Bykenore predicted an end to the famine and interpreted the gale-force winds that blew through Dublin on Christmas Eve as an omen of treachery among the rich and powerful. Knowing what lay ahead for Edward II, I could not count the archbishop wrong.

I only wished someone could foretell my own fortune.

Somehow, my heart and my impatience managed to survive through February. During another of my bread distributions, I heard that Roger Mortimer had returned to Dublin. And that this very night, a feast would be held in Dublin Castle where Mortimer, exercising his right as King Edward's Irish representative, would create a passel of new knights.

"How can Alaric?" I asked Sam later that evening when I was tucked away in my bedroom. Sam gazed at me with sympathetic eyes.

How long had Alaric been back? Why hadn't he visited or sent for me?

"You tell me you love me," I said, this time directly addressing my invisible lover. "And yet, I've not heard a word from you."

I moped around like Debbie Reynolds in *Tammy and the Bachelor*— falling in love with an unattainable man; gazing mournfully out her bedroom window while singing about her plight to various birds and trees and musical instruments; having her heart crushed and mooning about (image of myself sprawled on a chenille bedspread surrounded by movie magazines, sighing loudly between sips of my chocolate malt) until Tammy discovers her man does indeed adore her. After which, they skip off into their happy endings.

> **Observation to readers:** For all the reasons I hated my mother, her obsession with Debbie Reynolds, which intruded at the most inappropriate times, ranked near the top.

But Alaric did come, at least via an escort, and awaited my arrival in Castle DeLaMer's bailey.

Once in his arms, I was incapable of saying much beyond, "I missed you so." Words were puny substitutes for the enormity of my emotions. Still, when I was nestled in Alaric's powerful embrace, cocooned in his bed with curtains closed to keep out the cold, I recognized my primary emotion: *joy*.

"We heard about all the fighting," I said later after we'd physically reacquainted ourselves. With my head upon Alaric's chest, his chest hairs soft against my cheek, I added, "I did not fear for you because I know what a great warrior you are."

Alaric snorted. "'Twas not much to fear. The clans prefer throwing down their weapons if they canna flee into the bogs. I'll wager they've suffered more from the famine than most. Most would sell their birthright for a heel of bread." He said this with pity rather than contempt.

For me, these moments, when we chatted about mundane matters, were what I most cherished when Alaric was gone.

Which happened all too soon.

~

From our summer of 1318, from all our time together, one afternoon stands out.

"Have you seen Bog Cotton?" Alaric asked while we waited outside the stables for our horses to be saddled. When Alaric hawked or allowed his hounds to hunt, we included others in our excursions. More often, we rode alone or with Sam, who remained a frequent companion.

"Tell me," I said, slipping my hand through his. At Fair Green, I'd seen bolts of cotton imported from Italy, but Bog Cotton must be something different.

"'Tis the Irish wildflower, some say, and magical in its own sense."

"I'm surprised Gerald of Wales did not mention it then," I said, and we both laughed.

After a considerable ride, we reined our mounts upon a hillock opening onto a boggy meadow. While bogs were generally bleak, forbidding places, and dangerous to walk upon, today, a blanket of white, like puffs of clouds fallen to Earth, spread before us.

"Lovely!" I wished, as I often did, that camera phones had been invented. For with the shifting light, the cotton heads resembled a great scattering of the pearls I'd seen poor folk hunt when local rivers ran low and clear.

"'Tis a blessing to see this land producing something other than mud and misery," Alaric said before we guided our mounts farther inland. Since we rode side by side, he periodically reached across to brush my hand where it held Blixette's reins or to brush my thigh.

That was the way it was during those months when only moments passed before we each found a reason to touch the other.

We finally dismounted in a meadow carpeted with wildflowers ranging from palest butter to deepest citrine. After Alaric held up his arms and I slid from Blixette, he pressed against me, causing the stirrup to dig into my back. Fitting that here in this field of flowers, his kisses tasted like nectar.

This I will remember. This I must remember. Whenever I doubt you love me. Or that there is a God and life is more kind than cruel.

After removing his cloak from where he'd lashed it behind his saddle and hobbling our mounts, Alaric took my hand. As we explored, the flowers brushing our knees released a delightful mixture of citrus, spice, and sunshine. Upon finding an appropriate spot, Alaric spread out his mantle and pulled me down upon a bed soft as moss.

Covering my body with his, Alaric smiled down at me. Those eyes so dark, so impossible to describe—black or grey or brown—gazing at me with such love. Reaching up to curve a strand of hair behind his ear, I thought I'd never seen anything so beautiful.

"Does this please you?" he asked. "Our bed?"

Overcome, I could only nod.

We did little more that afternoon than rest contentedly in each other's arms. Occasionally, we spoke. More often, we enjoyed the breeze, the droning bees, the butterflies fluttering from flower to flower, and the birds passing overhead. When a covey of quail scurried like fussy schoolmarms past our makeshift blanket, we, in turn, giggled like their pupils.

I was full up with love. With quiet ecstasy. If poets could describe these feelings, they were far more skilled than I.

"Know what I wish?" I asked, nestled against Alaric's chest.

He kissed the top of my head. "What, ma Bel?"

"That we would stumble upon one of Gerald of Wales' islands out in the middle of a lake—"

"I've seen a few such on campaigns, though with no accommodations simply awaiting our arrival."

"But once we rowed out to said island, we would discover the perfect cottage. After making it our home, we'd live there forever, just the two of us."

"Aye, the Island of the Living."

Since we were woolgathering, we glossed over the more sinister parts of Gerald's tale, such as the island was referred to as the Island of the Living because, while no one there could die a natural death, they could suffer sicknesses so painful they chose to be transported to a larger island where they would die immediately upon touching the ground.

On our way home, the phrase "Happy, happier, happiest" repeatedly ran through my brain. As if it were an enchantment spell guaranteed to ward off evil.

If that were so, we'd soon discover the spell was yet another thing that played us false.

Twenty-Three

ALARIC

My time for dalliance was over. Alarmed by the growing power of King Edward's new favorite, greedy Hugh Despenser, Roger Mortimer had sailed for England. Therefore, in the fall, Archbishop Bykenore appointed me to lead one more campaign against Edward the Bruce. While Bruce's base was far north in Ulster, he had sallied forth to terrorize the populace. His brother, Robert, illegitimate Scottish king, was supposed to meet up with him, but Edward, ever the hothead, had not waited. I prayed Robert Bruce would indeed arrive by the time I reached Ulster so I might kill the Beast of Bannockburn with my own sword.

That September day, my mind was awhirl with all the necessities that went into a campaign...and, incidentally, how to say goodbye to Bel, who had returned, as she regularly did, to her Dublin residence.

I did not hear the footsteps on the stairs outside my solar and only spun around when the door was flung dramatically open.

"Jocelyn! What are you doing here?"

Throwing back her veils, Jocelyn Goodknyght rushed to me, fairly tumbling into my arms. Her familiar perfume, which I'd once found so captivating, enveloped me like a miasma. Undeniably, my former paramour remained lovely, the black of her mourning weeds complimenting her pale skin. I immediately noticed she was without a maid.

Alone with Jocelyn.

Once, I would have rejoiced.

"I had to see you," she murmured against my ear, as if James Lackford had just died, and she was in the first throes of grief. I removed her arms from around my neck and stepped back.

Jocelyn gazed up at me, lower lip quivering, eyes bright with tears. Vulnerable. Today's role was damsel-in-need-of-protector.

I stared down at her, mind tumbling back to someone who had been "out of sight, out of mind" this past year.

"Isn't it peculiar, the casting of our fates upon the stars?" Jocelyn asked. "'Tis near the anniversary of my poor husband's death, I've contracted my favorite astrologer, and he's assured me 'tis time we plan our future."

I had no idea what she was talking about. "I thought you were in England," I said dumbly. This...she, I did not need. "'Tis not meet we be alone," I added, though 'twas foolish to think propriety would be of importance to Jocelyn Goodknyght.

Rather than respond, she swept over to my bed and sank down on the counterpane.

"I have a chair," I said, gesturing to one of a pair positioned near the fireplace. Where Bel often sat nestled against my chest as we talked or I read to her.

Jocelyn's delicate hands stroked the counterpane, which was embroidered with plants and mythical beasts I'd chosen to amuse Bel. Conversing on a bed might be acceptable, but in this case, it felt too intimate. Particularly with Jocelyn eyeing me like a purse stuffed with pounds sterling.

"The stars are in alignment. Why else would we both be free at such a propitious moment?" When I didn't respond, she continued. "Rather than wait to be put under King Edward's protection and he grant me in marriage to whomever he pleases, we must seize the moment. You and me, my dearest. As we've wished for so long."

A chill went through me. Had this been Jocelyn's plan from the moment her husband collapsed?

I shook my head. "We were children. 'Twas so long ago." When I'd been a nobody. When I'd loved her and bedded her and obsessed over her while she'd callously pushed and pulled my affections. Now, here I was...and there she was. Out of a misty dream, our path had emerged. But that path had closed.

Jocelyn must have been displeased by my expression. From the folds of her gown, she retrieved what appeared to be an embroidered cloth folded in quarters.

"Come." She stood and carefully opened the material, after which she smoothed it atop the counterpane. "I've been working on this for years."

Reluctantly, I moved to stand beside her. Spread below us was a square of rich silk into which Jocelyn's face had been stitched. Strands of her own hair had been woven into the design. I'd seen such portraits, which didn't make hers any less exquisite. With such a face, how could it have been otherwise?

"You surprise me, Jocelyn. I didn't know you possessed such talent."

She traced the contours of her face, mapping it like a lover's.

"Touch it," she ordered. "It feels like the real thing."

Reluctantly, I brushed a palm across its surface, but the material caught on a jagged edge of my signet ring. When I drew back, threads came with me.

"*Merde*! Look what you did." The old Jocelyn would have stomped her foot, knowing I'd be undone by her tantrum. Then again, old Jocelyn would never have spent countless hours on tedious needlework in order to impress a nonentity.

I apologized for my carelessness, saying, "I can be clumsy around beautiful things." Jocelyn's smirk told me she wrongly interpreted my words.

"'Tis yours." She folded the square and held it out to me. "Put it in a special place. When you look at it, think of me and of what we'll soon share."

I didn't want it. Didn't want her. Thinking I would bury the cloth away in a linen chest or some such, I reached for it.

"Nay, take off your ring first. Lest you snag it again."

I did, carelessly tossing my ring upon the counterpane.

"Jocelyn, you canna continue this. I am happy with someone else. She is the one I love. And once I return from my current campaign, I intend to take her with me to England. Mayhap even marry her."

"What? Of whom are you speaking?" As if she couldn't see evidence of Bel with her mantle hanging on a peg and a pair of pattens below. Jocelyn must be telling the truth then that she'd been in England. Bel and I were hardly a secret.

The moment Jocelyn realized Bel's identity, her eyes turned winter cold. "But you know nothing about her, not her lineage. *Nothing*! Most likely, she is baseborn. She is not *me,* and you absolutely canna marry her."

"Enough." Jocelyn tried to shake my hand off her forearm, which caused me to tighten my grip as I dragged her to the door. "The one thing Bel possesses that you do not is honesty." Except for her tall tales. But not about *real* things, things that mattered. "You were always a mirage, Jocelyn. Be grateful you're a wealthy widow and will have no problem finding a new husband."

Of course, Jocelyn left in a huff, and I knew I'd made an enemy. I also knew Jocelyn would not cease her advances. Not because she cared for me but because she misliked losing.

I did not give a thought to my signet ring until later. Then, I searched all around the bed. I even had the floor rushes swept out and examined.

I never found that particular ring.

Of course, I did not.

Jocelyn Goodknyght, whose heart was as black as her mourning weeds, had snatched it.

Just one of many things she used to destroy Bel and me.

~

CLARABEL

Alaric promised he'd return by Christmas. "And I honor my promises," he said as the hour of our parting approached.

He pulled me from my chair next to his and into his lap. Facing him, I wrapped my arms around his neck.

"When I return, will you accompany me to England? Wendsbury and other family holdings are there. 'Tis my responsibility to make sure they are correctly managed." Alaric raised my chin, forcing me to meet his gaze. "Have you been to Wendsbury, Bel?" When I shook my head, he said, "'Tis settled then. We'll go together."

"I would like that." With those words, the remaining chains around my heart fell away. We would not be separated. Alaric craved me as completely as I craved him. Retrieving his hand, I kissed each fingertip. For the first time, I, the observant creature that I was, noticed his missing signet ring.

When I questioned him, he shrugged. "No idea where I lost it. I've not had time to have another made."

Hmmm. Signet rings were sometimes used as betrothal rings. Such an idea was madness. But then again, I was mad for Alaric DeLaMer. He wouldn't marry me. We couldn't marry. Yet the very possibility...

The following afternoon, Alaric personally escorted me back to my residence. Not caring who might see, he embraced me after we dismounted. "I canna know how long this will take, but even if we are in the midst of battle, if I must sprout wings and fly, I will stand here on Christmas Day. And if God so wills it, 'twill be the last time we part."

Fighting back tears, I clung to him. When had I become such a weakling? Pinning my happiness on another when every book, every relationship guru, and every self-help podcast preached we women were stronger and better and too enlightened to crumble without a partner. But they were wrong. That world had yet to be created, and here, Alaric was my *raison d'etre.*

Perhaps he would be regardless of the century.

◞

A few days later, Jocelyn Goodknyght appeared at my doorstep, presenting me with a sambocade. "In remembrance of my lord husband," she said, her smile sad. Jocelyn had only recently returned to Dublin from the royal court, she explained.

"I'd wanted to thank you for all those evenings we shared," Jocelyn said, placing the tart in my hands. "'Tis especially made for you."

My ever-hungry Sam plastered himself to my leg, trying to sniff at the treat. I called out to Elle, ordering her to remove him to the kitchen.

"When you enjoy my treat, do think of my lord husband. Sir James so loved his sambocade, didn't he?"

"How kind!" Now that I no longer feared Jocelyn's hold on Alaric, I could admit my animosity had more to do with jealousy than her shortcomings.

"'Tis for your enjoyment only," Jocelyn reminded me before departing. "My expression of gratitude, belated as it is."

After retreating to the kitchen and placing the sambocade on the wooden worktable, I ordered Sam to "stay!" near the kitchen fire. I was trying to learn the art of spinning, and Sam would be in my way.

"I'll be in my chamber," I told Elle. Tucked away in my room, I struggled with my new nemesis, which was way more complicated than it looked, requiring a ridiculous amount of coordination with fibers that were wound around a distaff, somehow being attached to a drop spindle and somehow being twisted into yarn.

"Forget this!" I finally muttered after several threads had mysteriously wrapped themselves around my fingers.

A sudden scream caused me to jump and snap the threads. I'd barely put aside the contraption when Elle burst through the door.

"Come quick! Something dreadful's happened."

"What?" I followed Elle through the hall to the front. "Has somebody been hurt?"

"Sam!" she said, which told me nothing. Until we reached the kitchen, where broken crockery and the remains of Jocelyn's sambocade were scattered on the floor. In the far corner, near Sam's makeshift bed, two kitchen servants were bent over the dog. Sam was stretched out on the floor, vomit beside his head, and diarrhea pooled from beneath his tail. Foam painted his jaws; his ribcage heaved as he struggled for air.

"What happened?" The scattered cheesecake told its own tale. Perpetually hungry, Sam had pulled it off the table and devoured it. Some ingredients must be toxic to dogs in the same way chocolate is.

"I should've been watching him," cried Elle, "but I did na hear a thing until Brigit and Tom finds him and comes yelling."

Even as I scanned the kitchen for something to ease Sam's suffering, he exhaled. One final time, Sam's ribcage rose and fell.

And that was that.

"Pretty Poison" is the title of one of Susan McDermott's most popular series. In Pretty Poison, my librarian friend's alter ego solves various murders by tracing them back to an array of poisons. Before each mystery, McDermott and I had discussed the poison to be used— antifreeze, wolfsbane, arsenic, and, my favorite, Botulinum Toxin, otherwise known as Botox. In *Pretty Dead*, a lethal amount is injected into the face of a social media influencer who refused to pay her cosmetologist bills.

Arsenic. Susan and I had weighed the pros and cons. Major pros— colorless, tasteless, odorless, and undetectable in most autopsies. So, unless one is as book smart as McDermott's amateur sleuth, the murder will go undetected.

Is this what had happened? Not so much to Sam, but to James Lackford?

Could he have been poisoned?

Late into a sleepless night, I mulled over the possibility, slotting together all of Lord Lackford's symptoms I had witnessed and how they fitted with arsenic poisoning. Fatigue, heart palpitations, nausea and vomiting, swollen face and limbs, lesions. The roadmap to murder had been right before me.

In my mind, I retraced our visits as best I could remember. Jocelyn had been clever. When Alaric and I visited, and sambocade was offered, Jocelyn would have foregone the poison or administered it in small doses. I remembered back to Michaelmas and Sir James' last day. He'd barely touched any food, but Jocelyn had repeatedly placed her arm around his shoulder and guided his goblet to his lips.

Had she given him wine laced with arsenic in front of hundreds?

In Lackford's weakened condition, it wouldn't have taken much to cause a total collapse of his organs.

Monstrous. But, with no scientific way to test my hypothesis, how could I prove *anything*? Even if I did, a nonentity such as myself would end up in the stocks or worse.

Still, James Lackford had not deserved such a death.

Nor had my poor, sweet Sam.

Round and round, I argued with myself. Poison? Coincidence? Confront Jocelyn? Stay silent? Investigate? Tell Alaric?

When the first hints of dawn leaked through my chamber shutters, I finally made my decision.

Jocelyn Goodknyght had poisoned her husband.

And she had tried to poison me.

Twenty-Four

If Jocelyn was surprised when my presence was announced at the entrance of her private chamber, she hid it well. I didn't waste time with niceties. "You poisoned your husband. Naga the Alchemist, said you purchased arsenic from him. You didn't use it on rats. You used it to poison Sir James."

Jocelyn continued folding one of the surcoats she'd been inspecting. She and a pair of maids were spot-cleaning her garments before returning them to her traveling trunks. "My lord husband had been granted a long life," she said, her gaze steady on me. "Even so, one canna live forever."

Not the reaction I expected. She reminded me of my mother, who treated the most outrageous as if it were ordinary. "You tried to poison me," I persisted. "That sambocade. 'Just for you,' you told me. It's a miracle I'm still alive."

Jocelyn studied me as if I were a particularly revolting species of insect. "You didn't enjoy the Cook's effort? When it was so difficult to obtain the proper ingredients."

We were obviously reading from different scripts. I experienced that old frustration when I was backed into a corner, hearing words one would never expect the other to utter.

"I'm going to tell Alaric," I blurted. "He'll have you arrested."

Carefully, deliberately, Jocelyn packed away her surcoat before dismissing her maids.

"Such naivete," she said, facing me. "Whose idea do you think it was to kill my husband?"

I stared at her, having no idea what she was insinuating.

A trill of laughter. "What a saddle goose you are! Alaric planned it all. From start to finish, every step of the way. So that finally, finally, we could wed."

It was my turn to laugh because what else could I do? Of all the explanations I might have anticipated, this wasn't one. It was beyond ridiculous. It was insane.

Jocelyn approached me, her expression placid, though, in the depths of those wide blue eyes, something flashed, warning a monster had been stirred awake.

"Who are you to intrude upon things you know naught about? Alaric and I pledged our troth as children." Jocelyn's hands drifted together, and she intertwined her fingers, her only sign of discomposure. "Which means my marriage to Lord Lackford and he to that simpering clodpate of a wife was sinful from the start."

"What are you talking about?" A frisson of fear ran the length of my spine. I'd been raised with a similar form of madness wrapped in a similar appealing package.

"Did you ever meet Alaric's wife? Nay, you did not." Jocelyn flashed one of her insincere smiles. "How I pitied Alaric, with that human leach ever clinging to him. Scarce able to form two words without looking to him for approval." Jocelyn tapped her forehead, the universal signal for "Not right in the head."

"Katrin?" I managed, insulted on behalf of someone I'd never met. "But Alaric loved her. Sir James said so. And how sweet and kind she was."

Ah, that shattered the façade. Hands balled in fists, Jocelyn paced before me. "All of life is artifice, is it not? And if we canna view behind the surface, how dangerous that can be."

What was she implying? Yes, much of life might be so, but not all.

Nor did I believe Alaric and Katrin's marriage was a façade, not from the tender manner in which he referenced her.

Jocelyn paused, her gaze unfocused, after which she squared her shoulders and faced me. *"Mon Dieu!"* She made a sudden, shoving motion. "Such a tragedy that the clodpate somehow slipped from the roof. An accident. One that was never questioned because if it was?" Jocelyn shrugged. "Had Katrin been mad enough to kill herself? A coroner would have to be brought in, and all manner of insalubrious things unearthed. Nay. Best to bury the body along with the..." her voice trailed off.

Sir James had said Jocelyn rode ahead of the rest of the visiting party. Had she enough time to maneuver Katrin to the roof and push her off? After which, she shaped her version of events by crying, "She jumped!" What a brilliant anti-heroine Jocelyn Goodknyght would make! Alaric would have quashed any investigation lest it ended in a finding of suicide. The consequences to his wife's reputation and her worldly goods, not to mention the state of her soul, would have been too dire.

Such a clever crime. Committed by a mind both nimble and diabolical.

"You pushed Alaric's wife?"

Jocelyn stilled and studied me. Her gaze swept my length, measuring what? "Katrin was not the only clodpate, Clarabel Lucy. Must I explain everything?"

"Yes, you must." In a contemporary mystery, I would be wired or recording the confession with my smartphone. Unfortunately, I was screwed and confused in equal measure.

"Alaric and I planned Katrin's unfortunate tumble. Together. Simple enough to do. First, we had to get rid of Katrin. Alaric often said he could not endure her a moment longer."

"I don't believe you." I'd been raised with the queen of gaslighting. Jocelyn Goodknyght's accusations were made up out of whole cloth. Whether I could bring her to justice, I would tell Alaric. If nothing could be done legally, at least he would *know*.

I veered around Jocelyn, intent on reaching the door.

"Halt! I am not finished."

Reluctantly, I obeyed.

Jocelyn reached for a chain that was partially hidden by her neckline and extracted a necklace with a large ring attached to it. A familiar ring. Alaric's signet ring. The one he'd said he'd lost.

Dread. How did certain people, those without a heart or conscience or morals, always have a way of surprising—and destroying—me? I braced myself for something...horrible. *I don't believe it; I won't believe it* ran around in my head.

"Alaric gave this to me—as my betrothal ring. Before we shared our marriage vows in St George's Chapel. On the heels of my lord husband's funeral."

"That's not true! How could you make up such a lie?"

I did know witnesses were not required for a valid marriage. Nor did one have to recite elaborate marriage vows in a church. But Alaric would never betray me so.

"So, you see, Clarabel Lucy, you were caught up in a dream you foolishly believed to be real."

"He would not wed you and bed me afterward," I said, though I felt myself crumbling inside, all my certainties dissolving. But that's what people like Jocelyn wanted.

"You do not know Alaric DeLaMer. These past few years, he may have been of sober mien and disposition, but before, he was a reprobate, bedding anything with skirts. His family despaired of him ever embracing manhood, which is why they forced him to marry that clodpate. Much good it did them—"

"I don't believe you. Alaric didn't marry you. Nor would he be so wicked as to kill his friend and his wife." My past had taught me never to expose my vulnerability or believe anything certain people said.

Jocelyn continued speaking, but it was white noise. On shaking legs, I exited the chamber, carefully closing the door behind me.

This wasn't true. Could not be true.

If only I could talk to Alaric.

What if he lied? He had loved Jocelyn once. Enough to kill?

As so many times in my life, it came down to a basic question: what is truth and what is fiction?

~

Word of Edward the Bruce's death reached us near October's end. To remind possible dissenters of the fate of traitors, Bruce's corpse had been quartered, and each part dispatched to Ireland's four corners. Knowing how proud Alaric would be of this victory, I ignored the brutality of Bruce's fate and exulted on Alaric's behalf. Sometimes. Other times, well...

Looking back on this period, it's fair to say I was not in my right mind.

I was obsessed with Jocelyn's accusations about Alaric. Yes, conspiracy and murder were horrible enough, but I'd found ways to rationalize much of that away because I wanted so desperately to believe otherwise. To be able to pretend so I didn't have to act. It couldn't be true. My childhood had been bathed in lies. Surely, that had given me a functioning b.s. detector. However, putting aside the truth or falsity of some diabolical plot, what if Alaric and Jocelyn were truly wed? That possibility had taken up fevered residence in my brain. In this century, kingdoms were shaped, and dynasties won or lost on the strength of similarly executed promises without witnesses or documented proof.

Even if Alaric provided a credible explanation, even if he was the man I'd fallen in love with rather than the mirror of my wants, needs, and desires, how could he explain away the signet ring? Such rings were used for betrothals. Alaric's ring was missing. Which circled me back to: If Jocelyn had told the truth about their marriage, might she also have told the truth about Alaric's complicity in murder?

What did I really know about Alaric DeLaMer? He was a creature of his time. What did love mean to him? I, of all people, should realize nobody knew what lay at the heart of another's darkness.

The only thing I knew for certain was that I was completely alone in this time and place. I'd been cast adrift on an ocean as infinite as the cosmos, doomed to wander forever, a hostage to forces beyond my control.

As if that wasn't enough, I suspected my life was in danger. First, while at the market, my purse had been cut. Then, the clay ovens we used for baking were smashed. Most frightening, St. Bartholomew's Hospital burned down. Yes, when most houses were constructed of wood and topped by thatch, fire was commonplace. But St. Bartholomew's had been arson; I was sure of it.

I no longer left my town house without a male escort. Unlike actual members of the nobility, I had no retinue of knights at my command, so I improvised. But could I trust locals, no matter how strapping, who were better trained for working the docks? My servants? While I'd tripled my makeshift "bodyguards" at night, I started at every rattling of the shutters, creak of the staircase, and outside noise. Was I overreacting? No. James Lackford and Alaric's Katrin were dead, and Jocelyn had attempted to poison me. Furthermore, my presence might endanger others.

November slipped into December. The Lackford town house appeared to be vacant. Yet, I could not shake the feeling I was being followed, that at any moment, I could be pushed into the River Liffey or receive a dagger between my ribs.

And my beloved?

By the time Advent arrived, I was convinced: Alaric DeLaMer had betrayed me.

I'd made my decision, and here we were: Naga the Alchemist's inner sanctum. The long, narrow room was properly atmospheric, with sinister shadows and lots of ancient-looking tomes on one wall of shelves. Drawings, scattered jars, and charts, including one similar to a periodic table of elements. Smells I couldn't identify. Overall, nothing to make my gut clench. Except for the huge snake in a glass terrarium, which was interesting since Ireland really did not have snakes or clear glass, for that matter. Naga's worktable was empty save for a carved wooden chest and a candle next to a leather-bound tome, its yellowed parchment pages opened to reveal writing resembling hieroglyphics.

"So, you do believe I provided your friend the means to embrace his destiny?" Naga asked, following the usual pleasantries.

I wouldn't have phrased Ollie's disappearance in quite that way, but I was too exhausted to argue.

Naga cocked his head to study me. Eyes I'd once been certain were amber now appeared black. "I have an object in my possession that will provide proof I was of service to your friend. Would you like to see?"

Rather than await my assent, he crossed to a side cabinet next to his snake. The light from the lone window shone upon his nimbus of hair, fine as dandelion puff, each color of his dragon's robe. After retrieving something from one of the cabinet drawers, he returned to the worktable.

Naga extending his right arm, palm extended. "You will remember this."

My missing Art Deco ring.

"Ah!" I'd forgotten how lovely.

"Do you doubt I can help you? Naga prodded. "The proof is here."

I stared at the ring, my mind whirling, my thoughts whipsawing. *Stay... Go...*

"Yours is a troubled spirit, Lady Lucy."

No shit, Sherlock.

Naga absently stroked the lid of the wooden box, his delicate fingers tracing its carved pattern. "You're a clever woman," he said, his tone implying the opposite. His gaze was calculating; in the uncertain light, his eyes gleamed like a cat's. The first time, I'd noticed that particular aberration. "Are you familiar with Albertus Magnus?"

I nodded, returning his stare. Cat's eyes. Not unheard of in humans but still disconcerting. "Dominican friar. Studied alchemy among other wonders." Some said he'd discovered the philosopher's stone, which transmuted lead to gold in endless amounts, rather like Rumpelstilt-skin, who spun gold on behalf of a miller's daughter.

"Albertus Magnus asked, 'Do there exist many worlds, or is there but a single world? This is one of the most noble and exalted questions in the study of Nature.'"

Well, this conversation just took an unexpected turn.

My gaze drifted to a sketch next to the elemental table—the ouroboros, the snake eating its own tail.

Naga followed my gaze. "A personal reminder that time is an

endless cycle, circling itself with past, present, and future. Only the uninitiated believe it to be linear."

Such a charlatan could not possess the key to endless wealth, to immortality, to expanding one's consciousness beyond human capabilities. But what if Naga wasn't a charlatan? Ollie's disappearance was proof of...something.

And I was such a terrible judge of character.

"You speak of the most extraordinary matters in such a mundane fashion."

"While they might seem fantastical to others, they're commonplace for one such as me. Would you like me to reveal how the process works?"

I continued to hesitate. Never see Alaric again? The price was too high.

You are an expert at creating heroes, mocked my wayward voice. *What if Alaric DeLaMer is simply another of your imaginary characters—Clarabel Lucy's Eternal Beloved?*

"Yes, Alchemist. Explain your wizardry."

With measured movements designed to heighten the drama, Naga opened the carved wooden box from which he lifted a square container made of glass and marked with faint etchings. Approximately the size of a pint-sized milk carton, it was stoppered with some sort of metal that shone like gold.

"You've heard of the philosopher's stone."

Could this be the holy grail of alchemy, the subject of thousands of years of failed experiments? If true, I was inches away from one of the world's wonders. I was fascinated and repelled in equal measure.

"A *soupçon* of the powder within whatever liquid you choose provides the fulfillment of man's desires, just as seekers claim."

Naga stroked the air above the container, causing the nearby candle flame to dance and play among its etchings. "I spent a lifetime uncovering its secrets. Followed by centuries perfecting them."

"It's a good thing you're immortal then," I mocked, annoyed at his theatrics. Naga the Alchemist provided a better argument for reincarnation. Died in the fourteenth century, reborn in the twentieth as Dottie Lucy-Flack.

"Immortality is an interesting state of being," Naga said, undeterred by my sarcasm. "While the uninitiated assume those so gifted will live forever, there is an escape clause, so to speak. Meaning, as we magi traverse our environment, we must exercise common sense. One cannot fling oneself from the Eiffel Tower and expect to live, for example. Or be run over by a convoy of tanks and emerge unscathed."

I swallowed. The Eiffel Tower? Tanks? With those two images, Naga confirmed the veracity of his claim. Yet he spoke so casually it was easy to miss their significance.

You can *time travel. You* have *visited other centuries.*

Naga folded his arms across his chest and drew himself to his full height. At that moment, he reminded me of one of God's angels—beautiful in that androgenous way. And creepy as hell.

"So, you see, Clarabel Lucy, I have the answer to Albertus Magnus's query: There are many worlds, and I have transgressed them."

My limbs tingled as if pricked by a million invisible bees. *Remember this moment.* I wanted to speak, to acknowledge the magnitude of his accomplishment, but found myself struck mute.

"I sense you are impatient to reveal the purpose of your visit," Naga said, switching subjects. "Can I, Naga the Alchemist, actually send you back to your decade and your abode?"

I managed a nod.

"I'll not bore you with details you wouldn't understand. Suffice to say I will supply you with a portion of the powder, along with the same instructions I gave your friend. While success is not dependent on the time of year, 'tis most efficacious when the veil separating the worlds is thinnest. Winter's solstice is optimal."

Three weeks away! Too soon!

I suddenly ran sweaty palms along the folds of my mantle. My heart screamed, *No! Don't do this!* But my heart was so easily fooled. Had I been writing this scene, I would have concocted a *deus ex machina* that would involve Alaric parachuting in at the last moment to save me, declare his everlasting love, and wrap our story up with a happily ever after.

Naga's voice was muffled noise. I was still mentally balancing the scales—stay or go? How silly when I'd already made up my mind that I continued with this pretend bargaining. *I don't want to leave. I would rather stay and risk all for love.* But that was more the purview of my heroines, not practical, cautious Clarabel Lucy, who couldn't manipulate happy endings. Who'd claimed she didn't believe in love. I could not change my nature to forgo safety over potential heartbreak. Nor could I bear to see Alaric's face when he confessed, "Everything Jocelyn told you is true."

The sound of a lid closing returned me to the moment. Naga locked away his container and returned the box and Art Deco ring to the cabinet.

He faced me across the worktable. Leaned toward me. Instinctively, I drew back.

"Do you think Naga the Alchemist would waste more than a breath in some nonentity square of dirt like Dublin?" he asked with a sudden intensity.

"I have no idea."

"While I've been round the world, I have a particular affinity for Britain."

I stared into those peculiar eyes. No doubt he was toying with me or perhaps trying to frighten me because he was a bully, amused by my discomfort, or for some other unfathomable reason. What would motivate me if I faced eternity and had seen, heard, and experienced everything? Wouldn't I be choked by the boredom of it all? Wouldn't immortality seem a curse rather than a reward?

Naga bared his teeth in an imitation of a smile. "I confess Naga the Alchemist could be responsible for making *Britannia major* the most haunted land on Earth."

I did not respond. Whatever game we were playing, I was ignorant of its rules.

"Have you ever wondered, Clarabel Lucy," he asked in a sibilant voice, "whether ghosts might simply be another form of immortality? Only whereas a magi's body will live forever, in certain circumstances 'twill be their spirits that are eternal?"

I was horrified by the very thought of such a thing, of ghosts like those flitting about Castle by the Sea being forever earthbound. An ouroboros of a most monstrous kind.

"I am interested in returning to the 21st century, not in immortality or whatever you're babbling on about."

"Many have expressed a need for that particular service. Some found themselves immortal, but as spirits or beings, as I prefer to call them. One must be specific with one's requests." That hideous smile again. "Mistakes made cannot be unmade."

"What will you charge for your services?" I asked, reaching for my purse.

"Bring me your Milanese necklace. Upon receipt, I will give you what you desire."

"My entire necklace? You hold your abilities dear." I would pay for it; of course I would. As Naga well knew.

"One last thing," he said as I readied to leave. In the light from the lone window, his face flickered from youth to age and back again. Goosebumps rose on my arms. "Here, in this time, the winter solstice falls on Christmas Eve. Being the scholar, you know all about the difference between the pre and post Gregorian calendar, do you not?"

I didn't. I had no idea, actually.

"You should book your travel plans for Christmas Eve."

Naga the Travel Agent. He was mocking me. I hated him.

And I would do as he said.

Twenty-Five

ALARIC

I had promised Bel we would celebrate Christmas together, and I meant to keep that promise. Currently, we were many miles to the north, near Carrickfergus Castle. We'd completed the final mop-up against the Scots, who'd been considerably less anxious to fight after losing Edward Bruce. Now, my men and I rode hard for Dublin.

As impossible as it seemed, as impossible as Clarabel Lucy *was,* I missed her more with each moment spent apart. And with each such moment, I realized how much I loved her. Not in the way of Jocelyn Goodknyght. That had been a boy's yearnings, the randiness of youth which had died with age. And Katrin? I could not and would not delve too deeply lest the pain and guilt rise to destroy my present happiness. Aye, I'd loved Katrin in my fashion. She'd been kind and gentle, but she was half my age and not so much a helpmeet as an obligation I'd pledged to protect and shield. While my feelings for Bel might not qualify as a lover's madness, as relayed by minstrels, where a man sometimes resorted to suicide upon being denied his prize, my emotions ran deep and strong. When not occupied with the business of soldiering, I contemplated how well Bel fitted in my arms, how I relished resting my chin on the top of her head, how sweetly she sighed and melted in my embrace, though she could yet revert to that prickly creature I'd first encountered. I enjoyed that Bel, too, enjoyed me teasing her and goading her into displays of unladylike temper accompanied by the peculiarities of her speech, which I did not always understand but found amusing all the same.

Despite my determination and my men's uncomplaining obedience, the weather mocked us. Unlike England, Ireland was devoid of the wondrous roads those clever Romans had constructed centuries ago. We maneuvered our horses over boggy tracks or faced rivers arising in the most unexpected places. Ireland's waterways were said to spring from the bowels of the earth, from the veins of wells, and from the heart of lakes. That I could believe. One moment, our pathway would be clear, and the next, we faced a menacing rush of water. Each one, whether crossed by ferry or upon our mounts, increased my impatience. Endlessly, I glanced at the sun, gauging how many more hours until sundown and the need for shelter. The days were short, the nights long, and the weather miserable, but I would bend nature and time itself in order to keep my word to Bel.

On Winter's Solstice, I pushed my men to travel through the night. The countryside seemed unusually still, though not as if it slept, but remained awake and watchful. I imagined invisible eyes upon us, though mayhap 'twas only the stars monitoring our progress. My squire Charles, who was young and more superstitious than most, had pinned a clump of mistletoe to his mantle in order to ward off evil spirits.

An image of Bel flashed through my mind, standing in the darkness at Castle DeLaMer's bailey. Had she sensed my nearness? Even now, was she anticipating my return? Such would not surprise me, for we seemed to have that primal a connection.

Around midnight, we passed an abbey where the Angel's Mass, in honor of the very hour our Savior arrived to redeem humankind, was being celebrated. Near dawn, we passed villagers creeping from their cottages to attend the Shepherd's Mass, the second Mass on this most sacred of days.

"Only a few miles more," I said to Charles, who'd been softly snoring beside me on his palfrey. The rest of my knights were more campaign-hardened and, truth to tell, as eager to reach Castle DeLaMer as was I.

When the sun had inched its way to be on a level with the machicolations atop Castle DeLaMer's keep, we crossed its draw-bridge. I meant to rest a few hours, bathe, have my hair and beard trimmed, attend King's Mass in order to fulfill my Christmas obliga-tion, and strike out for Bel's. But before that, I called for quill pen, ink, and parchment in order to send her a missive.

"To Mine Eternal Beloved Bella," I wrote, noting that my pen shook from exhaustion and emotion. After promising to attend to her as soon as I'd made myself presentable, I added one of the lines I remembered from her many poetical musings. *'I would not wish any companion in the world but you'* and felt the truth of that with a depth that was almost painful. I found myself smiling while pressing the new signet ring I'd had made to replace the old one into the wax sealing my letter.

After ordering one of my household knights to deliver the missive, I flung myself on my bed.

And did not awaken until the afternoon of Boxing Day.

I'd slept through all of Christmas!

Goading Charles to hurry, hurry, he attended to my dress, and we struck out for Dublin. But upon reaching Bel's town house, we were informed no one had seen her for two days. After questioning everyone and being told, aye, their mistress had been acting strangely though they could not give a proper example, I learned Bel had left funds to maintain the town house in case "I do not soon return." I learned that Bel's "escort," which possessed about as much worth as a pack of puppies, accompanied her to Castle DeLaMer, where they swore they'd watched her cross the drawbridge.

Which meant what? Bel was hidden somewhere in my keep? Had she planned to surprise me and somehow gotten lost? That I wouldn't put past Clarabel Lucy.

I searched all of Castle DeLaMer and its grounds. I found Blixette placidly munching hay in her stall, though the groom who'd tended her couldn't tell me more than that Bel had arrived soon before the portcullis had been lowered. We interrogated everyone, even the scullion who rose before dawn to light the cookhouse fires. No one had seen anything.

My men and I combed the surrounding countryside in all directions: every alley, hovel, church, and grand residence in Dublin.

I tamped down my dread, a premonition of something terrible, as I'd felt the night before Bannockburn.

There is an explanation, I reassured myself throughout the weeks. Bel could not simply have vanished.

I ordered masses said in St. George's chapel and continued riding out into the year of Our Lord 1319 and beyond.

Aye, I had obligations across the channel, but I also had seneschals and bailiffs to oversee DeLaMer properties. At least until Bel returned. We'd first met at Castle DeLaMer, and it was here she would return. I knew that down to the core of my soul.

Perhaps the minstrels were right; perhaps I *was* suffering from love madness.

I didn't care.

I would continue my vigil.

Clarabel Lucy would not forsake me.

Though, in my darkest moments, during the many nights when sleep eluded me, I feared whether it might be so: that our path had emerged for a while before closing within a dream.

Part Nine

ALARIC AND CLARABEL

2019 AND BACK AGAIN

Twenty-Six

CLARABEL

My first impression was that everything looked impossibly pristine. While I'd just arrived from a land famous for its magnificent edifices, most of Dublin's buildings were slapdash, jumbled together like crooked teeth. And always that dreary woolen sky. Here, beyond the Duchess's turret, I spotted a dazzling patch of Colorado blue; everywhere, a dusting of snow like powdered sugar. I inhaled a crisp, fresh lungful of air, blessedly free of the unpleasant odors so ubiquitous these past months.

The area around my feet was undisturbed, so I must have somehow been plunked down in front of the Duchess's porch. Like pole vaulting across centuries. The Duchess herself was decked out in all her holiday glory with icicle lights hanging the length of the veranda, swags of artificial holly below each window, and pine boughs anchored with red bows woven through front porch banisters. The only jarring note was the funeral wreath on the front door.

I was too exhausted to contemplate that or anything else. I'd carefully followed Naga's instructions—ingesting the red powder I'd mixed with wine in the bailey of Castle DeLaMer as near to midnight as I could gauge. I'd concentrated on my desired destination, just as Naga said, waiting for what seemed like forever in the bitter cold. Praying the elixir would work. Praying it wouldn't.

"When you see the door, step through it. It's that simple," Naga had said.

It *had* been that simple.

Despite the decorations, the mounds of plowed snow lining the driveway, and the red Tesla parked near the neatly swept steps, an eerie silence blanketed everything. Perhaps it was a weekend. That would account for the lack of activity at the old carriage house, the original site of Bella Publishing.

But the holidays were always busy.

The lone sign of life was the twinkling lights from the huge Christmas tree positioned in front of the bay window, which cast cheerful patterns upon the lawn. The scene reminded me of a *Twilight Zone* episode where the protagonist stumbles into a normal, everyday town, but *Hold on! Where are the people?* An uneasiness, a heaviness, pervaded the atmosphere.

Aftereffects of my journey, I decided.

At least the cold appeared to be real. I pulled my mantle closer. *Mantle.* How would I explain my clothing? Costume for another romance character? What about my absence? How would I answer, "Where have you been these past eighteen months?" Unless I had only been gone...minutes?

"Time is an endless cycle, circling itself with past, present, and future. Only the uninitiated believe it to be linear."

Cautiously, I ascended the steps and, after a final glance at the out-of-place wreath, turned the doorknob, fully expecting it to be locked.

Instead, it opened to the foyer and the muted sound of Christmas music.

The Duchess smelled like pine, cinnamon, and wassail. I was home. No, I'd left my home. Ute Creek felt like the loneliest place on earth.

"Hello! Anybody here?" Why was it so ungodly quiet?

Pivoting to my left, I stepped into the museum. Dear old Blix, sporting a Santa hat, greeted me.

"I'm glad you're still here," I whispered to Blix, who was inexplicably surrounded by bouquets and wreaths in every shape and form. As if he'd died and was being officially mourned.

What?

Ute Creek's Historical Museum's paraphernalia, ordinarily displayed on the visitors' table, had been replaced by an open guest book edged in black. Behind it was a smiling photograph of my mother in full Debbie Reynolds mode. Off to the side pamphlets "In Loving Memory of Dorothy Lucy-Flack."

I blinked, my senses too dull to immediately grasp the obvious: I had returned to celebrate my mother's funeral.

I have no idea how long I slept. When I first awakened, my disoriented self imagined I was in Castle DeLaMer's bailey after I'd drunk the potion, when the area had glowed like a thousand candles, soft and mellow and buttery. After which, I'd faced the proper wall, and there it was, the door Naga had referenced. *No.* The brittle afternoon sun filtered through lemon-colored curtains to pool atop my eiderdown duvet in a bedroom that was too warm and too silent save for the tick-ticking of the Duchess's old-fashioned radiators.

Still feeling sluggish and dull, I stared up at the familiar twelve-foot ceiling with its hairline plaster crack meandering about as if unsure where to start or end. Remembering when I'd been sheltered beneath Alaric's canopy, encircled in his protective embrace, skin to skin, overwhelmed with the revelation, *This is love. This is what I've been seeking.*

My eyes filled. *What have I done?* How could I survive here, anywhere, when my beloved was denied to me?

Intermittently dozing, trying to shake a smothering ennui. Until something clicked, and I couldn't recapture sleep no matter how desperately I tried. My mind raced like a hamster on a wheel.

How had this sorcery happened? Was there a throughline from Camelot Faire to Hearts Afire to Castle DeLaMer to Naga the Alchemist and back to Ute Creek? I felt like a pinball zipping around the cosmos.

Look, I'm no physicist. But Albert Einstein was, and he'd said,

"The distinction between the past, present, and future is only a stubbornly persistent illusion." So, if it was an illusion, did that mean we could alter the seam of events? And if we could, would the timeline we referred to as history effortlessly shift from one track to another so that once the shift occurred, historical archives, collective memories, and every trace of the events, along with their aftermath, would simply be erased? Or was that where parallel universes came in?

Did we exist in a clockwork universe where the clockmaker occasionally got drunk and tinkered with the gears?

Or was time a balled-up piece of paper with parts touching here and there and in all sorts of peculiar places, without rhyme or reason?

A tentative knock interrupted my endless mental circling. Before I could respond, "Go away!" a familiar face peeked inside. Lizzie Trahern-Wahlberg, red curls as unruly as ever, entered.

"The security cameras picked you up, and once we figured out who you were, I figured you'd returned to mourn your mama."

Security cameras? Oh, yeah, and how could I have forgotten Dottie was dead?

After some awkward hugging, Lizzie perched atop an antique toy chest, her forever favorite spot.

You shouldn't be here.

Correction. I shouldn't be here. None of this seemed real.

Lizzie dove right in. "Ollie told us you ran off with a knight. Is he an actual lord with a title and everything? Does he own a castle? Are you going to bring him to Ute Creek so we can meet him?"

My knight. Why hadn't I waited to hear Alaric's side? *How could I have been so stupid as to abandon you out of petulance? Fear you didn't really love me when I knew you did?*

Rather than attempt to explain the impossible, I changed the subject. "What happened to my mother? How did she die?"

The facts were simple enough. Dottie had accidentally overdosed, mixing anti-depressants, other medications, and booze.

"Ollie found her. She'd been dead almost a day."

So, my former partner was also back in Ute Creek. I'd think about the ramifications of that, of my mother. Later.

Lizzie turned out to be my personal town crier, catching me up on the last eighteen months. Ollie's and my disappearance had made international news, and when Ollie turned up claiming amnesia, it had been dismissed as a publicity stunt.

"Your mama had already taken over Bella Publishing, so it was a war between the Narcissist and the Psychopath." Lizzie paused, twisting a strand of her springy red hair in the way I remembered. "Though I'm not sure which is which."

All the locals had been fired "without severance or anything." After which, Ollie had brought in his own stable of toadies, and Dottie had become the new public face of Bella Publishing I and II.

Lizzie giggled. "And I do mean new face. Your mama's facelift made her look like a cross between Debbie Reynolds and Sylvester Stallone."

That tore a laugh from me. "So sorry I missed it."

Should I feel guilty for laughing at a dead person? For feeling only relief that my mother is gone?

After finishing with Bella Publishing, Lizzie switched to local gossip. The best news: Bad Box Max Dockerty and Seraphina had wed and were the proud parents of a baby girl.

After Lizzie left, I slumped back in my pillows.

Rather than attempt to digest so much new information, I went back to sleep.

The next day, I forced myself to get up, shower, eat, and explore a house that at least remained familiar and welcoming. More light than I remembered, but that probably had to do with the paucity of windows in the fourteenth century.

"I missed you, old girl," I said to the Duchess while moving from room to room. She responded with her usual creaks and groans, her bones settling for the winter. Before long, I needed to do something about all those wreaths and bouquets surrounding Blix the Wonder Horse...

My ruminations were interrupted by the front door chimes. Before I could respond, Ollie Scott barged into the foyer.

"Just a little constructive criticism, C.L.," he said by way of greeting. "You look like hell."

Upon hearing of my return, Ollie had driven over from Vail in some shiny vehicle resembling a tank, all waxed, prepped, manicured, and coiffed. Both the tank and Ollie. As though he'd never been a pile of rags begging outside Castle DeLaMer, had never wagered on cockfights, or drunk himself silly in the dives on Winetavern Street.

By unspoken agreement, we retreated to the third floor, which had long ago been converted into my personal office, writing space, and library. Where Dottie had danced to Debbie Reynolds' show tunes while readying herself for a future that never materialized.

This was the first time I'd been here since my return. Judging by the chaos of papers on my desk and the lingering fragrance of Jovan Musk, Dottie had commandeered the entire area.

Why aren't you sad at her passing? Why don't you care?

Crossing to the library area, I eased into one of a trio of leather wing-backed chairs.

After carefully closing the door—as if we were in danger of being overheard by Christmas mice?—Ollie settled across from me, propped his feet upon a matching ottoman, retrieved a cigar from the pocket of his Burberry check shirt, and lit the tip.

Cigar? Since when had he started smoking? Since when had I allowed smoking in the Duchess?

"Condolences about Dottie. We had our differences but never figured her for a junkie."

"Heard you two were fighting. Makes her death mighty convenient, doesn't it?"

Ollie drew smoke into his mouth and held it, all the while raking his gaze over me. "Didn't think I'd see you again. What happened with your knight? I figured you'd found true love."

Unable to muster any real emotion, I simply stared. I kind of hated him; kind of felt indifferent. This didn't seem real. *That* didn't seem real. I was caught between here and nowhere.

When I didn't respond, Ollie waved his cigar in front of him. "What was the price you agreed to pay?"

I knew to what he was referring. "My—your—necklace."

He raised an eyebrow. "What else? What did you decide?"

I had no idea what he was talking about.

Ollie licked his lips. "This changes everything, doesn't it?"

"Me returning?"

He shook his head. "Not so much. I don't see you taking an interest in Bella Publishing, do you?"

I didn't see myself taking much interest in anything. I continued staring, remembering now why I hated him.

"Been marking out a new plan. Easier now that Dottie's outta the picture. Take Bella Publishing public. Or sell. Or expand, maybe become the next Amazon. Haven't decided now that I've got the whole world by the you-know-whats. Right now, I'm leaning toward politics."

It was too much effort to push, "You've never even registered to vote" past my lips.

"The power behind the throne," he continued. "That's where the deals are made."

"Deals," I echoed. Because Oliver Harrison Scott wouldn't care anything about policies, easing suffering, or making his surroundings better for anyone but himself. Regardless, he couldn't do anything with Bella Publishing without my consent.

Ollie placed his cigar in an ashtray that had not been there during my tenure, rose, and crossed to one of those huge globes hiding a liquor cabinet within. Also new.

Poured himself a drink. Didn't offer me one.

I studied my former friend. He'd put on weight, which made sense since we didn't have to worry about food in 21st-century America. Wearing shiny leather pants, ironic Doc Martens, a puffer jacket, and with Gucci Aviators shoved atop his lacquered hair, Ollie appeared not so much ridiculous as irrelevant. A boy playing a man. Apparently, I'd come to equate "man" with chain mail, surcoats, long hair, and, yeah, okay, a broadsword belted low on muscular hips.

Ollie returned, swirling liquid in a brandy snifter while he stood above me.

"Will we be enemies, C.L.? Clash of the titans?"

Another time, my interlocutor and I were reading from different scripts. "The only thing I'm sure of is I'll never forgive you. The rest I'll figure out later."

Ollie laughed. "Never's a very long time, Clarabel Lucy. To people like us."

I blinked. Still impossibly slow-witted. "What are you talking about?"

"Forever." He bent over until we were eye level. "Immortality."

I was about to call b.s., but time travel was also impossible, and Naga, if not immortal, had to be pretty fricking ancient. "You may have made that bargain with that charlatan. I didn't."

Ollie settled back in his chair, crossing his legs, stretched upon the ottoman at the ankles. "Think about it, C.L. Forever."

I'd never discussed any such thing with Naga. Maybe all his cryptic remarks had been meant to pique my curiosity, to make me ask, "How can I be like you?" Didn't happen. One normal life with the man I loved was all I wanted.

I studied my former friend in his faux relaxed pose—cradling his brandy snifter, puffing his cigar. Now that Ollie didn't have to worry about his expiration date, he could try on and discard a thousand costumes and indulge in whatever virtues and vices he pleased. But he was in the beginning phases of his adventure, which meant he remained the Ollie Scott I'd grown up with—he of the fearless fly glasses, gangly limbs, and twelve-year-old "It's all about the Benjamins" pretentiousness. If he thought to impress or bully me, that would not happen in *my* lifetime.

"I can't think of a worse fate than to have everybody around you die," I said. "Over and over again."

Ollie placed his drink on the nearby end table and rearranged his features to indicate he was contemplating weighty matters. "Not the most conducive atmosphere for forming lasting bonds, I'll grant you." He tapped the side of his temple with a finger. "But I'm the man with the plan and plenty of time to carry it out."

I rolled my eyes. When Ollie's master plan had consisted of begging for scraps outside Castle DeLaMer, I wasn't concerned he could transform into Dr. Evil, no matter how many centuries at his disposal.

"I kinda like the term 'demigod.'" Ollie leaned his head back against the leather cushion and released a cloud of smoke. His cigar smelled like dried prunes and coffee grounds. "What if I did help your bitch of a mother move it along? A little too much booze, crushed pills, you know the drill. Did I tell you I've expanded our mystery line? 'Murder More Graphic,' I call it."

Wasn't surprised by Ollie's semi-confession. If someone someday wrote his biography, they should title it *Diabolical*.

"Wouldn't it be ironic then if you were arrested, convicted, and sentenced to life without parole? How appealing would immortality look to you then?"

Ollie returned his cigar to the ashtray, retrieved his brandy snifter, and studied me over its rim. "You never answered my question, C.L. What happened to that Neanderthal knight of yours? I was sure you'd be rattling around in that fricking Dracula castle forever."

With those few words, all thoughts of Dottie, of Naga, of Ollie and his megalomania disappeared. I was plunged back into my pit of despair.

Oh, my beloved. What have I done?

Twenty-Seven

~~

I felt like a ghost. Upon awakening, I raised my arms to stare at them and remind myself that, yes, I was corporeal. Still, I felt insubstantial, flitting through each day with my feet skimming the ground, hovering instead of walking. Suspecting that when I stood before the bay window in the parlor that had housed the Christmas tree, sunlight would pass through me.

I holed up, not in my Bella Publishing office, but in the turret room opening onto the Duchess's balcony where I'd written *Robin of the Rood*. On cold days, I curled up in one of the window seats beneath the trio of windows rising to the copper and beamed ceiling. I imagined cutting a laser beam through Roja Mountain. On the other side, I pretended, lay the Ireland of *Topographia Hibernica* with its mythical beasts and enchanted islands. Where, on calm days, church spires could be glimpsed beneath the surface of lakes. Where stags grew so fat they could not escape a hunter's arrow; where priests granted shapeshifting wolves Extreme Unction. Where frogs did not exist because they couldn't be born out of Ireland's mud; where birds never migrated but in winter survived in an ecstatic middle state between life and death. Where a half-man, half-ox attended court in Wicklow and fed himself using his cleft hooves as hands; where a youth named Fantasticus foretold the future by gazing into the past.

I could relate to Fantasticus. All I did was gaze into my past—without seeing anything but the bleakness of my future.

With the first hints of spring, I hauled up an outdoor lounge chair to place upon the tower balcony, though not too close to the wrought iron railing, which only came up to my belly button. Our remodeling contractor had complained that, while the railing had been grandfathered in, it wasn't up to code. Because replacing the ornate ironwork would have been prohibitively expensive, not to mention an insult to the Duchess, I'd compromised by maintaining a respectable distance from its edge.

Day and night, Alaric haunted me. Across the centuries, I felt the pull of him, knew when he thought of me and sensed him as clearly as though he stood beside my bed or awaited me in the next room. I imagined him wandering Castle DeLaMer, heard him whisper my name the way I'd so often heard Daddy's singing. In the wee hours, when the Duchess slumbered and I drifted in and out of sleep, I swore I heard Alaric call, "Bella, Bel. Come out and play!"

The Duchess had her own share of ghosts, didn't she?

Sometimes, I pondered the actual mechanics of a haunting. How did it work when the lovers' physical bodies had long been reduced to shavings from a grindstone? Were the sightings some sort of hologram? There but not there? Echoes that could only be released into the current dimension under certain conditions? Or was it something entirely different? What if the Knight and his Lady weren't even dead? What if they were immortal, living a parallel life we only occasionally glimpsed? Some physicists believe all existence in time is equally real. Maybe the Knight and his Lady had no idea of the passing centuries but assumed they'd only been together a handful of days. I liked the idea of that: to awaken each morning believing in the newness of their love. Or, if the Knight and his Lady did realize they were permanent residents of a haunted castle, they simply shrugged.

So much more pleasant to contemplate such matters than do anything productive, to concoct some sort of plan to...what?

I wasn't sure. Yet.

I did trust I would eventually experience that psychic click I always did when wrestling with a problem. That out of the inchoate mess of my unconscious, a plan would arise.

~

CLICK!

Twenty-Eight

ALARIC

By my reckoning, Bel had been gone four months.

Still, I would not abandon my post.

"Mayhap she is dead," Jocelyn said, during one of several times she intruded upon my vigil, always coming back around to her obsession regarding marriage. Though I schooled my features, I imagined strangling her, happy thought that that was. Bel was not dead, and I hated Jocelyn all the more for uttering such blasphemy. I was familiar enough with death to recognize the circumstances surrounding it. Always before, I'd experienced premonitions, in dreams or other signs (though oft times, I only understood them in hindsight.).

Knowing how my words would cut, I responded, "I'd advise you to travel to His Grace's court. There, you can avail yourself of a husband. I told you before, Jocelyn, I do not love you, and I'll not marry you no matter how you recast our childhood infatuation."

Jocelyn sometimes reminded me of a dumb ox. Staring and blinking and staring some more.

Then, she licked her lips as if she had some secret to impart before flouncing away.

Immediately forgotten.

At times, I despaired.

Still, I waited.

CLARABEL

April had arrived. Patches of snow nestled beneath the Blue Spruce lining our property and painted the Wet Mountains a glistening white. From my front porch or even the tower balcony, I fancied I could smell Maurice's roses. Before their falling out, Ollie and Dottie had totally restructured Bella Publishing, which included abandoning the carriage house that had been our original headquarters, so the grounds were blessedly peaceful. I hadn't seen Ollie since our Christmas encounter. Which he'd translated to: *I can do whatever I want cuz C.L.'s too distracted to even notice.*

His mistake.

Lizzie had become my placeholder, taking care of all the mundanities of my life, such as reminding me when I really *must* visit Seraphina, Bad Boy Max and their baby, or Susan McDermott and other locals. Most importantly, I was grooming her to take over Bella Publishing after I implemented The Plan. Not that Lizzie knew. Yet another secret I kept to myself.

During my initial weeks back, the wall separating me from everyone had seemed impenetrable. Now, it was more a fog—sometimes lifting, occasionally settling in so thick I found myself in a psychic limbo. Still, it was comforting to know how effortlessly Ute Creek had moved along in my absence.

That made implementing The Plan so much easier.

When Ollie and I had started Bella Publishing, I'd hired the most highly respected accounting firm in the state. Next, I'd retained Johnson, Pasquale & Erikk, a corporate law firm recommended by the local attorney who'd handled Daddy's trust.

"Eye wateringly expensive," he'd said. "And worth every penny. Crackerjack attorneys'll keep you and your business on the straight and narrow. Trust me on that."

I did.

Oddly, Ollie had never taken any interest in the actual structure and legal intricacies of Bella Publishing. After making sure the language regarding his salary, bonuses, and percentage of profits was ironclad, he'd focused on perfecting and expanding Bella Publishing's brand. More corporate profits equaled more personal profits. Beyond that, Ollie depended on me to summarize our quarterly meetings with our attorneys, which, if extending beyond five minutes, had him mugging and yawning and making elaborate "wrap it up" gestures.

That turned out to be his downfall. After becoming disillusioned with the expansion of Bella Publishing, I'd consistently made changes to our corporate structure, some subtle, some not so much, just in case...

Lizzie spent endless hours with our attorneys and accountants, learning the financial and legal side of Bella Publishing. With each bullet point I crossed off on my mental whiteboard of Things to Do, I experienced a renewed sense of purpose. One step closer. One day closer.

Now, I was ready to cross off the trickiest bullet point of all.

~

"Clarabel Lucy!"

I had been sprawled on the chaise lounge, tapping away on my laptop. Hearing Ollie's bellow, I stood, placed my computer on the lounge and faced the tower door, steeling myself for our confrontation.

Footsteps stomping up the third floor, a glowering Ollie scuttling across the wooden floor. No doubt he'd figured out my coup after receiving notice of his firing, unsuccessfully trying to access Bella Publishing's bank accounts, and being refused contact with our accountants and attorneys.

I felt *fabulous*.

"C.L.!" Ollie bolted onto the balcony and, bully that he was, crowded me until we were nose to nose.

"What the hell d'you think you're doing? You can't fire me. We're equal partners, you stupid bitch."

"Guess you didn't read the fine print," I said, refusing to step back.

"Maybe you should hire a really good lawyer. Oh, wait. I already hired the best. I can do whatever I please with Bella Publishing, and that'll be...well, that's no concern of yours."

For once, Ollie had tossed aside his mask. His entire face was puce, his expression undiluted hatred.

"What's the problem, Ollie? You've got all the time in the world to create a thousand publishing houses or Amazons or Teslas or become the first trillionaire. Or conquer the world. But you're done with Bella Publishing."

Ollie snorted like a wounded bull. Mindful of the railing, I edged away from him.

"You should've stayed gone," he said. "You fucked up everything."

"Yes."

"With enough time, I'll figure out a way to beat you."

"The way you beat Dottie?" I nearly blurted. Instead, I shrugged, pretending indifference. If The Plan worked, I'd be gone. If The Plan worked, Ollie Scott would assume the appearance of an unpleasant dream.

Ollie seemed to shake himself. I could almost see the wheels turning in his head, struggling to snap into place so he could adjust his strategy and regain control. *Whir. Click. Hover. Descend.*

"So you never bargained with Naga to live forever?"

Should I answer truthfully, he might pitch me off the balcony. "I have a feeling Naga gives us what we *think* we want rather than what we really do. And we don't bother reading the fine print." *Such as addendums regarding immortality.* "Kinda like you and Bella Publishing's paperwork."

Watching him malfunction like a short-circuiting robot, I suddenly realized how I might rid myself of Oliver Harrison Scott.

Turning my back, I faced Ute Creek, spreading below us while remaining a safe distance from the railing. I thought of Alaric's Katrin, pushed to her death. How foolish I'd been to believe Jocelyn Good-knyght. Fleeing Alaric the way I fled so many unpleasantries rather than face them.

I remembered that day when Sir Lucan and I had stood atop Castle by the Sea's keep, and I'd realized I'd stood there or would stand in a place very like it gazing out, not at the sea of water, but a sea of rooftops.

Time is a chimera. With a blinding flash of insight, I realized that truth. Simple enough: time was no more, no less than a fabrication of the mind.

"...I will beat you, C.L.." Ollie's voice from behind me.

I forced myself back to the present. Here I was—a reverse Satan taking Christ up to the top of the temple, tempting Him to jump so He might be caught by angels. Only Christ hadn't been blinded by hubris.

"Remember when we were in kindergarten, and we came up here after watching *Superman?*" I softened my tone, faking reminiscence. "Picnicking on one of Dottie's old tablecloths with peanut butter and jelly sandwiches and Orange Crush. In glass bottles, no less." None of that was true. But I was winging it; gambling Ollie's boundless egotism would lead to his fatal mistake.

"You were more a fan of *Swamp Thing* than *Superman*," Ollie said, acting as if we indeed shared a memory. In reality, the only time we'd ventured up here, Daddy had scolded us and installed deadbolts on all relevant doors.

Forcing a relaxed smile, I faced Ollie. "I tied the tablecloth around you as a cape."

"Good times," he agreed enthusiastically. Both of us were working at something, I suppose.

"You wanted to jump off, to fly like Superman. I jerked you back from the railing. Five-year-old Ollie Scott could have been snuffed out right then before ever having a chance to be what you've become."

Ollie cocked his head, studying me.

"You do know that if you stepped off the railing now, you would die, don't you? That you're not really immortal?"

"Ever the buzz kill, aren't you, C.L.?" Ollie held out his arms as if embracing the panorama below. "D'you think I'm stupid? You're the one who fucked up coming back. Especially if all you got was some stupid powder for your trouble. Whereas I..." he smirked. "One 'borrowed' ring in exchange for all this? Not so clever, are you, Clarabel Lucy?"

"Don't stand too close. You could fall."

"What difference would that make? Don't you get it? Look at me, shitkickers!" Ollie shouted at Ute Creek's invisible inhabitants. "Ollie Scott: ten feet tall and bulletproof!"

Here we were—me, the product of my fears, and Ollie Scott, the epitome of what passed for an American success story.

"Should've read the fine print, Ollie, before you signed away your soul," I said, silently praying my awkward manipulation would work. "Step over this railing, and you'll go 'splat' like a bug."

Ollie's expression morphed yet again, and I knew I had him. Like all of us, Ollie would remain true to his nature.

He stepped up to the wrought iron railing.

"Don't," I said, feigning alarm.

Ollie smirked. "Watch this, you fucking bitch."

And plunged off the railing.

~

Ollie's memorial service was held a week later.

It was poorly attended.

Twenty-Nine

Lucan DeLaMer's chauffeur picked me up from Dublin's airport in a Rolls Royce that looked like something out of a BBC period drama. I wasn't surprised by Lucan's five-star treatment. I'd rented Castle by the Sea at a price that should pay its utilities and taxes into the next millennium.

As we drove, my exhaustion from the long flight was replaced by a thrumming in my veins, as if even my blood had been shaken awake. *I'm here!* Tomorrow was Midsummer's Eve. Tomorrow, God willing, I would rest in Alaric's arms.

Before leaving Ute Creek, I'd changed my will, gifting the Duchess to the town of Ute Creek with Lizzie and her family, its live-in caretakers. Johnson, Pasquale, and Erikk had drawn up all the necessary papers to restructure Bella Publishing as a co-op with Lizzie at its head and all the locals rehired. Beyond that, I was satisfied I'd fulfilled my obligations to those in my current/past life.

Upon my first glimpse of Castle by the Sea, I allowed myself a moment of pride, which, damn it, I deserved. Pulling myself out of my malaise and charging forward like Edward III leading his knights against the French—which he never actually would have done because that wasn't the way medieval battles were fought. And okay, some days

I'd more inched forward. But I'd completed my task. The rest was up to the philosopher's stone.

Once inside Castle by the Sea's courtyard, I was greeted by Lucan DeLaMer, looking appropriately shabby in a tweed jacket and Ghillie hat.

"Such a pleasure to see you again, Ms. Lucy!" After shaking hands, Lucan's gaze swept my face as though seeking something. Confirmation I was a crazy American? Surely, he wondered why I'd rented a place the size of Buckingham Palace for one person.

"You are no doubt exhausted," Lucan continued. "You'll be ensconced in the Cavalier Suite again, per your request. And I had all the things you left from your original booking unpacked and replaced, hopefully, to your satisfaction. Dinner will be served at eight."

I unpacked, showered, dressed, and happily reacquainted myself with *Haunted Castles of Ireland,* which had been left on the bedside table where I'd originally placed it.

At the appropriate time, a servant arrived to guide me to a formal dining hall which contained a table enormous enough to accommodate an entire platoon.

"I gambled you'd enjoy eating in grander circumstances," Lucan said. Once seated, he at the head and me to his left, we were served a surprisingly plain though delicious meal of bangers and mash with a side dish of braised red cabbage.

While my host opened a bottle of Guinness Draught and handed it to me, I studied him, unsuccessfully seeking some expression, mannerisms, and physical connection to Alaric. Or did the current Lucan DeLaMer resemble the Lucan who had died at Bannockburn?

I must remember to ask Alaric. I felt a shiver of anticipation. In a matter of hours...

"We were questioned after your disappearance," Lucan said. He drank from his own bottle, which I'd learned was the proper way to enjoy Guinness Draught.

"The resultant publicity revived those old tales of people disappearing in our maze. Curiosity seekers flocked here seeking UFOs or black holes or whatever paranormal fad causes people to vanish.

Vandals carted off so many souvenirs our hedges appeared to have been afflicted with a blight."

"Strange things do happen in old places," I said, sidestepping any fake explanation. If Lucan hoped I'd confide even the sketchiest version of my adventure, he'd be disappointed. "The truth was quite boring. Sometimes, one simply needs to get away."

We continued our meal in companionable silence. The lighting was dim enough to blur the details of the various paintings strategically placed upon the walls, though a tapestry within my sight line portrayed a stag being downed during a hunt. A servant entered to light a fire in the marble-manteled fireplace gracing the middle of the room. Somewhere beyond this dining hall, beyond the vast jumble of rooms, the original Castle DeLaMer existed as a pile of rubble. But if Naga's powder worked, tomorrow, it would be magically reconstructed while our current surroundings would vanish like one of those islands from *Topographia Hibernica*.

"I sometimes do think about what it was like when Castle by the Sea was Castle DeLaMer," I said. "When knights practiced their martial skills in the bailey and the solar was small and quaint with rushes smelling of lavender and our—the bed—was covered by a velvet canopy such a deep blue it was nearly black—" my voice broke, and I stumbled to a halt. What had triggered that river of words? You could feel it here, the residual of all the DeLaMers across the centuries, settling over your consciousness like dust in an abandoned house. Perhaps that accounted for my blurting out things better kept safely locked away.

Lucan cocked his head, studying me like a watchful hawk. Rather than directly address my ramblings, he asked, "Have you visited St. George, the family chapel?"

I shook my head.

"One of our most prized effigies is of the survivor of Bannockburn, Alaric DeLaMer."

An icy hand reached inside my chest to freeze my heart. Because I had a lifetime of rationalizing away or refusing to face unpleasant facts, I'd conveniently forgotten about Alaric's tomb chest. During online research, I'd clicked on a virtual tour of St. George's Chapel, which had revealed his carved marble effigy, gauntleted hands clasped in prayer, legs crossed, and not really looking like Alaric at all. Maybe that's why its implication hadn't registered until the camera had lingered on the brass plate of his birth and death: 1280-1319. Alaric died in 1319? That knowledge had left me panicked. What if he was dead before I could return? What if he would die soon after? Here I was, desperate to spend my life with him, risking it all for...a handful of days? To return to a corpse? I'd finally explained it away by deciding my return would alter events. I refused to believe that all this wizardry would reveal itself as a cosmic joke. *"Guess I forgot to mention, Clarabel Lucy, your lover, yeah, well, he doesn't even exist!"*

"—show the several tomb chests tomorrow if you like."

Yanked back to the present, I answered, perhaps too forcefully, "No! Maybe another day," I added more softly. "I'll have the entire week to explore."

Sir Lucan and I continued chatting, though I'd become aware of an unsettling undercurrent. Perhaps it could be explained away as the awkward differences occurring between people of different cultures and social strata. Was Lucan a member of the impoverished nobility forced to cater to wealthy outsiders to help pay his bills? Did he resent me or feel obligated to entertain me because of my financial "gift"? Or was he simply a gracious host determined to make his guest feel at home?

"A *legacy* such as ours, a *responsibility*..." Lucan was saying. I arranged my features in what I hoped was an attentive expression. Somehow, during my daydreaming, he'd veered off in an unusually personal direction.

"I often think of it—the DeLaMer obligation—as a wax seal impressed upon a royal decree. When opened, it reveals a whole-life order. Meaning I, the present DeLaMer heir, am condemned to serve what Americans would refer to as a life without parole prison sentence."

I stared at Lucan in surprise. What happened to the famous English stiff upper lip, their legendary taciturnity? Personal confessions were supposed to be an American specialty.

Lucan carefully laid his knife and fork to the right on his plate, signaling he'd finished. I was simultaneously unnerved and irritated by his likening centuries of privilege to prison. A vintage Rolls Royce? Castles? Holdings across Ireland and England? Seat in the House of Lords? Really, Lucan DeLaMer! Could you be more self-absorbed?

My host must have sensed my disapproval, for after dabbing his mouth with a linen napkin, he explained, "My family has striven to live by the concept of *noblesse oblige*. Though to those who do not measure worth by bloodlines, especially you Americans, that might seem a weak justification for..." He waved his hand as if encompassing his wealth.

"We have our own royalty, though that might run more to sports figures, movie stars, and musicians," I responded. "Or now, social media influencers who I'd be hard-pressed to determine what they actually contribute to society."

"Perhaps the scales are balanced somewhat by my family's military tradition."

"Yes." I thought of Alaric and Bannockburn, but the DeLaMers' service had extended before Evesham through the Hundred Years War to the Battle of the Boyne, Waterloo, the Somme, D-Day, and beyond. Castle by the Sea's website had listed Sir Lucan's military service during the Iraq War even before his appointment to the House of Lords.

My search for some innocuous comment or change of subject was blessedly interrupted when a servant appeared to remove our dinner plates and replace them with lemon-colored sorbets exquisitely framed in crystal dessert cups.

Gratefully, I sampled the sorbet, which tasted like the citrus slushes I'd so loved in Italy.

"Please excuse my melancholy," Lucan said between wafer-thin bites. "Parliament is in recess, so I recently returned from London. My former wife has a flat there. Too much time together reminds me..." He raised his shoulders in a Gallic-style shrug. "There is truth in the aphorism 'Those who cannot remember the past are condemned to repeat it.'"

I forced my hands to rest lightly atop the linen tablecloth, forced my body to remain still when, internally, I squirmed like a fish on a hook. I *did* remember the past; I was racing to it. *What do you know? Is this entire conversation some sort of veiled wink and nod? Are you trying to warn me? Aid me? Destroy me?*

"Sometimes my forebears seem to be just there, in the other room," Lucan continued in a reflective tone.

Perhaps it was the long flight and lack of sleep, but my host increasingly spoke in riddles. Dutifully, I finished my sorbet while mulling various excuses for making an exit.

Almost as if speaking to himself, Lucan continued, "I expect to enter and to see them and not be at all surprised. I will recognize them from the faces and forms staring down at us from these walls or that have been so carefully documented in our family annals, and I will say, 'How have you been?' and they will respond or not, as they choose, and then we'll all go about our business."

He paused. Our eyes met, held. Shadows from the fireplace flames danced upon the air; the hound in the tapestry of the stag hunt appeared to move.

"I'm not surprised one such as you senses their presence, Ms. Lucy."

But I'd never admitted to that, had I? I opened my mouth to contradict him, but once again, it betrayed me. "Have you seen the Knight and his Lady recently?" I silently cursed the faulty wiring of my brain, which was causing me to behave like a malfunctioning self-driving Tesla. Yet, I could scarcely refrain from questioning what the Knight and his Lady looked like, from ordering Sir Lucan to describe their clothing, from clasping his hand and pulling him to my suite where I would show him the *Haunted Castles of Ireland* painting. "Do your ghosts look anything like these two?" I'd ask, tapping the page. "Who do you think they are? And why, out of the parade of humanity inhabiting these rooms, are the Knight and his Lady the only ones who've stayed?"

"I only returned from London to welcome you," Lucan said. "Things have been quite ordinary these past few days. No spectral visitors to speak of."

We stared at each other. *What do you know? Are you toying with me?* Lucan spoke so openly about ghosts and a maze that gobbled up people; maybe he also knew about time travel. Maybe Lucan DeLaMer *was* a time traveler. Or had our entire peculiar exchange been leading to this, his *J'accuse* moment? *"I know all about that red powder you have hidden in your luggage, Clarabel Lucy, and I'll have no part of it. Using my home as some sort of time travel merry-go-round or substitute matrix."*

Abruptly, I pushed back my chair and stood. "I'm very tired. If you don't mind, I'm going to say goodnight."

Sir Lucan rose with me. "Tomorrow morning, I will give you your tour," he said. "And then you'll be left to your pleasure."

Indeed.

~

My destination: the room adjacent to the DeLaMer museum. I'd replicated my original experience as best I could, including the time of day. I did exchange Veronique Vixen's costume for the gown I'd previously worn. And okay, I had a cloth bag fashioned from a tapestry material hanging off my shoulder. I'd sewn the bag myself, attempting to make it appear "medieval." Inside, I'd packed the equivalent of a first aid kit, a pouch of loose jewels to be used as currency, and the remainder of the philosopher's stone.

Fluorescent lights, casting a ghastly glow upon the limewashed walls, hummed overhead. I crossed to the passageway from which I'd first stumbled into the fourteenth century and peered inside. Black as a moonless night. The way I remembered.

Despite the fact I'd already drunk the powder mixed with wine, nothing out of the ordinary had occurred. Shouldn't I be feeling *something*? I couldn't really remember much about my first experience. A glow had suffused the bailey; I'd seen a door. The rest was hazy.

"Concentrate," Naga had instructed after I'd purchased the potion. "Focus on your desired destination."

Alaric, standing in the bailey. Yes, the way I'd first seen him, half-naked and swashbuckling around like some throwback to the seventies. *No. Erase that. Alaric, fully dressed and moderately tidy.*

"Be there waiting for me, Alaric," I ordered, staring into the passageway. It was then I realized the room had grown unnaturally still; even the fluorescent lights had ceased their humming. My hands began tingling, then my feet. *Yes!* I'd forgotten that detail and the way it had crawled throughout my body until my entire being had seemed to vibrate.

Closing my eyes, I whispered, "Alaric, Alaric, Alaric," and focused my thoughts. When I opened them, the light had altered. Like turning a dimmer switch—changing from a chalky white to a soft yellow, gradually intensifying until it was the color of aspen leaves in the fall. The air had become so thick I struggled to breathe.

As if moving underwater, I advanced one step and then another into the passageway. The area pulsated with light. I struggled through a handful more steps. Paused. Sensed I was moving through the liminal space between now and then.

Another shift, and I could breathe more easily, more effortlessly move forward. I increased my pace until the light became a sentient being beckoning me. "Come closer," it whispered. Invisible arms reached out to spin me through time.

I became aware of a muted roar that sounded impossibly like the sea.

"Bella, Bel!" Alaric whispered.

Through the roar, I discerned voices, too low to distinguish: the ringing of a smithy's hammer, the neighing of horses, and of dogs howling.

"I'm coming, Alaric!" A final burst of adrenaline and I was running. "Wait for me!"

The light winked and danced before my vision, urging me forward. Only a few more steps.

I saw it—the spot where one light, that unnatural luminescence, ended...

And a second, that of a fourteenth-century Irish afternoon, began.

Thirty

ALARIC

It was my habit each day to stand in the bailey at the time I'd first met Bel. Whether fair weather or foul, I did my duty, which doubled as my private penance. My household was used to my peculiar behavior and had ceased to question it since we are each of us peculiar in our own ways. While I told myself I didn't really expect to be successful, I was ever disappointed after I closed my eyes, prayed to Christ and all the saints that Bel would reappear out of nowhere—and opened them to emptiness.

But today was my birthday, the day I'd first met Bel, the day of so many happenings that I marked June 23rd as the ideal time.

Magic was real. As were miracles.

I closed my eyes.

CLARABEL

Upon stumbling into Castle DeLaMer's bailey, the first thing I saw was blue sky. Not Rocky Mountain blue, but blue enough. My gaze dropped down, and there he was, standing in the middle of a deserted bailey. At least it seemed deserted because my entire being was concentrated on Alaric. The moment my beloved spotted me, his eyes widened. I didn't read astonishment there; more relief. He held out his arms, and I crossed to him, my movements slow, deliberate. Savoring each moment before the one most sacred to us both.

Alaric enveloped me in his embrace, first tentatively, as if wrapping his arms around a dream. Gradually tightening until how could either of us know where one ended and the other began?

We stayed that way, holding each other. Both of us so very grateful we were home.

It seemed I slept forever. Upon awakening and reassuring myself, I remained safely encircled in Alaric's arms, I drifted off again. While traveling across centuries was certainly exhausting, I think these last miserable months had added to my enervation. Finally, after the fog lifted, Alaric and I were fully together, both of us experiencing a tsunami of emotions impossible to describe.

Of course, he questioned me about my absence, but how could I explain? Instead, I deflected.

"It was dreadful. I don't want to talk about it." True enough. "I fought my way back to you as best as I could. It was a long journey, but I can promise you this. I'll never leave you again."

"Nay, you will not." Alaric made it sound like a threat, which left me secretly delighted. How I'd missed the Neanderthal part of my knight. Later, to quote J. Alfred Prufrock, there would be *"Time for you and time for me."* Maybe then, I'd concoct a fantastical tale he'd pretend to believe.

Hoping for my return, Alaric had continued paying the lease on my town house and kept watch over it. During my long sleep, he'd ordered everything packed up and removed to a castle storeroom.

I was grateful for that, happy he took charge. I felt incapable of ever again making a decision, large or small.

Still, we had one giant obstacle threatening our happiness. The date of Alaric's death. Thirteen-nineteen was half over. Any day, he could be snatched away. But with me returning and altering events, would that date hold? One time travel trope was that your very presence in another century rearranged outcomes. Which was why returning to the past was impossible. If you kill your grandfather, then you could never be born. If you'd killed Hitler, well, you get the idea. Dominoes would fall one upon the other, rippling across the universe until what we label history would be no more than sand dunes endlessly reshaped by the wind. But others theorized if you tried to kill your grandfather or Hitler, something or someone would intervene to prevent it. Minor details could be altered, so they postulated, not major events.

Regardless, I was proof of the veracity of time travel. And there was only one person who could provide me with the answer to how I could save my beloved.

So it came down to this. A showdown for which I was woefully unprepared. Naga the Alchemist, it turned out, held the gun and all the bullets. I held empty air.

I found Naga in his inner sanctum while an apprentice in the Elixir of Life's storefront packed his merchandise into traveling chests. His master, the young man informed me, was moving.

Naga did not appear surprised at my appearance, though that might be because he'd had centuries to school his features.

"Ah, Lady Lucy. Disenchanted with life in the future?"

My gaze slipped to the nearby terrarium, where I fancied his hideous snake studied me through eyes identical to Naga's own.

As if responding to a question I hadn't asked, Naga said, "My work in this unappealing place and time is completed."

"Where are you headed?" Small talk, as if that would disguise my desperation. As if I still believed I could fool him.

"Londinium. Home of Big Ben."

Since Big Ben was a nineteenth-century landmark, Naga was providing an in-your-face reminder of his ability to century-hop.

We stared at each other. That peculiarly flawless, preternatural face, downy halo of hair, the intense scarlet, blues, and purples of his voluminous gown all added to his theatrical persona, though I'd learned to my sorrow Naga the Alchemist was far more complicated than appearances suggested.

"I'm particularly fond of His Majesty's Royal Palace and Fortress of the Tower of London."

"You mean the Tower of London?"

"Aye."

Naga sets out his elixir for Anne Boleyn as she faces execution. "I will make you immortal," he assures her. A desperate Boleyn also skips the fine print. Which accounts for the many tales of her haunting Tower Green.

"Then, I'm glad I caught you before your departure." Taking a deep breath, I plunged forward. "Do you have any sort of potion, not for time travel or immortality, but as an antidote? Like an amulet that can protect you from poison or...witchcraft or, say, what if someone was going off to war so they'd be immune from harm? So they'll die of old age. Of natural causes." I trailed off.

"That is not it at all. That is not what I meant at all."

"Anything is possible," Naga said vaguely.

"Can you be more specific?"

Naga turned to face the wall, which still held his esoteric books and charts. Reaching out to unpin one of the charts, he spread his cape, causing his dragon's wings to dance their unsettling dance, as he knew they would. You'd think someone immortal could come up with a few new moves.

He swiveled his head over his shoulder to address me. "This morn, an acquaintance of yours visited. Lady Lackford. I was pleased to supply her with more arsenic powder. Regardless of the century, rodents remain a problem."

As if I were a toddler who could be distracted by a shiny toy! Still, Jocelyn Goodknyght? Hadn't Alaric mentioned she'd sailed to England?

Carefully rolling up the chart, Naga crossed to the worktable and secured it with attached ribbons. "Lady Jocelyn spoke of your return."

How would Jocelyn know? Most likely, she was staying in her town house and had observed Alaric's men removing my things.

I shrugged, pretending disinterest.

"How is my previous client, Master Scott?" Naga asked suddenly.

"Dead."

Before his expression settled into its usual mask, I registered his shock. So, Naga must not be omniscient. Or, if he'd foreseen a different future, that meant outcomes weren't predetermined.

Unless he was indulging in more performance art.

"Hmmm. Unexpected."

"Ollie didn't read the fine print," I said, proud of that particular turn of phrase. Okay, well, no one would accuse me of being William Shakespeare... except for that whole fake husband bit, but...

"Neither did you, Clarabel Lucy." Something flickered across his face.

"Excuse me?" I imagined Naga's snake studying me out of glittery eyes, calculating the optimum moment to strike. "What do you mean?"

"We all hear what we wish to hear. You scoff at your...deceased friend, but you did not *hear* the words I spoke upon your previous visit. *You* did not read the fine print."

I stared at him, uncomprehending.

"Before I relinquish any portion of the philosopher's stone, there is a process I must follow, an immutable contract, so to speak. When a potential customer appears, I listen to their needs, spoken and unspoken, before agreeing to provide the requested service. Though, it always comes down to one demand. They all seek that elusive fountain of youth. No one wants to grow old. Or die, do they?"

"No one wants to die before our time," I clarified, though that wasn't why I'd purchased his services.

Naga tapped a finger upon the worktable as if considering. "I am dutybound to detail the consequences of imbibing my elixir."

"Which are?" I experienced that first faint coil of dread, a fore-boding that my personal universe was about to implode.

"Alchemy means transformation—not only of physical ingredients but of the alchemist himself. Because we magus have the patience and the skill to uncover the secrets of the philosopher's stone, we trod loftier realms. Our obligations are not yours; our pleasures are not yours."

"Tell me about the fine print," I prodded. I had listened that day, hadn't I? Naga spoke in such flowery terms, spreading so much b.s. it was easy to tune him out.

"One such as Oliver Scott, if he is so *careless* as to expire, will simply pass in normal fashion. To await Judgment Day if you believe such things. Or to sleep. Or to awaken in Paradise."

Naga, sensing my vulnerability, sinks his fangs into my exposed neck. I forced myself to appear calm, to pretend a scream wasn't rising inside me.

"The major revelation for a magi such as myself is that humans in all their diversity aren't diverse at all. Nor are you a particularly inter-esting species. You will have a reaction to pain, to pleasure, to betrayal, to love, which is all quite predictable."

"I don't understand."

"To wit: it all becomes excruciatingly dull. So we magi must snatch pleasure however we can." Propping his elbows atop the worktable, Naga leaned closer. "I am your puppet master. When I cut the strings, you crumple to the stage. The illusion is broken. You are no longer a strutting, gesticulating marionette but rather poorly painted and carved pieces of wood. So do not come looking for compassion or answers or anything else you seek. I am incapable of such considera-tions, of such emotions. Of doing anything save view your struggles." Naga's eyes were pools of blackness. "Let me correct myself. I do find pleasure in one thing. The pain of others."

"That doesn't seem very enlightened," I said, covering my alarm with bravado.

"When you came to me, when you commented you did not wish to be immortal, you referred quite specifically to your body."

While I didn't remember that precisely, I nodded.

"The philosopher's stone grants two types of immortality. One is of the body; the other is of the being."

"You mean the soul?"

"*Being.* 'Tis not quite the same thing." Naga held out his hands, palm extended, mimicking an invisible scale weighing invisible contents. "Body or being? Those who shun immortality of the body will find themselves—" He bared his teeth, and I experienced the terror Ted Bundy's victims must have felt upon realizing the nice man on crutches seeking their help was a serial killer.

"When certain clients discuss their needs, they fail to specify they desire immortality in the *corporeal* sense. They, like you, hear only what they wish to hear. Which inevitably leads to the series of events that brought you, Clarabel Lucy, back to me. Complaining you did not hear what I actually said. To paraphrase: you neglected to read the fine print."

"I don't want to live forever if that's what you're implying," I said, fighting down my horror. "I'm sure I made that plain. That I only wanted to return to the 21st century. I didn't ask for all the rest. "

"'Twas your *implied* choice. Your former friend was more forthright. I much prefer the straightforwardness of men to the dithering of women."

So, this is how a cobra hypnotizes its prey. Frozen. Struggling to breathe.

"That day, we spoke of immortality along with the rest of it. Since you did not specifically state, '*I do not wish to live forever as a "being,"*' that is your default state. Nor are there any escape clauses, such as enjoyed by those like your friend. No fall from a tower. No atomization from a weapon of war. You, Clarabel Lucy, are fated to live forever." Dramatic pause. "As a ghost."

Whatever Naga saw in my expression, surely it pleased him. For, I literally felt the blood drain from my face. I probably did resemble a ghost—or the stag woven into Lucan DeLaMar's hunting tapestry, bleeding out after its throat's been cut.

"Life, death, and rebirth." Naga pointed to the chart of the ouroboros, the snake that eats its tail. "Unfortunately for you, Clarabel Lucy, you will be forever stuck somewhere in between them all."

Thirty-One

ALARIC

When Jocelyn Goodknyght was announced, I was staring out the solar window opening at nothing, my mind whirling with plans for Bel's and my future.

"Jocelyn!" I was surprised enough to greet her familiarly, noting in passing she appeared more frayed around the edges. She, in turn, did not bother with the customary bow but swept forward.

"I am betrothed now," Jocelyn said without preamble. Once, I'd dissected every fluttering of lashes, every gesture, curve of the lips, vocal intonation, seeking validation that she, this illusion to which I'd once attached the word "love," might please marry me. Thus, I instinctively interpreted the smile Jocelyn bestowed on me as false.

"'Tis an advantageous match." Jocelyn still wore her widow's weeds, though the richly embroidered damask shimmered prettily in the afternoon light. "While Richard is a second son, he is first cousin to Hugh Despenser, 1st Lord Despenser."

"Ah, the Despensers. They have risen high in His Grace's favor."

Hugh Despenser, Edward's new favorite, was a greedy piece of work, though I dismissed him as a substitute for Piers Gaveston. Since we generally charge forward repeating destructive behaviors, I wagered His Grace would do the same.

"My Richard is very handsome," said Jocelyn, placing her gloved hand familiarly on my arm. I studied her carefully as if her motivations could be written plain upon her face. Jocelyn was not a stupid woman. Despite the close family connection, a second son made her dependent on King Edward's continued favor. Her Richard might indeed be handsome as Adonis or ugly as a goat and one step above a beggar, for the truth of it. Should the Despensers become too ambitious and pose too great a threat to those like me, we would rise up. We, too, would simply be following our natures. No matter her cleverness, Jocelyn's fate might ultimately be determined by others.

Moving away from my former lover, I angled myself to enjoy a better view of the bailey. Bel should be returning soon, and I wished Jocelyn gone before that.

A rustle of fabric signaled my former lover's approach. "'Tis not too late for us, *mon amour*. 'Twould be completing the circle of our lives—"

"Do not!" I said sharply.

I turned to face Jocelyn. Her mouth had thinned to an angry slash.

Who was that young suitor, that coxcomb naïve enough to pine after such vapidity?

"How I thought I loved you, I do not know," I blurted, immediately sorry for such brutal truth-telling. 'Twas not meet to be deliberately cruel, no matter how Jocelyn vexed me.

Hatred flashed in her eyes before she turned away. After hesitating as if considering her next move, Jocelyn crossed to the table beside my bed, where a jug of wine and two goblets had been left. Jocelyn's back was to me, her cloak hiding her movements. I assumed she was pouring herself a drink.

"All my holdings here are in capable hands," Jocelyn said. Rather than rage or throw a tantrum, she discussed mundanities. "And I closed up the town house. I can think of no reason to ever return to Ireland." Her back remained to me. "The banns will be posted upon my return to court. King Edward himself has agreed to attend our wedding."

"God grant you many years of contentment," I said, meaning it.

Experience had taught me our lives could shatter in the space of a heartbeat. Now that I'd found happiness, I wished something similar for those around me.

"You have no idea what sins I've committed on your behalf," Jocelyn said to the wall.

Was she referring to sins of the flesh? But those were easily erased with confession and penance. Puzzled, I debated questioning her, but before I could, she spun to face me again, holding two goblets. Closing the distance, she handed me the one brimming with wine.

"For all the memories," Jocelyn said, raising her goblet in a toast. "I'll not forget you."

"Aye." I followed her, draining its contents.

"Goodbye, Alaric." Jocelyn returned both goblets to the table and readied to leave. "We'll not meet again."

I was relieved she did not ask for a goodbye kiss.

~

CLARABEL

Shadows had crawled across the mews, stables, and other buildings by the time we crossed from Castle DeLaMer's outer bailey to its inner. The realization that a fair amount of time had passed registered somewhere, though had it not been for my escort and Blixette, who obediently followed the lead rider, I might have ended up in the River Liffey or beyond the pale, for all I noticed.

Dazed. Numb. Mind frozen. One moment, I was incapable of processing the implications behind Naga's revelations, and the next, they exploded inside my brain. Obliterating all hope for Alaric and me. For me, period...

This can't be true... something out of a horror novel...impossible. Denial, rationalization, the way a patient does following a diagnosis of a terminal illness. *No, no, no.*

An endless future stretched before me, peopled by nothing. I, insignificant as a tear, faced the endless maw of the universe above, below, and before me.

You did this, Clarabel Lucy, because you did not read the fine print.

Doomed. But Naga wasn't more powerful than God, and God always provided escape clauses. *Believe in Christ. Repent your sins.* But what if Naga and God had some sort of arrangement the way He had with Job. Or Lucifer?

God would not do that. God is loving. Naga is a liar, blathering about bodies and beings and the rest. Taking cruel pleasure in scaring you.

But Naga hadn't lied about the potion. And he, at least, had lived a very long time.

I looked up to the solar windows where Alaric often stood, hands behind his back, surveying the bailey.

I will lose you to death.

I might already have lost him. During my absence, he could have tripped over one of his hounds and cracked his skull, suffered a heart attack or aneurysm, been delivered a fatal blow during swordplay, or choked on a chunk of bread. While Carl Sandburg had written that fog came "on little cat feet," it was death that arrived so. Offhandedly casual or offhandedly cruel. Shouldn't our passing be acknowledged by a fanfare of trumpets, fireworks, a Greek chorus, or a "Breaking News" alert?

Rather, it slipped like rain down a windowpane. Or padded about on tiny cat paws, scarcely marked, scarcely missed.

But not for me. When I passed, my being would wander forever in some hellish form of Limbo.

We are shooting stars, you and I, flaming out as we enter the atmosphere. We are the moment between the bullet leaving its chamber and smashing into our brains.

Already dead, and we don't even know.

On impulse, I retreated to St. George's chapel. Alaric was conventionally devout, me considerably less so, but since my return, I'd happily attended daily Mass. I was profoundly grateful to God and enthusiastically added my prayers to Alaric's, to those of the household and our priest, Father Crispin.

Someday, this modest space would hold Alaric's tomb chest. Visitors would pause to ponder this marble knight with his crossed feet, crossed arms, and stern profile.

1280–1319

Shadows were deeper here. The scent of wax candles and incense lingered, as did the prayers and petitions and the presence of God and goodness. Even in my despair, I experienced a flicker of comfort.

I approached the garishly painted rood in its place above the altar.

To every thing there is a season, and a time to every purpose under the heaven.

So Ecclesiastes had stated, but not for such as me, consigned to eternal winter.

Remember this, Clarabel Lucy. You did this to yourself. Had you not been so impetuous, had you trusted Alaric's love, you would never have felt the need to flee all the way back to the future.

Even in my despair, even in my self-pity, I realized the weaknesses in my character that had brought me to this moment.

"What am I going to do?" I asked the rood, and beyond that, my dad and Maurice and the pantheon of Catholic saints and angels. "And don't tell me life isn't fair. I know it isn't, though this is a little beyond the ordinary."

Closing my eyes, I breathed in that fusty odor so ubiquitous in ancient places, forced myself to stillness, forced myself to imagine Daddy murmuring, *"Down in the valley,"* and settling his hands on my shoulders. As if to remind me, "This too shall pass."

I guess it's true we can be convinced of anything. I left the chapel clinging to the faint hope that some way out would present itself. Perhaps Alaric and I could stay locked in a tower until 1319 passed, and since we'd beat that, he might live into old age.

Something.

When I entered the solar, the fireplace had been lit, as had rush-lights on either side of the bed. I did not immediately spy Alaric slumped in his great chair.

"My love!" I hurried to him.

When he turned his head, I noted his complexion was grey, and his forehead, upon feeling it, was slick with sweat.

"What's happened? Are you ill?"

"Stomach."

Immediately forgetting my problems, I studied him with alarm. What could have laid low a man who, in all the time I'd known him, hadn't suffered so much as a cold?

Alaric slumped back. It was then I noticed the covered chamber pot beside his chair.

"Have you vomited?"

"A bit." He closed his eyes. "I'll be fine after I rest."

"When did you last eat?" I glanced toward the bedside table with its wine and goblets. "Would you like something to drink? You must stay hydrated." Fighting down panic—*Is this the day Alaric will die?*—I hurried to the doorway and ordered a waiting page to bring Alaric's squire and his chamberlain, whose primary job was to tend his lord.

"And a basin of warm water. Cloths."

After pouring some wine, I returned to Alaric. He scarcely wetted his lips before grimacing and turning his head away. "Must have been something I've eaten."

"When was that?" I detected a faint odor of garlic. A combination of spices—medieval cooks delighted in bizarre pairings—that had disagreed with him?

"Regular dinner. And later, a bit of wine with Jocelyn."

"Wait! Jocelyn Goodknyght was here?"

Alaric waved his hand lethargically, signaling she was too unimportant to contemplate. "Said goodbye. She's betrothed... sailing for England."

I hesitated. If I questioned him too intensely, he might accuse me of jealousy. But why would Jocelyn suddenly show up? And odd that Naga had mentioned her visit... Might he and Jocelyn have concocted some sort of revenge plot? But Naga wasn't God, capable of orchestrating events or implementing conspiracies. He'd probably been unaware of my return. He certainly didn't know I would appear at his shop this morning...

Focus!

"When was Jocelyn here?"

Alaric managed a shrug.

"How long after her departure did you start feeling poorly?"

Rather than respond, he closed his eyes and leaned the back of his head against the cushion.

I heard sounds on the stairs, signaling the page's return.

Don't go borrowing trouble. But how could I not be suspicious?

Lady Lackford... arsenic...rats overrun everything...

Poison appeared to be Jocelyn's default choice.

Charles, Alaric's squire, appeared, trailed by the page carrying a basin and Geoffrey, Alaric's chamberlain, with cloths draped over his arm like some medieval butler.

"Please help me put Sir Alaric to bed," I said to Charles. "He'll be more comfortable."

Alaric was growly about being assisted, but his face paled with the effort, and he leaned heavily against me. After we settled him atop his mattress, I said, "I've some medicine that may help." I hurried across the room to the chest where I'd stored my tapestry bag. After retrieving it, I searched through my makeshift pharmacy containing various remedies for colds, flu, diarrhea, and the like, all neatly labeled and placed in cloth pouches so as not to arouse suspicion.

But what if Alaric is suffering from arsenic poisoning?

There was no treatment for severe poisoning, not in any century. If my suspicions proved correct, Alaric had not months but hours.

After gathering a few medicinal pouches, I returned to Alaric. His chamberlain had helped him settle against the pillows.

I reached out to smooth Alaric's hair. "Better?"

He gagged. Grabbing the chamber pot from the page, who'd retrieved it from beside Alaric's chair, I raised it to his chest so he wouldn't have to bend over.

Afterward, I wiped his mouth with the wet cloth Geoffrey handed me.

"What do you think is wrong?" asked Charles, his youthful face pinched with worry. "Should I call Father Crispin? He is good with potions."

"Aye," Geoffrey and I said in unison.

And with administering last rites, if it comes to that.

After Charles scurried away, I placed the pouches on the table next to the wine and goblets. I studied the tableau. One cup appeared full or nearly so; the other empty save for what I had poured Alaric. I remembered the way Jocelyn had poisoned her husband, slowly, methodically, until the *coup de grâce* at Michaelmas.

Jocelyn could easily have dumped a fatal amount of the odorless, tasteless powder into Alaric's wine without risking exposure. And if someone else came along who happened to drink from the jug—most likely me—so much the better.

I saw it then, a trace like spilled salt upon the table's surface next to the jug. And experienced such a wave of despair.

Murder number three.

"Oh!" I envisioned the scene. Simple really. Jocelyn had calculated that today would be her only chance. Already planning her final if-I-can't-have-you-neither-can-anyone-else act, she had visited Naga. No doubt, hoping I would also drink from the poisoned wine. Knowing she might be celebrating at the royal court by the time word reached her of our deaths.

"So these are the cards we've been dealt," I whispered.

I studied Alaric. His eyes were closed. His chest rose and fell strongly through his tunic. Such a fit man, it might take him long to die. The suffering he would endure...

"I will not lose you," I whispered. Geoffrey had left his lord's side to throw more logs upon the fire. Alaric's eyelids fluttered. His fists atop the counterpane clenched. Another spasm? I waited until they relaxed, all the while slotting my plan into place. The solution came to me. With it, my terror was replaced by a deathly calm.

Leaving Alaric's side, I returned to the chest and my tapestry bag. Inside, I retrieved what remained of Naga's elixir.

"Bella, Bel," Alaric called, his voice quavering. I refused to think of the anguish awaiting him. That, too, would pass. What was a matter of hours when compared to eternity?

"I'm coming!" Before I reached him, he'd vomited once again. Once again, I wiped his face. Now that I knew what must be done, there wasn't any reason to search for more signs of deterioration. The outcome might be inevitable, but I wasn't helpless.

To Alaric's page, I said, "Bring me a fresh flagon of wine from the buttery."

To Geoffrey, "More blankets, please. In case he's chilled."

To Alaric, "Everything will soon be fine. I'm going to mix you something to ease your discomfort."

Alaric's fate was unfolding just as the dates on the brass plate had promised.

What has been is what will be,
and what has been done is what will be done,
and there is nothing new under the sun.

Ecclesiastes was right. Alaric and I weren't new. We weren't unique. Not even my fate, if what Naga said was true since the British Isles teemed with ghosts.

Stepping away from Alaric to the table, I tossed Jocelyn's wine on the rushes on the off chance it wasn't poisoned and refilled it with wine from the jug. The poisoned wine.

I stared down at it. Such a mundane act. Death arriving on little cat feet.

I drank. Detected nothing beyond the usual slightly vinegary after-taste. No wonder arsenic was referred to as the poison of kings.

Ears attuned to the page's tread upon the stairs, I stood beside our bed, fingers laced with Alaric's.

A groan escaped him.

When the page returned carrying the flagon, I ordered him to place it on the table. Lifting the poisoned jug, I handed it to Alaric's chamberlain. "Please toss the contents out the window. Then leave us. Wait outside until Father Crispin arrives, or I call."

Geoffrey frowned. "I canna leave my lord. He might have need of me."

"If he does, I promise I'll let you know."

Once Alaric and I were alone, I poured wine from the new flagon into his goblet. Opening the jar containing the elixir, I poured the remainder into the goblet. The powder quickly dissolved.

I pray it's enough. I pray this works.

Our future, such as we might be granted, hinged on this being successful. Would we be thwarted by yet more fine print? If you did not seek out the alchemist, if you did not ask for the philosopher's stone, would the elixir be rendered ineffective? What if it reacted with the arsenic in some bizarre fashion?

"Since you did not specifically state, 'I do not wish to live forever as a "being,"' that is your default."

So said Naga. So be it. I had to trust my scheme would be successful. If we were blessed, Alaric, too, would live on as a ghost. With me.

I fancied Alaric's breathing had become more labored. My thoughts drifted to Jocelyn Goodknyght. How filled with hatred she must be, how corroded her soul. If I could hurl curses like lightning bolts, it would be tempting to do so. But in the end, our actions are what curse us. I didn't need a notation in some obscure annal to know that Jocelyn would be done in by her own private demons.

You lost. Alaric is with me.

If Naga's elixir didn't work, my triumph would be short-lived. If it did, we would share eternity.

Another groan.

Too early yet for me to feel anything.

I approached my beloved with the goblet containing the elixir.

Alaric's face against the pillows appeared flushed. His mouth had thinned, signaling his distress.

"Drink this, my love." I held out the goblet.

Alaric shook his head.

"You must. I promise it will ease your pain."

Helping him to a sitting position, I felt the first twinge of discomfort. Our deaths would be difficult, but they should be quick. The best we could hope for would be to slip into a coma from which we would not emerge.

All go unto one place; all are of the dust, and all turn to dust again.

Our bodies would, but Alaric and I would not. And since time was really nothing more than a fabulist's tale, our eternity might pass in a handful of hours or days. An irrelevancy, or more properly, a gift. So long as we were together.

"Enough, Bel." Alaric shook his head and pushed the cup away.

"Please drink it all. I promise 'twill soon be over."

Our eyes met, held. He could not possibly know what was happening, but something stirred in their depths, some recognition perhaps, and he obeyed.

Alaric had drunk the elixir. I had drunk the poison. Hopefully, the two would work properly, complementing each other. After which, we would strike out like knights in a chivalric romance, seeking new adventures.

"I'll lay beside you." I kissed Alaric on the lips before sliding in next to him.

If I were writing an ending for one of my heroines—who would never be allowed to die, but let's pretend—she would look ethereally beautiful as she slipped away. "More beautiful in death than ever in life," mourners would marvel.

Such would not be the case with arsenic poisoning. Alaric and I would not be the stuff of a Bella Publishing novel.

"Rest, my beloved," I said, holding his hand. "I'll not leave you."

Silence save for Alaric's stertorous breathing. I wondered what Father Crispin would find when he arrived. Most likely, we still had hours to go before our end.

Turning to view Alaric's profile, I experienced a wave of such gratitude. Not a curse, but a gift, to be able to view it and all of him into eternity.

"We're going to lie here, you and I," I whispered. "And we're going to think about how beautiful this room is, how beautiful is all of Castle DeLaMer."

Eyes closed, he nodded, his lips upturned in the ghost of a smile.

"Now we're going to concentrate very hard and imagine us being here together, you and me, ...forever."

"Forever," Alaric rasped. "I like the sound of that."

Epilogue

LUCAN DELAMER

Lucan ran a gloved hand across the ancient parchment. There it was, the story of Alaric DeLaMer, a short entry noting his date and cause of death. "A bloody flux."

Every time he was around the American, Lucan found himself thinking of the ancestor he privately referred to as Bannockburn Alaric. But perhaps that also had to do with his recent interaction with his ex, who he privately referred to as the Nutter.

Lucan carried the leather-bound book back to his private library, where he returned it to his specially designed and modified safe. Well pleased, he looked about. Nothing more pleasant than a night sat in his well-worn armchair close to a cheery fire, sipping Jameson whisky and revisiting beloved classics like *Topographia Hibernica*. Though it had taken him years to forgive himself for willingly allowing Rhonda into this, his hallowed space. When she'd pretended his interests were hers, correctly guessing she could bedazzle him into an impulsive marriage.

"We're distantly related," she'd said upon their first meeting. "One of my ancestors, Jocelyn Goodknyght, wed your Alaric DeLaMer, Fourth Baron DeLaMer of Wendsbury."

Lucan had been so captivated—and who could remember every jot and tittle concerning a family stretching back a millennium—he'd never doubted her confident assertion. (Rhonda was so confident about everything he'd only gradually realized his wife was a pathological liar.) After which, he'd endlessly flagellated himself by checking out every questionable statement he could remember and, when possible, tracing it to its source. Bannockburn Alaric had certainly not married this Jocelyn Goodknyght woman, who, it turned out, had been drowned when the cog in which she'd been a passenger had sunk during a channel crossing. The only commonality had been the year of their death: 1319.

Shaking off unpleasant memories the way his favorite Labrador shook off water, Lucan strolled past the warren of rooms in the direction of the kitchen. Tossing aside all that formal "dining" nonsense, he looked forward to enjoying a Shepherd's pie and Guinness with his cook for company.

Lucan paused outside the door to the room he simply referred to as the "hall," which had largely been constructed from the stones of the original keep. 'Twas a curious thing. He'd noticed that whenever he thought of *them*, they were more likely to appear.

The hall being one of their favorite places.

Savoring the sense of anticipation he always did before greeting old friends, Lucan entered. His gaze fixed upon the minstrels' gallery in the far corner. Soon, it would be twilight, their favorite time.

The pair entered silently, holding hands as always. Since the American's visit—and subsequent disappearance—they'd been shy, more often hiding themselves. But now, here they were as if his thoughts had indeed conjured them—the Knight and his Lady, facing each other and apparently in intense conversation. Then, the lady threw back her head and laughed, soon followed by her knight.

Their laughter drifted down to Lucan. As always, he smiled in response to sounds of pure happiness.

"Wonderful to see you again, Clarabel Lucy," he called.

The lady, dressed in old-fashioned clothes, her hair loose and tumbling down her back, turned to gaze at him.

"You too, Sir Alaric."

The Knight and his Lady looked from him back to each other. Then, this medieval Clarabel Lucy tossed her head in the way he'd noticed when she'd been the visiting American.

After which, the Lady and her Knight disappeared through the gallery door.

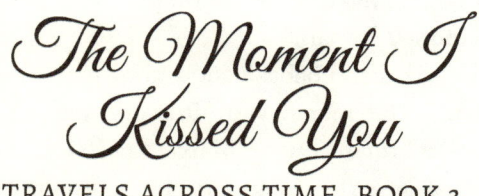

The Moment I Kissed You

TRAVELS ACROSS TIME, BOOK 3

"Gentlemen!" Horace Strank clapped his hands, bringing the assembly to silence. Strank was dressed in a velvet smoking jacket designed to emphasize his impressive girth, because in 1903 thin was definitely not in.

Gazing around the dark paneled drawing room, I recognized most of the guests. Mine owners in expensive evening dress, who complained they couldn't afford to pay their workers three dollars a day. Among them, I spotted Governor Peabody and James McParland, the regional head of the Pinkerton's—the undercover detective who'd once infiltrated the Molly Maguires in the Pennsylvania coal fields and whose testimony had resulted in the hanging of nearly two dozen.

The man my Ronan hated most in all the world.

What were Peabody and McParland doing here? Surely they hadn't traveled all the way from Denver to listen to some moderately talented piano player perform songs that wouldn't be composed for decades.

"May I present the lovely Miss Maeve Mooney!"

Polite applause. I bowed my head demurely, aware of the figure I cut in the cream-colored damask gown with its rhinestone and lace bodice that Strank had purchased for me. "Just an added perk," I'd explained to a fuming Ronan.

"Whose side are you on, Maeve?" he'd demanded. "You can't pretend you support us while eating from the rich man's table."

Squaring my shoulders, I took my place on the bench before the Steinway grand piano—a far cry from the battered Shaw I performed upon at the Pickaxe Saloon.

Maeve Mooney, on display for the rich.

"I need the money, Ronan."

"So do all the wives and babes widowed by men like Strank."

I drowned out the memory of Ronan's and my quarrel with a particularly spirited rendition of Maple Leaf Rag. After that, I ran through my usual repertoire—a mix of contemporary ballads and ragtime pieces, along with songs composed by artists not yet a twinkle in God's eye.

Beyond the great bank of windows, sunset had set the mountains ablaze. If I were entertaining at the Pickaxe, I would wrap up my performance with "Danny Boy," since Ronan's largely Irish clientele loved a heap of weeping along with their music.

But not here.

In my barely passable tenor, I launched into John Denver's "Rocky Mountain High," which was probably the reason most of these men had attended. I sang of Colorado's cathedral mountains, our clear mountain lakes, our starlight "softer than a lullabye." And here in this drawing room, with its imported Italian fireplace mantel and ceiling beams wrested from a Tudor manor house, the robber barons, who were tearing down the mountains and scarring the land, sipped their Jim Beam, smoked their Cuban cigars and blinked away sentimental tears.

"We are the appointed stewards of this magnificent state," they would say.

Because we can justify anything...

As I'd justified my presence here today?

I had picked a side, Ronan's side. I did believe, I did. But I knew the ultimate winners of this war. Governor Peabody would call out the National Guard, and in the end both the Western Federation of Miners and the strike would be crushed. In his speeches, Ronan often reworked the quote that would someday be made famous by Martin

Luther King: "The arc of the moral universe is long, but it bends toward justice—except for America's working class."

He had no idea how right he'd be proven.

I finished to enthusiastic clapping. Horace Strank embraced me in what I suspected was an inappropriate public display of affection. But Strank wasn't signaling affection, was he? He was signaling ownership.

"I'll have a carriage pulled round," he said.

Once outside, I shivered in the cooling air. In my other life, this glorious mansion had been a stone foundation, overgrown with grass and disturbed only by the occasional wandering cow. The mine shaft into which I would someday tumble down into the past was currently marked by a structure resembling a giant praying mantis.

Movement near the shaft. The electric lights Strank was so proud of did little to penetrate the darkness, but I still recognized James McParland. Next to him was a much smaller man, a man barely topping five feet, a man Ronan had nicknamed "Leprechaun."

My heart dropped to my stomach. No, it couldn't be. But as I watched the pair, their furtive, conspiratorial manner gave them away. Ronan was forever worrying about infiltrators betraying the movement.

He'd been right.

Paddy Mooney was not only a union leader, Ronan's right-hand man and my sainted ancestor, who, according to family legend, was the hero of the Cripple Creek strikes.

Paddy Mooney was a Pinkerton spy.

∾

Available in Paperback and eBook from Your Favorite Bookstore or Online Retailer

About the Author

On my first visit to Ireland, I visited Malahide Castle near Dublin. I was captivated by its stunning grounds and interior and its fascinating history, which so often aligned with the fate of Ireland itself. And once I learned of its ghosts, I knew Malahide Castle, now the fictional Castle by the Sea, would provide the perfect setting for my second time travel, *Eternal Beloved*.

Before I Wake is the first novel in my four-book time travel series, *Travels Across Time*. *Before I Wake* deals with a pair of star-crossed lovers reuniting and fighting in thirteenth-century Cornwall during the time of Simon de Montfort's rebellion against England's king.

I am the author of the six-book *Knights of England* historical romance series, plus *The Landlord's Black-Eyed Daughter*, based on the Alfred Noyes poem, "The Highwayman," which was published under the pseudonym Mary Ellen Dennis.

Upon completion of *Eternal Beloved*, I will say goodbye to my beloved Middle Ages and turn my *Travels Across Time* attention first to the Colorado Labor Wars in *The Moment I Kissed You*, and finally, to a haunted roadhouse on Colorado's eastern plains that *may* bear a close resemblance to a tavern owned by my grandfather.

When not writing, I enjoy my children and grandchildren and Karma the Wonder Dog, my German Shepherd who helped me survive COVID and numerous other adventures.

www.maryellenjohnsonnauthor.com

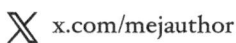 x.com/mejauthor

www.ingramcontent.com/pod-product-compliance
Lightning Source LLC
Chambersburg PA
CBHW021045030726
47496CB00006B/1695